Gambler's Rose

Gambler's Rose

a novel
G. W. Hawkes

MacMurray & Beck
Denver

Printed and bound in the United States of America

2 3 4 5 6 7 8 9 0

Library of Congress Cataloging-in-Publication Data

Hawkes, G. W., 1953-
    Gambler's rose : a novel / G.W.Hawkes.
        p. cm
    ISBN 1-878448-96-X
    I. Title

PS3558.A818 G36 2000
818'.54--dc21
                                                                99-048428

MacMurray & Beck Fiction: General Editor, Greg Michalson
Gambler's Rose cover design by Joni McLane, Y:1080, Inc.
Text was set in Janson and Bernhard at Professional Book Center

For my brothers, Gale and Gil, mirror twins,
and the whole damn family

Certain coasts are set apart for shipwreck.
—Loren Eiseley

It didn't seem possible, even to Halloran, that this many crooked games could go wrong. *A handful in as many months.* This time he'd been found out in a back-alley crap game, throwing bones in a Honolulu laundry at the foot of a huge steam press. He was crowded into an open space by men he didn't know and bundles of dirty clothes knotted with their own sleeves. Around the edges stood high, square stacks of clean shirts in butcher paper and string. He leaned against one and watched a kid throw dice against a pale green wall while rain hammered on the tin roof.

Halloran was losing. The kid, a black Marine in a white Panama hat and a lot of Louisiana in his voice, was taking everybody's money. He wore his dark blue silk shirt like a uniform. One gold front tooth had a ruby in it. To give the Viet Cong something to shoot at, he'd said, if he ever saw them. In 1971 it seemed to everybody that the war was slowing down.

"Little Joe. Got two hunnert in the middle."

Halloran laid two pairs of twenties, two fifties, a ten, and two fives on the back line. "It's faded. Lose."

"Gimme odds I make the foe the *bahd* way."

"How much?"

"Twenty."

Halloran added a hundred and sixty on the side. "Go."

The Louisiana Marine rattled the dice and tapped one of them in a closed fist against the ruby. He threw another four, but not deuces. He smiled, picked up his point bet, lost his twenty, and left the others. He tossed a nine. "New point's nine."

The Marine threw a six, then a ten, then another six. He threw everything but the seven that Halloran needed. He blew on the dice and grinned. He thickened up his Louisiana and looked into Halloran. "Ah'm gonna *dah* shootin' mah poin'."

Halloran almost believed him. They'd been gambling since before dark, and it was almost morning. The players and dice and money were tired. Halloran, scared, wished a curse on the Louisiana Marine and watched the dice bounce. They came up a seven, finally.

Halloran took them, the third set he'd seen in the game. White standards. Square corners. *Right-hand pocket.* He banked the dice against the wall with his left hand.

"Eight," said the Marine. "Fifty says he doan pass."

"This fifty down, too," said one of the others.

Halloran rolled again twice and got six for a second point. He threw a three and lost his bets. He rolled a four. Then a five. He wondered at the odds of hitting a natural progression, but was too weary to do the math. He put all the money he had left on the six and let the dice go, and as they climbed toward the wall, he knew that velocity and volume and distance were no match for the physics in the human hand. *This hand, anyway.* He willed gravity into being and got the pair of threes he needed.

No one but the Marine seemed to notice. "Five hunnert on the seven," the Louisiana Marine said. He grinned at Halloran. "Looks like you got to go through that to make your eight."

Halloran had dice in both hands now, the loaded bottoms from his right-hand pocket and the straight pair they'd been shaking for the last hour. He slipped the bad dice back and wished he could take his bets down. "Seven," he agreed without taking the Louisiana Marine's bet, and hit it.

He pushed them to the next shooter with the back of his hand and stood up. His knees popped.

The Marine got up without any noise and stood in front of him. Halloran concentrated on the kid's baggy pants and red high-top sneakers.

"Hey, Trick, what they call you?"

"Halloran."

"Other name."

"Charles."

"I got a brother Charles."

"Good."

The Marine shook his head. "Brother Charles is a cheat." His fingers tried to find the crease in his trousers. "An' not good, no way." He aimed three or four invisible cards at Halloran. "I ain't seen a straight befoe in that game."

"Neither have I."

"Weird, ain't it?"

"It's weird," Halloran agreed.

"Too weird, you ask me." He flashed his gold tooth, and one of his hands disappeared. "You got dice in your pockets, Charles, you're a dead crapshooter."

Halloran had two hundred dollars in his pockets, two pairs of bad dice, and a pain like needles in his groin. The door was a dozen long steps away on the other side of the owner, asleep in his chair. Halloran wasn't fast enough to get there and never had been.

"I rolled the same dice you did. Pick 'em up and look."

"I want to see what's in your pockets."

"You made money on that seven and I lost it."

"Doan' matter." He took a step.

Halloran toppled a stack of laundry between them and had time to notice that the bundles were tied with neat square knots before he rolled backward through the glass and dropped two floors to the alley. He landed on something soft enough not to kill him, got up shakily, understanding finally that he was trying to walk on plastic bags stuffed with garbage.

When he got free of them, he ran blind with rain in his eyes until the pounding of his feet on the pavement and the pounding in his head managed a synchronicity, and in between the thumps of feet, head, and heart he remembered what he should never have forgotten.

"Make sure you have a door handy," his father had told him more than once. "Know which way it swings, and what's on the other side when it swings open."

Halloran stopped running and threw up before he could bend over. He was in a part of Honolulu he didn't know, but at least he was alone.

When he found his hotel, he poured a bath and settled into it, adding hot water whenever he could stand it, staring through the bathroom's steam at the door. The first lesson a Halloran learned was to check for exits.

"Better that you don't get caught," his father had said, "but I think you always will. So look for ways out, first."

"What do you mean, I always will?" Halloran was ten, expelled from school for taking lunch money at a game of crazy eights.

"Look at you. You're faster than I was at your age, but your eyes light up when you make that move because you know you can." His father tapped the deck lightly. "You can get your fingers caught in those cards, Son.

"There was a man named Milo, a six- or seven-time Olympic champion wrestler, back in the real Olympics, eight hundred years before Christ. He was the strongest man in the whole Mediterranean. He was absolutely invincible."

"But," Halloran said, when his father didn't supply it.

"But," his father agreed. "Milo had that same pride. He was walking in the forest and came upon a stump the woodcutters had left, too tough to get out. They'd hammered a wedge into it, but the wood was as hard as stone and they'd had to leave it, unable to split the stump, unable to get their wedge back out."

His father turned a gray eye on him. "Milo thought he was stronger than the tree. He dug his fingers into the crack and pulled,

and the wedge popped out, but the stump closed on his hands."
That eye didn't blink. "A pack of wolves found him that night and
ate him alive from his feet up."

Halloran had stared down at the old blue diamond-backed Bee
cards he held to avoid his father's look. He clamped a thick thumb
down on the top card and dealt the second ones, trying to keep his
eyes dark.

"The first thing you worry about—after finding a door to go
out and keeping your eyes soft—is a player seeing that move. Hold
your thumb more to the side. That's it. The second thing you
worry about is a player *hearing* it. There's no way to get that second
card out without it sliding. Are you following this?"

Halloran nodded.

"Play in the big games without guns; they always go off backward. Know what sort of men you're playing against. Some will
throw you out if you get caught, some will simply pick up whatever
money you've left them and go, but there's some that will string
you up by the neck, or shoot you full of holes, or worse."

His father pulled at his bottom lip and tried to smile. "Take a
minute to look them over first and try not to play with that kind."

"You mean like Grandpa."

"Shaved dice caught him," his father said, and nodded. "The
old man was shooting for quarters in the Navy yard up at Norfolk.
Quarters. They killed him with a welding torch."

"I know," Halloran said.

"You *say* you know." His father handed him a new deck. "Old
cards are no good. They lose their slick. And cards are old after
they've been in play for an hour. Make your move with a new
deck."

Halloran's father had given his son unbroken packs of fifty
cards, or fifty-one or -three or -four, that he had manufactured, and
Halloran had to tell his father as he pulled the cards from their
boxes and weighed them in his hand how many there were.

"This is impossible."

"Do it by weight. The pressure of your fingertips is your whole life. A deck weighs three-quarters of an ounce, the same as your soul."

Halloran got instructions in marking, crimping, shuffling, stacking, and dealing seconds and bottoms.

His father had sat with his son at the table and pulled the cards into his own long hands. He shuffled them idly by running a thumb up their two halves. "You'll learn that you're almost never the only mechanic in the game. Watch the others. Wait for their specialty. If they're better than you, get out. Or team up; there's signals. But getting out's better."

"Honest games are that rare?"

"Honest games don't exist." His father dealt five hands, face up, a pat straight, three aces, a four-flush, three kings, three fours. "Pull out the discards."

Halloran did, and his father dealt the replacements. The three aces, the four-flush, and the three kings filled. The three fours caught a fourth. "That's a jackpot. You smile. You look sheepish. You say something about catching a break. You leave as quickly as you decently can afterward because you've made your money for the night. Or for the month.

"You keep a brand new deck in your pocket for that one. Save it for late in the game, when everybody's tired anyway. It helps if you're losing because it's hard to suspect a loser of anything but stupidity or luck."

"What do you mean honest games don't exist?" Halloran had asked.

"Think about it."

Halloran thought about it.

He'd given the boy a few minutes, then gathered the cards up, squared them, and handed him the deck. "Once *you* sit down to play in it, it's no longer honest."

Halloran held his breath now and sank under the hot water until it covered his eyes. He blew bubbles until he had to come up. "I need lessons," he said aloud and swore he saw his father in the steam, winking a clear gray eye and nodding. "Or another line of work."

He stood up, toweled dry, and stepped into his shorts, leaving the tub full. He spread open his sliced cheek with his fingers and looked for glass. The cut from the corner of his left eye to the corner of his mouth was clean as a razor's. "Another line of work," he said again, and tapped the mirror. He reached up and gave the broken ceiling fan a spin, then got into bed. *Marked.*

Halloran's feet hurt. He pulled the covers back to look, having heard stories of centipedes. When he swung his legs over the bed, he discovered that his knees ached. He stretched and got a pain in his back. He grimaced and felt the cut open. *I deserve this. I'm a Halloran.*

The Hallorans had a wrong gene in a wrong chromosome hooked up with another one for quick, one for shrewd, and one for patient, and was passed on from father to son (there were no daughters in the remembered Halloran history) just ahead of the Law—evolution, the only law—because it carried, too, the inevitable side-effect of self-destruction.

Halloran had never met his grandfather, or one of his three uncles, or his great-grandfather, Chesty, who'd had both his hands crushed on a blacksmith's anvil and then had died horribly by hanging himself, getting it wrong with those mangled fingers and slowly strangling. He had a brother he saw once in a while, and three cousins he hadn't seen in years. Only the brother, Reggie, and one of the cousins, Dex, mattered at all to him. Along with the wrong gene and the resulting solitude, the family history got passed down in anecdotes that were meant as lessons. But what he remembered, growing up, was that nobody in the long line of Hallorans had ever made an honest living.

He wished he could have grown up without life's wires and mirrors pointed out, without having always to figure the odds or developing in his own hands the magic that kept Hallorans moving between towns like gunslingers. Halloran pointed an imaginary gun at his temple and pulled the trigger, then collected his things for the beach.

Girl tourists were burning or browning. They turned to the sun like sunflowers, pulling at their tops and bottoms to blur sun lines. They flopped over onto their stomachs or backs, and, from afar, they looked like fleas jumping. Middle-aged men dotted the beach like round white stones.

Halloran spread his bamboo mat where the sun would hit his face square, hoping that sunlight would cure the cut. The scar would fade, but probably make him enough of a pirate to keep him out of the top league. *But top-league players stayed out of back-alley laundries to begin with.*

His brother had prophesied this just a month ago. Reggie had left a note at The Gardner, a Kansas City hotel the family used whenever they found themselves in the Midwest, saying he'd be in Jefferson City for the next week or ten days, and Halloran, with nothing much going, had drifted over.

"You're still playing for nickels and dimes," Reggie had said.

"Good to see you, too."

"I got into a game a couple of months back up in Denver, some newspaper people who flinched at my name when I sat down."

Halloran nodded. "I think I took five thousand before things started going wrong."

"Going wrong?"

Halloran nodded again.

"Five grand isn't much. Things shouldn't go wrong for you."

"For me?"

"I didn't get born with your talent."

"I don't want it."

"You don't have a choice. None of us do. What you *can* do is be the kind of player Dad made you."

"He made me a cheat," Halloran said.

"He made you a mechanic. There's a difference."

"It escapes me."

"It shouldn't."

"We're not getting anywhere here, Reggie." Halloran looked at his brother as if to confirm it. "I think I'll push on." But instead of going out, he'd walked across Reggie's hotel room to the windows and stared out at the hot, white streets of Jefferson City. With his back still to his brother, he asked, "Have you seen Dad?"

"Not for six months. He had a whole town in an immortal lock for a while."

"And then?"

"Then they ran out of money so he left."

"Left for where?"

"San Diego. Or maybe it was San Francisco. I hear he won a yacht, but I don't know if that's true."

"I doubt it is. He hates the ocean."

"How do you know that?"

"We've never lived near water, Reggie."

"Yeah, well, it probably didn't happen. Maybe it was some other fellow named Music."

"Sure, there must be dozens." Halloran turned. "Say hello for me the next time you run across him."

"Say hello, yourself. Leave a note for him at The Gardner. I know he'd like to see you."

"But I don't want to see him," Halloran said.

Reggie didn't push it. "Stay out of the cheap games, Charlie. You don't belong in them. You're not tough like Dex, and even Dex is in some sort of trouble."

"What?"

"I don't know. Uncle William hasn't heard from him in too long a while, and he's worried."

"Dex'll turn up." Halloran had waved goodbye, removed himself from the hotel and Missouri (but phoned in a note to The Gardner, anyway), caught a flight to Los Angeles and another to Honolulu, and then, apparently, managed to forget Reggie's warning. And everything else.

He rubbed his eyes, felt his face with his hand, and flopped onto his stomach, one more flea on the beach, and let his back burn for a while.

Music Halloran had only one eye. Charlie had sung that to himself as a child. It seemed as if it should be the beginning of a fairy tale or, at the very least, a song. *Music Halloran had only one eye. Ta-dum, ta-dum, ta-dee-dum.*

Halloran was twelve before he knew that one of his father's eyes was glass. Even then, Reggie had to tell him.

"He doesn't wink it, does he?"

"I guess not, now that I think about it."

"He doesn't even *move* it, Charlie."

"How'd he lose an *eye?*"

"I don't want to ask him; *do you?*"

Charlie didn't. "You suppose he takes it out when he sleeps?"

"Naw. Something might crawl in the hole."

Of all the ways he knew his dad, it was that sentence of his brother's that left him with his picture of his father. Reggie wouldn't remember it now, probably, but it had stayed with Halloran for more than twenty years. *Something might crawl in the hole. Music Halloran had only one eye. Ta-dum, ta-dum, ta-dee-dum.*

He got up and plowed into the water. The salt stung, but he figured that was part of the cure, too. And besides, he deserved it.

Charlie let the current carry him, as currents had since he'd made his first bad exit in a card game five months before. *Who are you kidding, Charlie? As currents have carried you all your life.* He felt the small tug of an undertow, and farther out there'd be a riptide waiting, but he knew what to do about those.

When the green water turned blue and the undertow tugged at him, he swam parallel to the shore, slowly working out all his aches. From time to time he'd ease in until the swells lifted him and a breaker shot him forward, then he'd swim out of the green and back into the blue again, where the hard work was.

He labored down the coast until he was opposite the nicer hotels. He let himself drift until he got tangled in families standing toe-reaching-deep in the surf. Nicely tired, he made himself heavy and dug his hands like anchors into the fine bottom sand. Each wave breaking above him dragged him a little closer to the shore.

Even as a kid, in some lake or public swimming pool, he had liked to sit on the bottom and stare back up at the light worming its way down from the surface in circles and spirals like liquid, hunting hawks. Hanging here, on the sea bottom, he saw children buoyed up and down like carousel horses, their fat little legs churning, their pink feet flashing in that marvelous light.

He rose in the last of his own last breath, a burst of bubbles, drew in another, and sank again, imagining for a moment that he was a shark, but dismissing that thought physically with a slow watery shake of his head. *Hallorans are clams.*

"Don't underestimate the poker face, Charlie," his dad said. "Don't overestimate it, either. There's men can read the corners of your mouth the same as if you spoke. In fact, we call those corners *tells*. And for God's sake keep your hands still. We've already talked about your eyes."

"Don't overestimate it?"

"If you can keep your face from talking, you can make it talk, too." His father's own expression flickered through half a dozen emotions like a sheet being shaken. "Poker is a game of deception, Son. That's the fun of it. You choose your deception to match the mark."

The water dragged Halloran onto the shelf, where he stood up. A small boy hooted with delight, as if a submarine had surfaced. Halloran reached out and gave the boy's head a rub.

He crossed the hot beach in a hurry, dodging the tourists on their blankets that looked like face cards scattered after a hand, and climbed hot rock steps up to a hotel's outdoor bar. He signaled a waitress.

"Dos Equis."

"Are you a guest, sir?"

"Yes."

"Your key, please."

Halloran patted the wet sides of his swimsuit and grinned sheepishly. "On the beach, with my gear. It's room five-eighteen."

She smiled, as she had been trained. "One Dos Equis."

"And a lunch menu."

"I'll be right back with it."

More people drifted up from the beach as he had. As if he'd started something, another swarm of tourists pushed out from the hotel.

The waitress delivered the menu and his beer, suddenly busy. "Give me a wave when you're ready."

Halloran watched her long tan legs move between the tables, and in a confusion, as if he'd blinked, another pair moved toward him.

The woman joined him as if they'd planned it. She held a glass of something long and white with most of a pineapple crammed into the top. "Do you mind?" she asked, shrugging helplessly at all the full tables.

"No. Please."

She settled into a white plastic chair made to look like wrought iron. Her coppery hair glowed blonde in the seconds before she ducked under the umbrella's shade. "Here on vacation?" she asked.

"Business. You?"

"Business, too, but I live here."

"At the hotel?"

"On the island. This is a conference for mathematicians. My school—Manoa—is hosting it. How about you? What sort of business are you in?"

Halloran gave her his best smile. "Mathematics." He left the smile there. "So help me." He held up an open palm, something he knew civilians took to mean, *Trust me.*

"You're registered, then?"

"No."

"What's your specialty?" It was almost an accusation.

"Probability theory."

She looked at him over her pineapple, unconvinced. "Mine's turbulence."

Halloran nodded as if he understood completely, but she'd be talking shop in thirty seconds and he'd be sunk inside a minute. "I know a little bit about that."

He thought of his dad. "You can run a bluff on anybody if you've done your homework. Know what they're experts in. *Check which way the door swings and what's on the other side when it swings open.*"

"Where do you teach?"

Teach? I'm not even a good student. "I don't."

"How do you put it to work then?" she asked. At his blank look, she said, "Probability theory. What do you do with it?"

"I cheat at cards."

"That's wonderful," she said, laughing. "But really?"

She should have a better laugh, he thought. She had a fine jaw, nice lips, white, even teeth, and a beautiful freckly nose, but her laugh had a honk in it. He'd like to hear it again, all the same.

"I'm a card sharp. That's all the mathematics I know."

She hugged herself. "I see."

"Let me buy you another one of those."

"Piña colada."

"Right."

"I haven't finished this one."

This was the sort of moment Halloran knew well. He'd spent his life manipulating people into and back out of them. The mark is brought to a decision, and so often what Halloran (or anybody else) would find to be a situation without peril or the need for conscious thought, was, for *that* mark, a matter of great importance. He'd seen it a thousand times. The decision at such moments was rarely as insightful as the moment itself. What was there in the situation that caused the conflict? That's what mattered. Understand *that*, manipulate *that*, and the mark was yours. Halloran put his smile back on and let the moment go as a gift to her.

"I've finished this one, now," she said, and Halloran raised his hand for the waitress.

"How do you like the hotel?" she asked him.

"It looks nice from here. Lunch?"

"No, thanks."

He ordered another Dos Equis, a steak sandwich, and "another one of those."

"Piña colada," she said.

The waitress nodded that she knew. "Five-eighteen, wasn't it?"

He nodded.

When the waitress left, she said to Halloran, "You're not in room five-eighteen, are you?"

"No."

"You're stealing."

"Yes. And when you told her *piña colada*, you were stealing, too. It's easy, isn't it?"

The moment was back, but it was a different one.

Halloran signed the bill that came with lunch, and somehow that restarted the conversation.

"What name did you sign?"

"Halloran."

"Is that your name?"

"Yes." He grinned at her surprise. "But my signature is illegible."

◆

Her given name was Lia, the feminine form, her parents decided, of Liam, her twin brother; her surname was O'Donel.

"Only one *n*, only one *l*. Don't ask why."

"Why?"

They were at dinner at the top of the hotel, Halloran in his only suit and a new, electric-blue tie. Lia wore a gauzy, peach-colored dress that made her hair shine.

"Grandfather thought that doubled consonants were pretentious, and two of them were too many, so he dropped both of them. I think he did it so his children and grandchildren and the children after that would have to explain themselves, bringing him into their conversations. It's exactly the sort of immortality he would like."

"Do you? Remember him?"

"Oh, yes."

During their meal and the coffee afterward, she pictured for Halloran a small girl being swept up in those huge arms and hugged to a warm, whiskey-smelling face and, along with her brother, *juggled*, tossed into the air from one hand to another. A Thanksgiving when she was fourteen remained as clear to her now, twenty years later, as it was then. Her grandfather had charged into the house spraying gifts and hugs and had taken her father—her father!—into his arms and cracked two of his ribs in his joy.

"My father is a large man, too," she told Halloran. "It was like mountains colliding, or so it seemed to me."

The two men were capable of violent arguments, even fist-fights, and their tempers sometimes broke windows and tables. Once, during the worst of them, her mother's lovely piano had been shattered, sat on by one or both of the men. The next morning, when Lia's father had brought out his tools to repair the aftermath, her mother had stood in front of it, daring him. As far as Lia knew, the piano still remained three-legged, its ivory keys a jumble on the slanting keyboard.

"But none of us got hurt, ever. And they were too big, too evenly matched, to hurt each other. It was the house that took a beating."

"That must have been something." Charlie thought of the quiet in his house, the discipline, the control that crackled like static between three unhappy bachelors.

Lia accepted a second cup of coffee from the waiter and turned it in her hands. "It was like living in a thunderstorm. And in the sunshine that follows. Grandfather died last year, on his eightieth birthday, and I miss him terribly."

"Mine died before I was born," Halloran said.

"Your father's father?"

He nodded. "But I've never met my mother's father, either. In fact, I don't remember meeting my mother."

"Is she dead, too?"

"I've often wondered."

"Brothers? Sisters?" Lia asked softly.

"No sisters. I have a brother, somewhere. I don't know where he is now. We move around quite a bit."

"That's awful."

He put a smile on it. "That's what happens when the whole family's thieves."

"That isn't possible, is it? Really?"

"It doesn't seem so, does it? Even the uncles and cousins are cheats."

They finished their coffees and Halloran stared at the check. He couldn't bring himself to reach for it and end the evening.

Lia misunderstood his hesitation. "Why do you do it?" she asked finally.

"I'm asking myself that lately."

"You're a strange man, Halloran."

"Yes." Hadn't she been paying attention? "May I see you again?"

She surprised both of them by ducking her head and nodding.

Lia spent a long night wondering what she'd gotten into. What sort of man tells you straight out that he cheats at cards?

A better question, she thought, might be why she'd chosen to sit next to him in the first place. She'd supposed, without really thinking about it, that he belonged with the conference—or at least there was a good chance that he did—but even as she thought that now, she shook her head. Actually, he was the sort of man she supposed *didn't* belong at the conference, and maybe that's why she had taken her drink to his table. She'd seen the cut on his face without really seeing it and had interpreted his troubled look as something other than scholarly.

That didn't explain anything, either. She wasn't attracted, necessarily, to troubled men. She wasn't often attracted to men at all. Dinner with one was usually more than enough. A breeze tugged at her robe, which she belted more tightly. She listened to the palm fronds in her backyard rattle with wind, watched the skin of stars ripple as if it were a sheet tugged by an invisible hand, and those two things together told her why she was drawn to Halloran: the conference was on turbulence, and here it was made real in this strange man.

She went inside and lay down in bed, but got up every forty-five minutes or so to look out at where the dark sea and the phosphorescent lines of breakers would be if it weren't for the houses in the way. An excitement was growing. Into her calm life had come a wind.

Lia almost slept through the one presentation she'd most wanted to hear in the next morning's schedule. Only by hurrying, climbing into jeans and a T-shirt, muttering, "Damn, damn, damn," racing through the streets, then parking where she shouldn't, and rocking her weight back on her heels in the elevator to quicken its drop to the convention floor, was she able to catch the end of the lecture. A tornado, imprisoned on film, was looping again and again through the dark-green streets of Lubbock, Texas, just as it had almost a year before. "And so it is here, in vortices like these," the speaker was saying, "at speeds probably exceeding three hundred miles an hour, that we hope to find the equation that has eluded us."

The enthusiastic applause exacted another "Damn," from her, and then she left to find breakfast. She found Halloran, waving to her shyly from a table draped in pink linen, and set for two on the lanai.

"How long have you been waiting?"

"Since six."

"It's nearly eleven."

"You had to eat sometime."

"I don't normally, you know. Not breakfast. I might have coffee, or a piece of fruit, or take a walk instead." *And I'm not staying at the hotel.* "It's nice to see you." She sat, wondering what she must look like. "I just left a tornado."

"It suits you. Is that mathematics?"

"Tornadoes? Sure. Everything is. Tornadoes are a laboratory of balances and vortices. I told you, didn't I, that turbulence is my specialty? Chaos?"

"I've been in one," Halloran said. "And I ran into chaos yesterday morning."

Lia took the last part to mean her and was pleased. She asked about the other. "Really? Which? I mean, where. When?"

"We were living in Arkansas City, in Kansas. I was fourteen. So that would make it, let's see, nineteen fifty-five. Dad knew it was coming so we spent the morning closing the house, shuttering the windows, boxing stuff up. A bunch of us—all relatives—were in chairs at a card table under battery-powered lights in the basement when it hit. My cousin Dex crept out in the dark while it was going on to steal money from the last pot."

"That's a famous tornado. It tore up Udall and killed nearly a hundred people. How could your father know it was coming?"

"He said the trees had an ambient light. If you knew Music, you'd know to trust that. Ambience is *his* specialty."

"What does music have to do with tornadoes or ambient light, either?"

"Music is my father's name. The only one I know him by, anyway."

"That's lovely—Coffee, please," Lia told the waitress, who nodded and left when Halloran doubled the order. "Strange, a little unsettling, but lovely."

"That's as good a description of my dad as I've ever heard. 'Strange, a little unsettling.'"

"But 'lovely,'" she corrected softly.

"No, he's not that."

The waitress filled their cups and left a carafe.

"You must have a pot of this stuff in you by now."

Halloran shook his head. "I waited for you."

"You've waited since six for a cup of coffee?"

"Waiting's *my* specialty. It's not a sacrifice. I can sleep with my eyes open. I have the patience of a stone."

"You would have made a heck of a model," she said, and colored.

"More like the sculpture. Or the painting. I used to wonder what I'd turn out to be, then I found out that I hadn't a choice. I'm the finished product."

"All fathers shape their sons," Lia said.

"Not the way mine has."

"You resent him."

"You bet. I learned young that we control accident, to a larger degree than is commonly believed, anyway, and that hope is what you've been manipulated into believing just before the cold hand's dealt."

"Then we believe the same things."

"How?"

"At the heart of this new science I'm studying is the idea that there's a rigid order in apparent randomness."

"So God stacks the deck too," Halloran said, and laughed.

"Maybe we all do. Or try our best to, given the opportunity. That's not cheating, that's sense."

"Then I'm the most sensible man you've ever met."

It scared Lia a little that he might be right. "What would you be," she asked gently, "if you'd gotten the choices you think you've been denied?"

"I can't imagine. To a gambler, people are no more than cards to be arranged as you want them, played when they're needed. We call those marks. Marks are what you put on the deck *before* the box is opened—an art in itself." Halloran smiled. "My family's taken it a step further. We no longer have in us any other possibilities. The double helix of our DNA is a gambler's rose."

"A what?"

"A gambler's rose. You must have seen one somewhere. Shops sell note pads twisted in a tight spiral like close stairs. If you take a deck by its opposite corners and exert pressure, the cards spin themselves into the shape of a flower. It's pretty."

"That sounds imaginative to me."

"I didn't invent it. It's also meaningless."

"But don't you see imagination working in anything you've said, Charlie? Isn't that all it is—the ability to envision a future and make it happen? Isn't that what you do—what all of you Hallorans do?"

"Why are you fighting so hard for the side of evil?" he asked quietly. "Not evil, maybe, but *wrong*. You're wrong-betting, Lia, hoping against a positive outcome. It's a smart move in craps, but dumb otherwise.

"The issue is *honesty*, not imagination. All of us can imagine wrong futures—even ugly ones—there's no trick to that. And there's something in all of us, too, that gets a little jump out of seeing them happen. But when that reality comes—and it's been doing more of that lately than it should—we sit back, horrified, and close our eyes." Halloran did that, now. *Too many close shaves lately. Why?* He looked into his empty coffee cup for a moment and carefully turned it over, upside down.

"You're human, Charlie. Nothing worse than that."

"I *look* human," he agreed. "There's a lot of us, these days, in that disguise."

"You're scaring me."

"Good."

2
♣

Music Halloran sat in the lobby bar of the Royal Hawaiian with a chimney glass of ginger ale and watched everybody equally, idly, not looking for action. He left marks on vacation alone as they tended to be more wary and less willing to spend whatever cash they had. And they were quicker to yell foul to the local constabulary. Back home they'd be ashamed to tell Sheriff Billy-Joe-Bob Watkins how they'd sat down in a game with a sharp and lost the savings account, but they had no such inhibitions in a town they'd never visit again.

"Wives," a stranger said, "who can figure 'em?"

Then again, some people can't help being marks. "I beg your pardon?"

"Wives. Mine's upstairs worried half to death about the kids, the same kids that she said if we didn't get away from she couldn't be held responsible if she killed with a rolling pin. Now she's on the phone to 'em—and let me tell you, that's *long distance*—and she's been on the phone for half an hour now with no end in sight. When she's not laughing like an idiot, she's sobbing and asking them to forgive her. Too many coconut-and-pineapple drinks, you ask me. You play gin?"

Doris Day, Music thought, *The Glassbottom Boat.* "I'm waiting for my son, but thanks."

"He going to show up soon?"

"I don't know." And Music didn't. He was in his fifties with two sons in their thirties, and he was still answering cries for help that came in the Hallorans' strange codes. *21.18 North. 157.50 West.*

"That's Honolulu," the clerk at The Gardner Hotel had said over the phone. "I looked it up."

"I got to get my head straight, as the kids say," the man was saying. "What helps do that is a little cards, something friendly, like a penny a point. Back home, I could go next door and chew Tom's ear and we could deal cards for an hour or two and then I'd be fine."

Music, in his light gray suit and carefully knotted tie, couldn't look anything like Tom. How many years has it been, he wondered, since a two-bit hustler had tried a move on Music? He smiled anyway, starting to appreciate a plight the man didn't yet know he had.

"Or I guess we could play for free, just to pass a little time."

"Cards without money?" Music asked, and puckered his lips.

"My thought exactly," the mark said. "I brought a deck down with me." He stuck out a hand. "Henry Brewster. Hank, or Brewsie, to everybody's who's not the IRS. I'm in insurance, but I promise not to say a word about it. Maybe we should move out by the pool."

"My boat could use some more insurance," Music said.

"Your boat?"

"The ketch, out in the harbor."

"Ketch, that's what—three masts?"

"Two."

"That's what? Forty feet?"

"Sixty-three."

"That sounds expensive."

"It is," Music said.

The light in Brewster's eyes was brighter than an amateur's, brighter, even, than his son's when he was ten.

"Well, I promised not to talk insurance, so I won't. And my state's landlocked, anyway, so I don't know much about boats."

"I don't know much about them, either. I just keep throwing money away on the one I've got." Music thought he'd have to shield his eyes.

They found a quiet table outside under a low-hanging, pink-lit palm frond, and Hank opened the worn box he had in his coat pocket and began shuffling. He went over the rules they'd play by—"If that's all right?"—while Music nodded and did his best to look as if he were concentrating.

"Penny a point? Spades are double?"

"That doesn't seem like much," Music said. "But if that'll take your mind off things, I guess it's okay."

"We can go more."

"Dollar?"

"That can get expensive in a hurry," Brewster said. "Just so you know."

"I don't mind. Money is—well—unimportant, just now. But if you'd rather—"

"Dollar a point's fine. Cash? I wouldn't want to have to explain this to the wife. She knows I like gin, but she has no idea I gamble on it. Ol' Tom, back home, and me, we have an arrangement." He looked, oddly, apologetic. "Cut?"

Music waved it away. There's a simple cut that can undo all but the very best of made decks, but as Music watched the man shuffle he was certain Brewster didn't have the skill to make a deck even if he were left alone for an hour under a fluorescent light.

The man had at least the minimum of smarts; he was going to play it straight for a while first to see if he needed to cheat. He did need to, of course, but by the time he figured that out, Music would have him in a hole too deep for light to creep into.

Music knocked early after three draws and collected the cards. Bicycles, but they'd been plastic-coated and washed. Marked, certainly. He could appreciate a good marked deck, but a good marked deck—by definition—never gave any signs. Henry Brewster had plastic-coated a deck he'd probably bought. One thing Music couldn't abide was a lazy crook.

Music fumbled the halves together and bent a card. Recovering, looking embarrassed, he bent another. "Oh, damn, my hands don't work right anymore. I'll get another." He signaled a waiter and gave him a ten to find him another deck. "Anything will be fine."

Brewster looked stricken.

The mark was down nine hundred dollars and didn't know how to escape when a young man took a seat at the next table, barely giving them a glance. Music, in spite of himself, felt a rush of pride and love. Even as a boy, and for all his faults, Charlie had never been underfoot.

Music delayed a double take, then said, "Charlie?"

"Hi, Dad. I didn't want to interrupt."

Music stood up and embraced his son, an act of such warmth it told Charlie this was the too-long-apart routine, the tearful homecoming, and that the old man wanted to be shed of this mark quickly. From the looks of it, that was just fine with the mark.

"Well, good to meet you," Hank said, rising to go. "Mr.—ah—"

"Halloran. Music Halloran. The number you're trying to forget is nine hundred and twelve."

Hank grudgingly brought up a roll of bills, and Music was glad to see that nine hundred took almost all of it.

"I know that name from somewhere," Brewster said, handing the money over.

"You probably do. And after you think about it for a while, you might even remember where you know it from. And next time you play the gosh-darn insurance man from Iowa, you might remember to get the marks to talk about themselves a little, find out who they are and what they're about. Sometimes they'll give you their money gladly, so long as somebody listens."

Music folded the money with one hand and put it in his pocket. "He's an idiot," he said, watching Brewster's broad, plaid shorts disappear into the lobby. "Idiots give us all a bad name."

Charlie had to laugh at that. "What are you doing in Honolulu?"

"I had to see if my new boat sinks. It doesn't, yet. Have you eaten?"

"I'm going to eat later."

"Come along with me, then."

"You thought my note was a cry for help, didn't you?"

"Wasn't it, Charlie? *Twenty-one North, one fifty-seven West,* for Chrissake? That's an S.O.S. in any language. Let's go eat. You can watch me, if you're not hungry."

They were tucked away in a back booth in one of the Royal Hawaiian's dark corners. Charlie watched the new way his father ate, pushing his food over the back of his fork with his knife, European style.

"So, did you have to kill a man to get your face sliced up like that?"

Charlie touched the cut and had to force his hand away again.

His father sighed. "You still light up like an aircraft's lights when you're lying?"

"This time it was chance."

Music coughed. "Chance? Bad brakes on a gasoline tanker? A hurricane? Am I chance? Are you? What sort of son did I raise that you believe in such things?"

"A straight in dice in five passes. Three through the seven."

"You got caught while you were losing?" When his son didn't speak, Music said, "Bad dice are dumb; you can't talk yourself out of that kind of evidence. How'd you get cut? It looks like a razor."

"A window, and they weren't bad dice."

"But you had tops or bottoms on you, didn't you? And that's what made you take the hard way out."

Charlie nodded, the student again, ashamed. *The hard way out.*

"You'll end up like Dex."

Charlie looked up.

"They caught him somewhere on the edge of Arkansas, near Missouri. They whipped him with belt buckles, Charlie, then hung him up in a sack on an old chain hoist and took turns with flat-nosed shovels."

"Is he dead?"

"They don't think he's ever going to wake up." Music sighed—something deliberate, Charlie knew—and laid his fork sideways across a clean plate. "I wonder if you will."

"I'm getting out of the business, Dad."

"Getting out? How about you try getting into it, first?"

"I don't have the talent you think I do."

"You've got more talent in one hand, Charlie, than the rest of the family together. You're a mystery. You're an evolutionary jump of some sort. I don't think getting out is a choice; I don't think you have any options but to start remembering what you've already been taught and start practicing what you already know."

"This is a sentence, then, without parole?"

"Is that how you see it?"

Charlie nodded.

"Listen to me, Son." Music waited for Charlie's head to come up. "Without me, you would have been Henry Brewster—that idiot I was beating at gin. All I've done"—*or thought I'd done*—"is keep you out of the minors. You couldn't have become anything but a sharp; someone or something else rolled those dice first."

"Genetics."

"I think perhaps what's on the other side of that."

"Which would be what?"

Music lifted his little finger. "Design, maybe."

"A woman told me something like that this morning. She called it 'an unseen order in apparent randomness.'"

"Listen to her, then, if you won't listen to me. Who is she?"

"A mathematician," Charlie said.

Music nodded, pushed his plate away, and smiled grimly. "*Design.*"

◆

Reggie took a little under four thousand dollars out of Jefferson City, but the week he spent doing it left him muscle-sore. He called The Gardner for messages and found that the whole damn family seemed to be vacationing in Hawaii, and that the last cousin, Dex, had got damaged in a game in Arkansas. He wrestled a little with guilt about not going down to the hospital in Little Rock—he was that close—checked the flights, figured his expenses, and thought he could just swing it.

Reggie didn't need to see Dex to know a beating or a coma. In one summer in Little Rock, all the surviving Hallorans had found themselves in an accidental reunion of two uncles, three cousins, his father, his brother. Reggie, along with his cousins Dex and Johnny, had prowled the alleys of North Little Rock in the evenings, sliding up and down the Arkansas River, getting into and out of small troubles, gaffing an innocent when they could find one, swindling the stupid, or just beating the locals in makeshift crap games. Charlie had been too young to take along and had stayed up watching the three adults and the eldest cousin shuffling and dealing slowly (the family custom at such gatherings), honing their skills in front of the world's sharpest eyes. Halloranhood, if nothing else, was a grindstone.

They'd come about midnight into a street that lay dark except for one weak green light too high up on a telephone pole to get broken. Under it, two black kids had been pitching quarters. The Hallorans got a dice game going, the neighbor boys went home for their friends, and they'd all squatted on their heels and rolled bones in the street on a night that smelled like metal. Within an hour, the Hallorans had most of the money.

Reggie figured that among the dozen or so players there must have been three pairs of shaved dice, but only one shooter had the bad luck to be holding the pair that was fixed for fives and twos when everybody bet the same way. Johnny called the seven before it was thrown and gave the shooter a look that was supposed to be *Welcome*, but it didn't work that way because the boy's friends hadn't a clue he was cheating them, even though the Hallorans had known it on the second pass.

They stood back while the boy's own buddies beat him. A kid who couldn't have been more than ten grabbed a pipe and socketed it into the back of his head. The skull had sounded like ice being crushed in a towel. Reggie had taken one long look as the boy was pitching forward, turned and ran, his cousins running with him, but he hadn't run fast enough to lose the picture of those blank-but-living eyes. He sure didn't want to see Dex that way now.

The Pacific lay under him like hot, wrinkled tin. The plane's shadow skidded across it somewhere, from wave to trough, but it was too far down to see it. Reggie, with his eyes closed and his head pillowed in the headrest, could imagine it, though, because every day in his life something not quite dark, thrown from a long way away, skipped unfelt across him.

He knew Charlie couldn't remember their mother, but Reggie did, or thought he did. He pictured her as a cast shadow across his life, when he pictured her at all, but mostly she was an unseen presence, an aroma. She smelled, for a reason he couldn't fathom, of chalk.

Reggie still carried an old photograph of her that he'd removed from his father's wallet. In it, her eyes, her smile, her hair, and the grainy texture of her complexion were all dark shades. She must have been about twenty-five when the picture was taken, about thirty at the time of his theft.

Reggie thought back, as Charlie had, to the day he'd straightened Charlie out about their parents. They'd been sitting on the floor, playing a two-handed card game—probably gin—and Reggie had been matching his brother's face with his mother's while he waited for Charlie to discard. Charlie had dark eyes, like his mother's, and light hair, but his nose and chin and thin mouth were somebody else's; not Music's, except perhaps the triangular dimples in his cheeks when he smiled.

"You're staring at me," Charlie had said.

"It's your ears. They're too big."

"Dad says they're Mom's."

"She should have kept them."

Charlie finally discarded.

"You don't remember her, do you, Charlie?"

"No."

"She's not too clear to me, either. I must have been about seven. That would make you three."

"Nearly four," Charlie said.

"Nearly four, then. Maybe I was eight, and you were nearly five. Maybe I was six, and you were two. What difference does it make? You want to see her picture?"

Charlie nodded, and Reggie handed it over. Then Charlie had asked, "How did she die?"

"Die? She's not dead."

"You're lying."

"She's not dead, Charlie."

"I went to her funeral."

"When?"

"When I was two, three, or nearly four."

"I don't remember any funerals, and you don't either."

That's when Music had walked in. He took one look at his sons and flashed through his emotional index file until he found *disgust*. Then he saw the picture Charlie was still holding, and his face changed again, to as close as he ever got to *sympathy*.

"Charlie thinks Mom's dead, Dad."

Music shook his head. "She's not."

"Then why isn't she *here*?"

No answer would ever be good enough for that one. The smell of chalk had closed around him—perhaps around all three of them—and Reggie caught the faint whiff of it again now. He drifted in it and wondered sleepily how many times he'd crossed over or through wherever it was that she lived without knowing.

He slept until the stewardesses moving in the cabin woke him. The big island of Hawaii unrolled underneath him in fields and cattle. Kahoolawe and Lanai rose up off the starboard wing, then Diamond Head on Oahu.

The passengers disembarked down rain-wet stairs onto the tarmac into a heat easier than Missouri's, so soft that it lay on his skin like powder. Breezes tugged at his shirt. He picked up a newspaper on his way to the taxi stand and found Charlie's hotel in the personals.

"Blue Surf," he told the cabbie.

But at the Blue Surf he learned that Charlie had checked out that morning. Reggie considered, then rented the room that had been his brother's and went out to look at Honolulu. This evening's paper would carry a change of address; he was probably rooming with Dad.

The evening paper carried a personal not from Charlie, but from his father. *Look for the Music Hall in the yacht harbor. MH.*

Once Reggie found the yacht harbor, he asked the white-haired man at the chain link gate what slip the *Music Hall* was in.

"Don't know that one. Visiting or member?"

"Visiting."

"Itinerant, then. When she come in?"

"I don't know. This week sometime, I think."

"Power, or sail?"

"I don't know."

The man gave him an exasperated look and leafed through the pages on his clipboard. He shuffled through them twice. "Here she is. Sail. Ketch. She's berthed in one-eight-five."

"Thanks." When the man made no move to open the gate, Reggie asked, "Let me in?"

"Can't, son."

"Can't?"

"Not without permission. The skipper of the boat has to sign you in or give permission."

"I'm his son."

"It's got to say so, here." He tapped the clipboard. "It don't."

"Can I call the slip?"

He looked on the sheet. "Ain't got a phone hooked up." He stared steadily at Reggie, waiting for the next question.

Reggie had one. "Got a ten-year-old kid in there somewhere I can give a dollar to, to run a message out to my old man?"

"Nope. I pretty much do that, but I don't do it for a dollar."

"Five?"

"Ten."

Reggie pushed a bill through the hole. "And tell him to hook up a phone," Reggie said.

"Right."

It took twenty minutes, and the man came back alone. "Skipper says he don't have a son, says you want the owner, and he's not aboard."

"But the boat's there?"

"The boat's there, all right. She must have come in last night, late, or I would have noticed. She's a beaut. Sixty, sixty-two foot, clean lines, teak deck. Half a century old; built in the '20s is my guess. Clipper bow, reverse transom, got to be full-keeled. They knew how to build them in those days. She's still gaff-rigged. Got double-planked mahogany over what's probably steam-bent oak frames. Masts are Alaska fir. Glad to have an excuse to board her. Bet she was built in Maine."

"But I can't go aboard?"

The man narrowed his eyes. "Crew says the man who owns it is in town with his son."

"My brother. A family reunion."

"Uh, huh." The eyes stayed hooded. "But you wouldn't know your dad's boat to look at her. Didn't know she was sail-driven, even."

"Didn't even know the name of it until an hour ago," Reggie agreed. "We're not a close family." He put his hands in his pockets. "That's why we need reunions."

"Well, if you want, I'll leave a note you stopped by."

"Tell him I've got my brother's room at the Blue Surf."

"Brother's room. Blue Surf."

Reggie could tell the man was still uneasy about something so he waited him out.

Finally, the old man said, "You know, you can get around the fence, here, if you're a strong swimmer. But these waters're full of sharks."

"You don't know the half of it," Reggie said.

3
♣

Reggie saw his father first. There's no mistaking that glide, Reggie thought, or the way the gray head swiveled with every other step to take in what was on his blind side. Few others would knot a tie in this heat.

Reggie stopped and bet with himself how many steps his dad would take before he noticed him—he figured six—but he'd forgotten how the combination lock of his father's mind worked, and that Reggie's stopping was enough to cause the tumblers to fall. Music flicked a finger in recognition but didn't shorten his stride.

"You're something else, Dad."

"You're late."

Reggie turned with him and they made their way back to the yacht harbor. "I didn't know we had an appointment."

"Something's up with your brother."

"I know. I talked to him in Missouri a while back."

"Seen the boat?"

"I tried to. They wouldn't let me in without a note from my parents."

"We'll fix that now. Move aboard, there's lots of room."

"I've got a place."

"Move aboard, anyhow. Charlie has."

"He has? Jesus." Reggie knew his brother's mind about their father, and his puzzlement showed. "I've never been able to figure him. I guess, then, I'll catch a cab and get my gear."

Music nodded, that settled. "Let me introduce you, first." At the gate he said, "I'm Halloran. On the *Music Hall*."

"Yes, sir."

"This is my other son, Reggie Halloran. Charlie and Reggie both come on board whenever they want."

"Yes, sir. I'll give 'em passes."

"That's that," Music said. "Let me show you my boat."

They walked for another quarter of a mile, sometimes their steps springing on a crosshatching of piers, past motor cruisers of all sizes. At the end of the longest finger pier lay a two-masted vessel nothing short of lovely.

"That's it?"

"That's it. She's got four staterooms, and one's yours. One's Charlie's. One's mine. I gave the other to the man who captains her. Named Walston. The crew sleeps forward, in bunks."

"How many crew?"

"Three, other than the captain. Only one other, now, and I'm a bit worried about him. Two said they'd get off here, and they have." Music looked at Reggie, figuring his size. "Having the two of you aboard will make me easier."

"What's she worth?"

Why didn't he pick up on my worry? Music, a little sadly, shrugged inside. "The best hand going, same as anything else. It was four queens against aces full when I got her. But she costs more than I can afford; I've had to come out of retirement to pay the slip fees."

"I didn't know you retired."

"Half. I played three or four times a year in the board room of a yacht club in San Diego. I was coasting into my golden years, then I got too smart for myself and won this." He laughed. "Funny all the ways this work can bite you."

"She's beautiful, Dad."

"She is. But I don't like the ocean."

"Charlie said that."

"Did he? How would Charlie know? All he's getting dealt is hearts."

"How's that?"

"He's in love." Music stopped at the gangplank and looked up at the empty masts. The rigging rattled as the boat rocked gently. "She is pretty, isn't she? Let me take you around."

The captain, Walston, trailed them through the staterooms and the salon and then up on deck, confirming everything the old man at the gate had said earlier. Built in 1923, in Portland, Maine, she had a double-planked mahogany hull and a full keel.

"Steam-bent oak frames?" Reggie asked the captain.

"How'd you know?"

"Masts of Alaska fir?"

"You know your boats."

"I don't know anything about boats," Reggie said.

The captain looked to Music for an answer.

"My sons learn things. That's what they're supposed to be good at." But Music felt another rush of pride.

"This is the damnedest family I ever met," Walston said.

"You haven't seen them at work, yet. I've got to talk to you about that. You'll be taking us out on day trips, or maybe a couple of days to the other islands. There'll be other gamblers aboard and a great deal of money. And nobody's to know that my sons are my sons."

Walston shrugged. "I don't talk to the guests unless you make me. My crew I treat like mushrooms." At Music's look, he said, "I keep 'em in the dark and feed 'em nothin'."

"I'm going to raise your salary by half."

"I've died and gone to heaven," Walston said. "Day trips out of Honolulu and time-and-a-half."

"Time-and-a-half's a bribe," Music said. "We're not a family of good gamblers, we're a family of *very good* gamblers."

"But we haven't played together in a long time," Reggie said.

"Too long, apparently. Your brother's forgotten whatever he knew."

"I know."

"He got cut."

"I'm not surprised."

"Three of you," the captain said. "That ought to make the odds more than even."

"They're more than even with just one of us." Music swiveled the dead eye toward him. "If that bothers you, let me know now."

"Boat's all that bothers me, Mr. Halloran. The business in it isn't mine."

"Get a crew that feels the same way."

"When?"

"Don't hire out of desperation," Music said, "but start hiring."

"Then I'd better go ashore."

"I'll go, too," Reggie said. "I'll check out of the hotel and be back for lunch."

"Starboard cabin forward is yours. Charlie's is port forward."

"Where is Charlie?"

"With a woman. He's supposed to bring her aboard tonight for supper."

"Oh, Jesus," Reggie said.

"She's a mathematician."

"Oh, God."

◆

Charlie had come aboard the *Music Hall* with his dad on Sunday night, still stiff-necked.

"You're falling in love, Son. You know how a bug in the deck skews the odds."

"That has nothing to do with the way I feel about my life. This has been coming for a long time, now."

"Move your things aboard and we'll talk it out."

"I've got a date I'm late for as it is."

"Then move in after, or tomorrow."

"I'll think about it."

Music saw that all his son could see were corners so he let it drop. "Let me show you the table in the salon."

He had it built in San Francisco from old cherry, and had the salon redone to match. Music spread his hands as if welcoming the octagonal table, its deep blue felt, the anchored, swiveling chairs upholstered in the same color. "Look at the trays." The chip trays were low and deep, like pockets. "You can remember how much a player has; Reggie can, too; most can't."

Charlie had been seven. He remembered his father saying, "Good chips are marked at their edges in another color. The gambler across from you wants to make a bet you'll call, he counts your stack and figures the highest number you'll accept. *You* know how much you've got, of course." With a look, he'd driven that old lesson home again. "When he wants you out, he makes that same count.

"Don't stack your chips in tens or twenties. Keep 'em ragged. Against the very best, it's an empty play—you worry about pot odds and card odds, not what's in front of you—but you'll find, Son, that you're not up against players like that too often. You can work most usually what I call money odds—the percentage of cash the man's got in front of him. Count the chips' edges. Fish'll make it easy for you."

Charlie, now, put his hand in a tray. "Deep enough to lay a stack on its side out of sight."

"Gives them trouble," his father agreed. "But the table's so damned beautiful, they don't care. Take my seat."

Charlie had to think. Every chair had space behind it and nothing on an opposite wall that distracted. But one got more light from behind, from the wide stairs going up to the deck. That seat would be facing forward with the boat. He looked more closely and decided the seat was a little wider, looked a little more comfortable.

Music smiled. "There's a drawer underneath."

Charlie felt with his hand and found a button. A rack of chips on either side of the chair slid out from under the table. At his left hand, twelve stacks in three pastel shades lay in their deep-blue velvety grooves: creamy yellow, rose, a powdery blue, all flecked at their edges in dark red. At his right hand lay another dozen stacks in darker colors: rich brown, maroon, and forest green, flecked with gold. Charlie ran a fingernail along them and pinched out half a dozen green ones. $1000 was embossed in their centers. He pulled out one of the creamy yellows and saw $5.

"An invitation to spend money," Music said. "The larger denominations are underneath."

He took his son through the staterooms, then up on deck. "There's a game in a couple of days. I'd like you to be in it."

"I've got to think about that, Dad."

"Didn't you say this evening that you wanted out of this?"

"Yes."

"What do you want instead?"

"You've asked before; I still don't know."

"A house, wife, children, honest living?"

"Something along those lines. Something that won't get me killed."

"That all takes money, Son."

"You're telling me to cheat so I can stop cheating?"

Music shrugged.

"You've already said I don't have any choices."

"I don't think you do. But what I think doesn't really matter. If you want to *try* something else—*anything* else—you've got to have a stake, and there's only one way you know of getting that, and the best place you'll ever have of getting it is on this boat in one of my games." Music reached over Charlie's shoulder and pushed one of the chip racks back in. "I'm looking for a game Thursday morning. Go on your date. Think it over. Bring your girl by and let me meet her."

"You want to show off your boat?"

"Actually," Music said, "I'd like to meet somebody who has found a use for math's *theory*. To me, math's always been as hard as concrete."

"If she wants to come, I'll bring her."

"There's not a woman alive, Son, and damned few men, who can resist envying expensive things."

♦

His dad was right. When he'd levered his father's sixty-three-foot ketch into the conversation, it had glittered in the air like a fishing lure. Lia's mouth dropped open, and Charlie half expected to see gills working under her ears.

"A sailboat?"

"It's a little big to be calling it a sailboat."

"A sailing ship?"

"I think it's a little small for that."

"What the hell is it, then?" She'd glowered at him fiercely in a way he was beginning to like.

"It's a yacht."

"Did he steal it?"

"He won it."

"But in your family doesn't that mean—"

"Not always."

"You mean you could make an honest living gambling?"

"It would be harder, but, sure. You've got to be pretty good at a thing before you can manipulate it."

"Well, then." She lifted her hands as if to say, *What's the problem?*

"It's not that easy. Honest gambling would be like carrying a shotgun to go birdwatching. If you've spent your life hunting, could you keep from bringing it up to your shoulder and blasting something pretty into goo and feathers?"

"I don't know," she said quietly. "Could you?"

They'd driven toward the mountains away from hotel lights. They found a small restaurant tucked under an ancient banyan, the last of the evening nestled in its crown in dark purples. The banyan sent its roots down from the upper branches in smooth, snakelike staircases, and a light rain rattled high up in the leaves, but the packed dirt underneath was dry. Charlie reached over the veranda's rail and stroked a polished root. He was at that moment of decision that he'd seen so many times in others, and he realized with some surprise that he was afraid to answer.

The hill was planted with banana palms, and they clattered like plates when a gust shook them. Lia shivered, and, as if that had caused it, the rain came down in a torrent.

Waiters scurried out onto the veranda and began pulling tables back and stacking them against the wall. "Sorry, folks," they said, as if the rain belonged to the restaurant.

"Are you wet?" Charlie asked.

"A little. I don't mind."

Her dress clung to her left arm and breast, and he could see, as if through a frosted window, the lacy top of her bra. She pulled at her dress to unstick it.

"I have to get back to work," she said.

"Now?"

She smiled and shook her head and didn't look at him. "Soon."

"I mentioned Dad's yacht so you'd come see it. It's—lovely."

"I've got a job, Charlie."

"Teaching."

"You say that as if it's not a job."

"I didn't mean that. It just seems that—I don't know—somebody could cover for a day or two. You could give your students another couple of days off. Something. I always thought colleges weren't tied to the clock like everybody else."

"We're tied to the calendar. The other teachers here, the ones from the mainland, have made arrangements for their classes during the conference, but I *live* here. I thought I could do both. I *should* do both." She looked at him shyly. "But I'm not doing either; I'm missing the conference *and* my classes. Somebody could cover in an emergency, certainly—"

"Then let's have an emergency."

She laughed, and he fell in love all over again with that honk. "Can you think of one?"

"I can think of several. There's lights and sirens going off in my head."

"Should I call the chair of my department and tell her that?"

"Would it work?"

She shook her head no.

"Sharkbite, then?"

"They'd want to see the scars."

"Do you have any you could show them?"

She shook her head again.

"A coconut dropped forty feet and landed on your noggin, and you're concussed."

"I'd be dead, and besides, I'm up for tenure next year. A bump on the head would make them worry."

"Even about a mathematician?"

She stuck her tongue out.

"Well, damn it, there ought to be some sort of trouble we can get into in Paradise."

"There's precedent," she said quietly, looking at her hands.

"But that won't keep you from going to work, will it?"

She shrugged.

"Jellyfish," she said, and stretched until the sheets slid off.

"I know, but Christ, Lia." He looked at his watch. "It's four in the morning."

She turned on her side and backed into him. "The excuse I need. Jellyfish would be just right and even somewhat accurate. They leave welts."

They sat at dawn on her small lanai with a breakfast of coffee and cantaloupe. The horizon had pulled up lavender- and peach-colored ribbons and was dropping them one by one like flares over the roofs and into the sea. She lived on the Ewa side of Honolulu, in Pearl City, on one of the steep streets that overlooked the naval base of Pearl Harbor. It was a street of dry, brown yards and bunches of yellow bamboo.

"Everything's scrubbed," Lia said.

Halloran had noticed it, too, when he'd arrived on the island. Mornings, in the soft steam rising from the night's rain, were freighted with garden scents. Somewhere in the black ocean or in the clouds that hovered at the base of the dark hills, a machine was silently at work copying yesterday's plans. It improvised a little, embellishing the original, then with a quiet whir and hum added another morning to its inventory.

"I need some sleep. Look at what dating you has done to my hands." They trembled when Charlie held them out. "You've ruined me."

Lia said nothing.

"And I think I've lost my concentration too."

"Is that bad?"

"It's fatal. What if I drop an ace of hearts into my hand and there's one already lying on the table? That sort of thing can get me killed."

"I guess it could."

"Or say I need a queen, and they're all gone, but I haven't been paying attention."

"Awful."

"Awful, yes."

"You don't really do that, do you?"

"Of course. Dad made us sit through drills every day, remembering which hands had folded which cards."

"I didn't mean that; I meant dropping an ace out of your sleeve."

"No. You want to do that sort of thing, you bring up a cold deck with the card you want on top, and then you just give it to yourself when you're ready."

"You just give it to yourself?"

"That's all."

"If you can concentrate."

"Yes. And you need some sleep, too; you're going to meet my father tonight."

"Music."

"Yep. Him."

"And I have to concentrate for that?"

"Everyone else who's ever met him has thought so."

♦

Charlie and Lia came aboard the *Music Hall* just before sunset. Music waited on deck. The captain had called down to him that guests were arriving, and he'd knocked on Reggie's door and gone up. Reggie joined him just as Charlie and his girlfriend stepped onto the gangway.

"Here's the whole family waiting," Charlie said in her ear. "Watch your purse."

She hit him with it instead, and Reggie groaned to himself and glanced at his father. *Too late*, Music's look said.

Music took her hand and kissed it.

"Oh."

"He turns his fork over when he eats, too," Charlie told his brother. "Where did these European manners come from, Dad?"

"With the boat." To Lia, he said, "The Hallorans are sort of social chameleons."

"It's a beautiful boat. Ship?"

"Boat. I'm not sure of the difference, but I think she has to displace more tons than she does to be a ship."

"How many tons does she displace?"

"I haven't the foggiest," Music said, and smiled. "The captain will know."

"That's an interesting way of looking at things, though, isn't it?" Lia asked. "Defining a thing—or a person—by how much of something else he or she or it displaces. He doesn't weigh a hundred and eighty pounds; he displaces a cubic meter of oxygen."

"We do it with cash," Charlie said. "How much money is that mark displacing?"

"And how much of it can we move from over there to over here. I'm Reggie, the big brother. I understand Charlie has shown you all our family skeletons."

She nodded, embarrassed for some reason. "I'm a bit surprised. I thought you'd be more—I don't know—circumspect. Secretive. That you'd deny it or something."

Music pointed the way to a table set up on the afterdeck. "We are, usually." Music gave his son a look. "More circumspect. But in this game, when the con falls apart, you take your lumps. Charlie's let the cat loose so all we can do now is stand here and say, 'Aw, shucks.'"

"You say 'Aw, shucks' elegantly, Mr. Halloran."

"Music."

"Is that a family name? I've never heard one like it."

"Do you know that my sons, in thirty-some-odd years, have never asked? It took you thirty seconds."

"I'm sorry."

"No, that's not what I meant. It's quite all right. It's a natural question."

"Isn't it just table talk?" Reggie asked. He said to Lia, "It's common to hear a winner say, when he hears the loser declare a lower hand, 'Music.' I always thought, Dad, that's how you got your name."

"It's not."

"Well?" Charlie asked. "How did you get it, then?"

"It's a nickname your grandfather gave me."

Lia's embarrassment was complete. "Please. I'm sorry I asked."

Music waved the apology aside. "My dad was teaching me to deal seconds at about the same age I taught you. I practiced for hours in what today would be called a parlor, much as a kid is forced to sit at the piano for his lessons. My dad liked to have the radio on—he couldn't bear silence—and so I dealt seconds with an orchestra at my back. I can't hear Mozart or Brahms without an immediate and intense memory of those grueling afternoons. Anyway, I was so damned clumsy at it that my dad said it was louder than the music."

Charlie looked at his father strangely. He'd carried the name all those years to remember the lesson.

"How noisy can it be, dealing cards?"

"Do you remember that ace of hearts I told you about?" Charlie asked her. "Keeping it on top until it's wanted?"

"Oh, Lord, he's teaching her," Reggie said.

Lia nodded.

"To do that, you've got to treat the second card down as the top of the deck and deal from there. That's what's called dealing seconds. It makes a noise when it slides out from under the top one."

"Then how do you get away with it?"

None of them spoke.

"Somebody's always rattling his stack of chips," Reggie finally said.

Lia looked at each of them, but stopped at Charlie. "What have I done, here?"

"You've only asked what we all ask. And we never know the answer. In our ears, those seconds come out like gunshots, and we never quite believe we'll get away with them."

"I'd like to hear it."

The sons looked to the father. "After dinner," Music said. "The food's waiting down in the galley."

"You have a cook?" Charlie asked hopefully. "Dad can't cook," he told Lia.

"I'm having it catered."

They ate on deck under colorful paper lanterns the caterers had strung up. Each course was served by small, dark, quick-handed men in white jackets and black trousers who leaped up the steps from the galley, grinned, nodded, and pulled a plate away with one hand while leaving a freshly loaded one with the other.

"I hope it all works," Music said. "I mixed things up a bit—Hawaiian, Chinese, Filipino, even a Gulf Coast dish or two—because I wasn't sure of your tastes."

"It's all wonderful," Lia said.

The center of the table was a jumble of bottles and glasses: white and red wines, champagne in flutes with pastel stalks, a bottle of sake amid a mushroom-jumble of tiny, ceramic, thimble-sized cups, beer in dark, sweating bottles. The food was a jumble, too: sticky, almost-purple poi in halved coconuts; sea anemone eggs on beds of kelp; slabs of grilled swordfish broiled in lemon; huge butterflied Ecuadorian prawns spread open like lobster tails;

a cold, fiery bouillabaisse that made Lia's eyes tear; thin, curling, dark leaves of mushrooms heaped with rice and vegetables; diced squares of chicken in hot pecans—and more and more and more. Perhaps it's how a gambler stacks a deck he's uncertain of, Lia thought. But all of it was heavenly with the champagne.

She looked up after a while and realized that she was the only one eating. The three Hallorans were sitting back from the table with beers in their hands, sitting as completely still as she'd ever seen men sit, with their feet planted solidly and their hands quiet on the bottles.

"Oh, my God, I've made a pig of myself." She hiccupped and put her hand to her mouth in a fruitless attempt to stop another.

Charlie belched quietly and smiled. "I think that was the idea, wasn't it, Dad?"

"It's the boat," Music said. "She seems to carry with it her own rules."

Something dark and furry jumped onto Lia's lap. She let out a little cry and spilled her drink.

"I don't know where he came from," Music said. "Maybe a Filipino dish that didn't get made. Just push him off."

"I will not." Lia reached to rub his ears and rubbed too hard. The cat got down again with a growl. "Oh, dear." Lia looked at Charlie who was wavering a bit at the edges. His left side was pink, his right side blue under those lanterns, and she thought that right down the center he was lavender. "I'm sorry."

"It's a party," he said. "You'll have to take my word for it that we're having a good time; I know you can't tell by looking at us. Hallorans never learned to drink."

"It's easy."

"Not for us. Something inside stops us when our control begins to slip."

"That's lucky."

All of them smiled.

"What did I say?"

"Luck is sort of a joke with us."

"I forgot." Another hiccup caught her, and she honked. They smiled for real this time, and she smiled back. "I want to see—or hear, or whatever—that Halloran magic."

"We can show you in the morning," Reggie said, "if you'd like to turn in."

She shook her head no. "Now, please."

When the caterers, like native bearers, had filed onto deck, balancing on their heads woven baskets that rattled with plates and silverware, and Music had paid them and they had gone, a mist gathered on the water. Music stared at it as if it had the answer and finally said, "All right."

"Oh," Lia said, when she saw the table in the salon lit by hurricane lamps. She sat immediately in Music's chair.

Charlie sat beside her, Reggie took a seat opposite, and Music walked to a cabinet and brought out a new deck. He broke the seal with his thumbnail, peeled the jokers from both ends, and spread the deck face-up in a fan in front of her. Then he walked around and sat next to Reggie.

Charlie lifted one edge of the fan and pushed it so the cards tumbled like dominos, their red backs up. He squared the deck and worked its diagonal corners away from each other until the deck spun on its axis into a gambler's rose. He placed it in her palm with the ace of hearts uppermost.

It swam a little in her vision. "That's it?"

"That's it."

"Now deal those seconds you were talking about."

Charlie took the deck back and waved a hand across it so it was square again. Then, with the deck still facing him, the ace showing, he dealt twenty cards from it. The ace under his thumb never moved.

"I didn't hear a thing."

"He's always been good at it," Music said.

"Did you hear it?"

Music nodded.

"You, too?"

Reggie nodded as well.

"Well, *I* didn't hear it." Then Lia, too, nodded, and put her head down dizzily in a fan of red hair on the dark blue felt.

4
♣

Lia woke to a soft rocking. Morning curled around petals of light that danced in blue patterns against the wall. Water slapped at the boat's hull like an open hand. A diesel coughed.

She scooped her watch from the night table and squinted to focus on its tiny hands. Just eleven. Another lecture—another class—missed. She stretched with the delicious knowledge of an unexpected vacation from everything, and in stretching she awakened a headache. It wasn't fair that something as delicious as champagne should carry such damage with it. She felt bruised.

Unfairness and pain brought the Hallorans to mind, and she got up to shower and dress. "A poker game's nothing more than a genteel mugging," Charlie had told her. "Nobody sits down in one with any other purpose than to take the other fellow's money. At its very best, it's a social occasion because you need people to play it, but it's never *sociable*. At its worst, it's robbery."

That poker was unfair (with Hallorans at the table), and that its unfairness bothered Charlie, was a part of her attraction toward him, but another was something that warred with that buzzer in her mind. "Every woman wants to change her man for the better," her father had told her. "But you never can, sweetheart." *That's probably so, Dad. But it's inviting, nonetheless, to be with a man who wants to change.*

Without knowing he was doing so, and in a different context, Charlie had repeated her father's warning. "The best hand before the draw is most often the best hand after. And the reverse is true, too."

How good was the hand she held now, before the discards? She found a man's white terry cloth robe in the closet, put it on and belted it tightly, aware with a sort of hypersensitivity that she was the only woman among strange men. She found the shower she'd been shown on last night's tour, bolted the door, and tried to let the hot water drive out the hangover.

Fair, unfair. Order, chaos. It was a jumble to her, but her belief in science encouraged another belief, that all of creation had its reason and a reasoning. Even love, perhaps.

Lia's father, standing like a boy in front of his wife's ruined piano and facing a fury she'd never before seen in her mother's face, had seemed to her with all his size to be outmatched. His wife could have toppled him with the right word, but she'd said nothing. And even long after the moment's anger had passed, the piano still hadn't been fixed. Maybe *that* anger, that particular rage, couldn't ever be soothed.

What had that to do with Charlie? Why do I have that memory so clearly in front of me now? If only the throbbing would leave her head, she thought, she could make sense of it.

The water pressure dropped for moment, strengthened once more, and she was reminded that she was on a boat and that water, ironically, was probably precious. She turned off the taps and squeegeed her hair with fingers that felt like paper. She hadn't thought to bring a towel.

The Hallorans were sitting in canvas chairs on the afterdeck in the shade of an awning. When she climbed the steps to join them, Charlie and his brother hesitated, then rose like gentlemen, following Music's lead.

"Good morning," Music said. Reggie nodded at her. Charlie smiled.

"Good morning." She shaded her eyes, then explained the gesture. "It's my brain's gentle reminder not to be so stupid."

"Maybe sea spray will help," Charlie said, pulling a chair out for her. "Dad says we're about to get underway."

She didn't sit. "Underway?"

"Just a trip around the block," Music said. "The captain wants to see what sort of crew he has."

"I should go ashore." Lia tugged at her damp clothes. "And get out of these."

"Bring 'em back and move aboard," Charlie said.

She glowered at him, but he apparently didn't realize she meant it. "I'm not ready for that. Meeting the family's one thing." She smiled with good humor she didn't feel. She supposed it had been logical to put her to bed in the cabin below, but she wished that Charlie had taken her home instead. Charlie should have noticed her embarrassment.

Charlie didn't seem to, but his father did. "I'm sorry that we trundled you off to a cabin last night. Charlie tried to wake you so we could get you into a cab, but—" He spread his hands.

Charlie grinned. "You didn't want your neighbors to see me carrying you over my shoulder through your front door at midnight, did you?"

Had any of that happened, or was Charlie merely playing the hand his father dealt? She smiled again, and tried to make it look as if she did it ruefully. "No, I guess that would have been worse. When I was taking my degrees, I should have taken one in drinking's aftermath."

"Every dumb move has its penalty," Charlie said.

She felt the heat at her throat rising to her ears. Their assuredness made this moment worse. Charlie, on his own, was as confused and uncertain as she, but around his brother and dad he took on an icy surety. She thought, charitably, that this must be the professional in him that even *he* didn't like.

"I'll catch a cab and go back with you, if you like."

The *if you like* undid all the rest. "I won't be good company for hours."

Charlie didn't put up a fight, and that made her angry too.

You're out of control. None of this is as bad as you're making it. She smiled a third time and put her hand out to Music. "Thank you for last evening."

"My pleasure." He shook her hand instead of kissing it. "I hope you do come back and visit."

So he, at least, knew.

◆

Charlie stood with his dad and Reggie as the *Music Hall* made her slow way out of the yacht basin, past the breakwater and the reef, and into the open sea. He thought it strange to be moving without any sound other than the luff of a sail and the clanking, chime-like boat noises. The smell of the sea that he'd always hated disappeared, and he was startled to discover that it was the smell of the *shore*.

When the boat had some sea room, the captain told them to keep an eye out and grab the rails because he wanted to put the crew through their paces.

"We'll be below," Music said, and the captain nodded as if he'd hoped for that.

The Hallorans sat without discussion at the table, the fanned deck still spread on its blue felt, and Music pulled the drawers out to deal those beautiful chips.

"Ten-thousand-dollar freeze-out. Play the cards as they come. Pretend, because you've screwed up recently, that your fingers are broken."

Music lifted out three stacks of yellows and peeled five off each, put those back, leaving twenty, and placed those stacks on the felt. "One hundred." He counted out twenty each of the rose-colored chips the same way—by lopping five off the top. "Twenty-five each for another five hundred." Twenty blue chips. "Blues are fifty; another thousand." Four of the brown chips from the right-hand tray. "Hundred each. Four hundred." Ten of the maroon chips. "Five hundred each; five thousand." Finally, three of the beautiful dark green ones. "A thousand apiece. Ten thousand altogether." He pulled his own chips into the tray in front of him and reached under the table to release a catch. He spun the table's blue center until the other two stacks had swiveled around to his sons.

Music drew a card from the fanned deck. "Cut for the deal."

Reggie won it and said, "Stud," then anted one of the yellow chips and dealt. The three chips lay like a summer cloverleaf on a pond. "This is a beautiful setup, Dad."

"Play cards. It's *meant* to be beautiful. How is it my kids have forgotten everything?"

Showdowns are rare in three-handed games with good gamblers; the hands aren't often contested to the last, as the shapes of them are apparent early, so the game teetered, oddly triangular, and stayed so for hours.

"You sandbagged too long if you had that third king," Music told Charlie.

"If I had it."

"You weren't holding the five of diamonds," he told Reggie.

"Maybe not."

The boat slewed around and began to buck in an uncomfortable chop. Reggie said he was getting sick.

"Walston's doing what he has to so we'll have a smooth ride when the guests arrive."

"It's set up?"

Music nodded. "It's definite for tomorrow. They'll come aboard at nine. We'll sail around the island a time or two, then drop anchor somewhere pretty until their money's gone."

"Who's coming?"

"Three of them. Fellow named Arthur—Vincent's his first name—and his daughter. And a business associate of his I don't know."

"He's bringing his daughter?"

"She plays."

"Christ."

"Family against family. I can't get away with disowning you, Reggie, you look too much like me. But Charlie can be somebody else. And it would help if my son were a little dumb at the game for most of it." He looked at Reggie. "Can you manage that?"

"The idiot son?"

"Distracted son would be better. Your heart's not in it. Get up and look out a porthole once in a while or go up on deck for twenty minutes. I want you to make some good plays late, but I want it to look like a combination of luck and belated concentration."

"You want them watching you."

"Yes. They have to be absolutely certain about me."

"So you're not going to cheat?"

"That's why I have sons. And I don't want you cheating either."

"You want me to do it," Charlie said.

"Unless we can pluck them otherwise. Always remember, boys, we might be able to take them straight up. Lunch?"

Reggie refused, but Charlie and Music built sandwiches in the long galley and took them back to the table. "We need a cabin boy or steward in order to do this right," Reggie said.

"What do you know about the Arthurs?" Charlie asked.

"The old man's a fine player. He's hard and brave. His daughter I only watched for fifteen minutes when she held a couple of hands for him while he was on the phone. She didn't make any dumb mistakes. Big money doesn't scare either of them. She plays to distract."

"Meaning she has a nice body?"

"And not enough clothes?"

"She's not that obvious. In fact, as I remember her, she's quite charming. And, as I never had much of a chance when you were growing up to round out your education with tips about playing against women, I can only hope you've picked up some on your own."

"Charlie hasn't."

"I told Lia I'm a cheat, and she didn't run. I see that as an accomplishment."

"For whom?"

"Did Mom know, Dad?" Charlie asked, ignoring his brother.

"It was pretty hard to keep it from her."

"But you tried, didn't you?"

"Until you boys came along, and I saw in you both our history busting to get out."

"That's what I thought. No wonder she left."

The *Music Hall* sawed around into a quartering sea and began pitching and sliding. They heard Walston bellowing orders, an answer of running feet, the jangle of metal and ropes like a cyclone fence in a stiff wind, then the *whuff!* of a sail filling, and the boat was level again and driving through the water.

"I'm going on deck," Charlie said.

"I did the best I knew how. With all of you. You, Charlie. Reg. Your mother, as well."

"You've never let *us* off that easy," Charlie said, turning from the first step. "You always told us 'I did the best I could' is a piss-poor excuse."

Reggie watched his father after Charlie had gone, looking for a gap in his face, for a clue, for a twitch, or frown, or even a narrowing of his eyes. *Eye*, Reggie reminded himself. But Music picked up the deck and began palming cards.

"What's your best move?" Music asked without looking up.

"The crimp before the cut. And I'm pretty good at seconds."

"Let's see it." He spun the table so the deck stopped in front of Reggie.

"Tell me about Mom. And call Charlie down and tell him, too."

"I hardly remember her."

"Who do you think you're talking to, damn it? You haven't forgotten a losing hand in forty years. I'll bet you could still open your high school gym locker." Reggie even brought a hand up to twist an imaginary dial. "Don't you see, Dad, that Charlie's right? Shucking civilians is one thing, but you can't shuck *us*. *Shouldn't* shuck us."

Music turned so he could fix Reggie with his glass eye, which meant he might be looking somewhere else entirely. "Your mother left when she saw the education I was giving you." Music sighed, though no sound came out. "Bring your brother down here."

Music had kept only one secret from Margaret, and it wasn't gambling. Her father had played in Friday night poker games with the town's power structure, and in a matter of weeks she had from her father's own mouth the sheet, as he liked to call it, on Music Halloran.

She'd known from their second or third date that his engine was cards, that he'd probably won his bright yellow coupe and his nice clothes in poker or dice, that he was too successful, considering the profession he'd chosen, for simple chance to allow.

It had excited her. The test of his love would be his telling her how he made his living and ask her, anyway, to join his life. But they'd married while she was still so much in love that she could forgive all faults, even the one of silence, and then she was a mother almost before she was through being a bride. Secrecy, she understood correctly, was as much a part of Music as his long, delicate hands. And the test of *her* love, she decided, was accepting that.

She'd been able to do that until one evening when a policeman had come to the door to tell her that her husband's father had been murdered up in Norfolk. She called her father, who called a councilman, who told him, who told her, that Music was most likely sitting in a game in The Gardner Hotel, and so she'd gone there and given a bellboy ten dollars to take a message up to him.

She followed the bellboy at a distance, turning one corner after he'd turned another, for the maybe silly but wifely reason of wanting to see her husband at work. If she stood outside the door, she reasoned, she'd be able to see the game in progress through the gap when he came out.

The bellboy knocked and slipped the note under, and Margaret had taken his place and waited. When Music opened the door a long five minutes later, suspicion had already crawled into her mind, and so she pushed it all the way open after he'd begun it and marched past him into a dark room lit only by the hotel's sign outside, up to the rumple-sheeted, sweat-scented bed and the naked, skinny, homely blonde who sat in it, smoking.

The two women had stared at each other silently, then Margaret had turned away, sick.

"'God, Music, she's *ugly*,' your mother said to me, then went home and packed." Music looked at his nails, picked a scab of blue felt from under one, then raised his head and stared in turn at his sons. "And she *was* ugly. I think that's what hurt your mother the most."

"She deserved better," Reggie said.

"Of course she did!" Music lowered his voice. "Of course she did."

"And she's deserved better all these years since," Charlie said. "Her sons should have heard what happened long before now."

"Perhaps. I'm not convinced of that. In any case, that hand's played."

"I never even knew she came from Kansas City," Reggie said. "I've spent half my life coming and going from there."

"We all have."

"She still lives in Kansas City, in her father's old house," Music said. "Under her maiden name."

"Which is?"

"Losen," Music said, pronouncing it like the beginning of lozenge, and laughed softly. "None of us get free of our names."

♦

Vince Arthur took a two-bedroom suite at the top of the Ilikai for himself and his daughter, while Bill Groton rented one a dozen floors down.

Arthur called. "You got ocean or street out your windows?"

"Parking lot. You've got more than one window?"

"Come on up here and see how you ought to be living."

Vince Arthur's suite was the southwest corner of the thirty-second floor, a crescent-shaped curve of rooms that looked out onto the beach at Waikiki and colorful Kalakaua Avenue.

"Down there in the yacht basin there's a boat with my name on it."

"It's got Halloran's name on it, Father," his daughter said. She made a face. "The *Music Hall.*"

"It's going to be *Divine Scent* before long."

"Don't underestimate Halloran," Groton said.

"If I were going to do that I wouldn't have brought you along. You're as good as he is, right?"

"I doubt there's a handful of men as good as Music Halloran. What I told you is that I'm good enough to catch him if he tries something, but you won't need me to do that. He knew my dad, and I'll be sure to tell him that. You'll get a fair game, Vince."

"You're damn right." Vince Arthur turned back to the center of the room and took the three steps down into a sunken seating area. "Pour us some drinks, honey."

"But don't underestimate him, Vince," Groton said again. "He can fleece most of the people you know without cheating."

"Okay, okay. I'll be cautious. But if it's a clean game, I'll win the *Music Hall*."

"I didn't say be cautious." But Groton let it drop.

Vince Arthur had been after Stace Woods for twenty years to sell him that ketch. She was the most beautiful boat at anchor in a harbor city of beautiful boats, and her lines and rigging spoke of more than just money. She was art. At one time, she'd been owned by a senator. Crowned heads had walked her teak decks. And, more than that—though that was a great deal—Vince Arthur had been smitten by her shape in the water the morning he first saw her.

Stace Woods had dangled that boat in front of him at every good chance and had even risked her twice before in card games over the years (although Vince was certain the second time had been a bluff—but what a bluff!), but then he'd had the bad luck or poor judgment to put her up against a pot a third time, against Music Halloran. That time Music Halloran had the goods, and now Stace was in the hospital, dying. The causal relationship between the two events was not lost on Vince.

"Stace had aces full of tens." Vince shook his head. "Only one ace and the two tens showing."

"And Music had four queens. Three of them down. You've told me."

"And you say he did it honestly?"

"You said he wasn't dealing."

"No, *I* was dealing, damn it. But *he* cut."

Groton shrugged. "Great hands happen, I've been trying to tell you."

"I'll have another, Bobbie, if you're still making them." Vince handed her his glass and noticed that Groton's was still full.

"You're Margaret, on this trip," Groton reminded her. "You ought to call her that, Vince. Get used to the feel of it. Get her used to hearing it."

"I don't look like a Margaret."

"Everybody looks like a Margaret. All you have to do to look like a Margaret is to say you are one."

"I don't see why the name of a woman who left him twenty-five years ago is going to shake him up."

"It might not. It probably won't. I doubt you'll shake up Music Halloran with anything less than an earthquake." He shrugged again and walked to the window and looked out. "I worry that you're not taking this game seriously enough, Vince. When he sees me, his eyes are going to get very, very cold and he's going to want a big piece out of each of us."

"It's my money; let me worry about it."

"He'll do his best at that point to help the other players beat us, too. He'll get you in a whipsaw whenever he can. He's going to be *pissed.*"

"There's three of us," Vince said. "Bobbie—"

"Margaret."

"Margaret, then, plays a pretty mean brand of poker, too. He wants whipsawing, we'll give him one."

"Okay, Vince." Groton put his glass on the windowsill. "I'm going down to bed. But think about this overnight: Music Halloran hasn't done anything else with his life but deal cards. He learned it from his dad, who learned it from *his* dad. While you were in college, then on the phone making deals, and later when you were turning the glands of small, furry animals into something a woman would put behind her ears, or while you were on the golf course, or screwing your brains out—excuse me, please, *Margaret*—Music

Halloran was sitting under a bare lightbulb at a green baize table playing poker."

"Then he ought to have a lot more money than he has," Vince said.

"He's got the *Music Hall*," Groton said quietly, then said good-night.

Back in his own room, Groton stared out at the parking lot that was beginning to shine with rain. He wished Vince would let him stay at his own house, just twenty miles away over the mountain in Kailua. "You meet a man with one rain-colored eye," he remembered his father saying, "you watch with both of yours because that's Music Halloran, and he's quicker than a charitable thought."

"He's only got one eye?"

"He only needs one."

Music Halloran was the bogeyman in Groton's childhood, one of the devil's many shapes that looked into a boy's bedroom window or hid in his closet. It was Music Halloran, not his own father, that he had to learn to be good enough to beat.

Groton had met him once at a sort of sharp's jamboree, a mechanic's convention in St. Louis, in 1959. It would be like this in hell, Groton had thought even then, everybody in the same trade needing to beat each other up for a living. Halloran had had a son along with him, or maybe two sons—it was hard to know with all the Hallorans how many there were. The boy Groton had been had looked into that eye, had shaken that skinny hand, and had gone cold. He doubted it would be any different now.

Groton had lied to Arthur that Halloran would know him—he might not even recognize the name—but he had to find a way to convince his employer to take the man seriously, even if that meant inventing a relationship that didn't exist.

Groton hadn't seen Halloran since. Then this perfume magnate had hired him through a friend of a friend to sit in on a big game and keep his eyes open. Groton had learned years ago how to do that.

♦

Music sat with Walston in canvas chairs on the afterdeck, watching Honolulu's lights. The new crew sat cross-legged in a triangle at the bow, playing blackjack on the hatch of the sail locker. Halloran, even at this distance, could hear the slap of the cards.

"Who's winning?" Music asked.

"What's that?"

"The blackjack game. Who's got the money?"

Walston squinted. "One of the new men. Jackson. But he won't have it long. I think Bruman and cards is the reason the other two left, but they didn't say so."

"Could just be Honolulu," Music said.

"Could be."

The *Music Hall* rocked gently, the wind warm even with the light rain that tocked on the canvas awning, and Music felt he could sleep right here. He closed his eyes and breathed in the pipe smoke that hung around Walston's hands.

"You hire him, Captain?"

"Who, Bruman?"

Music nodded.

"Mr. Woods did, just before he handed her over to you." Walston tapped the stem against his teeth twice. "Good sailor."

Music nodded again. He felt a bump at his ankle, then the long body of a cat against his calf, and looked down to see a black cat bang its head again against his ankle. He looked at Walston.

"Ship's cat. Cracker Jack."

"I saw him at dinner the other night." Music remembered Lia's surprised delight.

"He came with the boat."

"So did you. Is he yours?"

"I guess he is," Walston said slowly, "though I've always thought of him as the boat's. But I named him, and I feed him, so I guess he's mine, if cats belong to anybody."

"Cracker Jack?"

"He's got a surprise inside."

Music turned in his chair so he could train his good eye on the captain. "What sort of surprise?"

Walston was uncomfortable now, and Music could tell he wished he'd said nothing. "Mr. Woods didn't like that cat, and the cat knew it. Maybe that's why he stays in the sail locker like he does."

"Why haven't I seen him before now? Why didn't Woods like him?"

Walston drew on his pipe, the red glow of the bowl lighting his palm. He took his time to answer. "He said the cat gave him the creeps."

"How so?"

This new owner, Walston knew, had the patience to go through an interrogation, and locked onto half-answers the way eels did dinner. *Well, why not just say it?* "He's psychic."

"All cats are psychic," Music said, reaching down to rub the cat's ears.

"You believe in that stuff?"

"Of course."

"I don't know whether or not you're pulling my leg, Mr. Halloran."

"There's no money on the table, Captain." Music probed around the cat's neck with his fingers. "He's got some thick scabs. He fight with the rats in the hold?"

"He goes ashore. Fights other ships' cats. Mixes it up with dogs, for all I know. He's a brawler." Walston looked down almost paternally as Cracker Jack rolled over and boxed at Halloran's hand. "I thought, him being black, and you being a gambler—"

"I'm not superstitious, Captain. I never have been. Luck's something you can narrow with skill. Luck's something you can remove entirely in the right circumstances."

"But there is luck."

"Yep. And it comes evenly to us all."

"You like cats," Walston said, pleased.

"My dad said they'd play poker if they were people." Music looked at Cracker Jack, and Walston supposed he was thinking of his father. "They're nothing but patience and deception, and they're the laziest creatures on earth."

"Is that you, Mr. Halloran?"

Music smiled. "Pretty much. My sons have been reminding me lately that I've been a little too lazy, too patient, too deceptive all these years." He sighed. "But at least I didn't raise stupid kids."

"We're of an age, Mr. Halloran. This is the time in life when a man sits on deck under the stars and wonders if he's done just one damned thing right."

"You want a drink, Captain?"

"I didn't think you drank, Mr. Halloran."

"I don't. But the bar below is open, for now. You could bring me up a ginger ale."

The cat, like a dog at his heels, followed Walston below. "You've got some fine scotch, here, Mr. Halloran," Walston called back.

"Whatever you want."

Walston put a ginger ale in Music's hand, and the ice popped and cracked open. "Your sons are giving you hell for the lives you've given them."

"You must have children."

"Three. All girls."

"You get that same grief from them?"

"Every time they have a fight with their husbands, and I'm ashore somewhere they can reach me. 'If we'd grown up like normal people, in a house with a yard somewhere,' they tell me, then whatever troubles they're having would go away."

"Married?"

"The girls? All of them."

"You."

"Not in a long time. Just that once. My wife was swept overboard in a storm."

"I'm sorry."

"So am I. It was my fault. I had too small a boat and too big a sea and too much faith in myself. I should have put in sooner." Walston tasted his drink and let the glass rest in his lap. "You must have been married, too."

Music nodded. "I lost mine the same way, Captain, the way all wives are lost, swept overboard in one storm or another. Or maybe it was the boys and me who went over the side."

"They think so."

"Yes. They think so."

"The younger one—"

"Charlie."

"Charlie. He's got a—disturbance, let's say—inside him, like the cat does. You can see it in the way he holds his hands."

"You could be a player, Captain."

"He's not happy with himself."

"No."

"Had a girl and lost her."

"Yes."

"The other one, though—"

"Reggie."

"Reggie. He's more like you, isn't he?"

"Yes. It's Charlie who's like his mother, even in his looks. They both want to see her again, now, as I guess they have for all these years. They're mad that I've kept her a secret from them. They haven't stopped to wonder why she didn't take them with her when she left, why she chose as she did to leave them with me. Why she hasn't told them where she lives. They should stop and wonder that, shouldn't they? She left everything on the table and walked away, even though the boys—then—were innocent."

Walston's pipe was out so he put it in his pocket. "We're all hard on each other, Mr. Halloran, even when we don't mean to be. And we're even harder on ourselves. The fault we recognized in Eden wasn't pride—hell, it wasn't even disobedience—but that we are the image of God, and God doesn't forgive. He didn't then, anyway, not that one. That's the lesson: *to forgive*, but very few can. How can we imagine ourselves to be more—to be better—than our creator?"

Music stared at Walston for a minute, but when Walston didn't look back, closed his eye. "I guess I hoped she'd try. Or they would. A man's children is all he's got."

"Maybe we're all *God's* got."

"In that case," Music said, "we must break his heart."

The captain had gone to bed and the foredeck was empty when Reggie and Charlie came back aboard. Their father was asleep in his chair. A glass of melted ice he held cradled in his lap had stained the crotch of his slacks.

"We ought to get him up," Reggie said. "We've all got work in the morning."

"He's awake."

Reggie looked again. "His breathing's too regular. He's still asleep."

"No, he isn't. I bet he woke with the first footstep on the gangplank, and now he's listening to us talk about him."

"You ought to have this paranoia looked at, Charlie."

"I'm staring right at it. It looks back at us with one eye. It's the Halloran infection. Always take the edge, no matter how insignificant, so you can do unto others first."

"Dad?" Reggie asked.

Music opened his eyes. Starlight glinted from the glass one. "What time is it?"

"Late," Charlie said.

"Guests come aboard at nine."

"*Guests?*"

"Fish, then."

"Fish coming aboard." Reggie shook his head. "Jesus, Charlie, why can't you see the beauty of this? We can pirate every port in the world."

"Give Dad an eye patch. I've got a scar. If you're lucky, Reggie, you can get a wooden leg or a hook."

"He's been this way all night," Reggie told Music.

"How'd you get that glass eye of yours, Dad?"

"How'd you get all that hatred, Son?"

"We might as well take our money at gunpoint."

"Do you think so? A fish sits down with me, he gets what he deserves, because he is a fish. If a player knows what he ought to—what to look for, what to listen for—then you've got a game with an opponent instead of a victim. That's life; you don't like it, jump over the side."

"I'm going to, when tomorrow's game is over."

"Why not go now?" When Charlie didn't answer, Music said, "It's not me you're angry at, Son."

Reggie turned from one to the other.

Charlie was silent for a minute. "How'd you lose your eye?" he asked again.

"You don't have a right to know everything, Charlie."

"If you've hammered one lesson home to us time after time, it's this one: *Know everything*. Well, now I want to know where your eye went."

"How does a son lose his fear of his father?" Music looked to Reggie for the answer. "I was still scared of mine a year after he died."

"Ever think maybe a son shouldn't be?" Charlie asked.

"That's wrong. Raise a kid that way, and he's afraid of everything else."

"Maybe one day I'll find out. Maybe one day I'll give you a call and say, 'You were right, Dad. My kid's scared of shadows, but he loves me. I think that would be a good trade. Unless Reggie has kids—and it doesn't look like he's going to—I'm the last Halloran, and the next Halloran is going to be honest."

Music had to force the words out. "And what's he going to do with all that stuff in his fingers? What's he going to do when he sees a deck of cards, or a pair of dice, or a *Racing Form*? He's going to itch to gamble, and he's *going* to gamble, and if you haven't done your job to prepare him, he's going to lose.

"You'll have sent him to face the lions without so much as a stick to beat them back with. Being a Halloran, *he has to go to the lions*, Son, even if he goes empty-handed."

"You're not going to tell me, are you?" Charlie pushed away with his hands the disgust he could almost see. "We used to wonder, Reggie and me, how you lost it, but we were afraid to ask. We even used to wonder if you took it out at night, if maybe you dropped it into a glass of water by your bed like a set of teeth so it could look at you while you were sleeping, but we were afraid to go into your room to see. Now, when I need to know, when I'm not afraid of you anymore, you're not going to tell me."

Music stood up, frowning as he did it at a vague pain somewhere, looking tired. "It was poked out with a bicycle spoke when I was six. It had nothing at all to do with any of this." He brushed at the water stain in his lap, then fixed his one good eye on his son. "And you were right, I was awake when you came on board tonight. But you're more right about some things than you are others."

He went below, and after a moment his sons heard his stateroom door close with a click. Then Reggie went down, too, leaving Charlie standing alone on the softly rocking deck with a black cat that had come from nowhere to become suddenly visible.

5
♣

"Guests arriving, Mr. Halloran."

"Thank you, Captain."

Music looked his boys over as they stood in the salon, much as a mother might before she sent them off to make a good impression at a birthday party. "You look good in a tie," he told Charlie. "Decided who you are, yet?"

"Liam O'Donel, a mathematician."

"Damn it, Charlie, you need a job with some money."

"My family's loaded. New money. You know, upstarts."

"Hello, *Music Hall.*"

They heard the captain on deck greeting the players, then their footsteps clattered like a herd of heavy mice as they walked to the companionway. Music, exasperated, said, "We'll have to make it work."

Vince Arthur introduced his daughter, Margaret, and Music blinked and introduced his son, Reggie, noticing with dismay that she, through a feminine or gambler's radar, had fixed his son with *the look*, and that Reggie, in ten seconds, was already two stages into smitten. *My sons are being blown away like chaff.*

"This is a business associate," Vince said. "Bill Groton."

Music stared at the face, but in fact he was staring at the name. "In that case, you're in the same business I am," Music said, and smiled. "I thought you made perfumes."

"I do."

"And do you make perfumes, too, Mr. Groton?"

"We've only met once; I wasn't sure you'd remember me."

"I knew your father. He had quick hands."

"Not quick enough, to hear him tell it."

"Mr. Groton's my insurance policy," Vince said.

"I understand. Is he going to play or watch?"

Groton was angry that he'd already been labeled a piece of furniture, and that his presence hadn't stirred a moment's interest in Music Halloran except for his father, who had just as quickly been dismissed.

"Play," Groton said.

Music's eye wandered across Groton's face like a light. "Very well." Music turned to Charlie. "This is our other guest, Mr. O'Donel."

Sure and begorra, Charlie felt like saying. "How do you do?"

Vince shook his hand. "You might as well know right away, Mr. O'Donel, that I'm playing for this boat. Everybody else here knows it."

"She's a fine-looking craft. If I win it, I'll sell it to you. We don't have a lot of use for boats in Wichita." Charlie grinned to himself; he *would* sell it to Arthur, too, given the chance.

And what do you do in Wichita, Mr. O'Donel? was the question the Hallorans waited for, but it passed unasked. "Are you a gambler, Reg, like your father?" Margaret asked.

Reg. Charlie gave Music a look, but his father's face was stone.

"I'm a gambler, but not like my father."

Vince looked at Groton. Groton's look said, *I told you.*

Walston stuck his head in. "Excuse me, Mr. Halloran. When would you like to get underway?"

"Whenever you like, Captain."

"The tide's right, now."

"Then let's do it."

Music mixed drinks and handed them around, and they went up on deck to watch the *Music Hall* move slowly through the traffic and out of the harbor. Boats hooted at them, and Vince put a proprietary hand on the rail and almost believed she was already his.

"Stud," Margaret said, and dealt the cards. Reggie got the king of hearts; Margaret got the queen of spades. "King bets."

Pay attention to the cards, Music thought desperately, pushing the warning like a mental nail into his son's brain. He wished a curse on the young lady.

She paired her showing queen and the other hands dissolved.

Vince pulled a flat, battered, brushed-aluminum case from his breast pocket and opened it, exposing half a dozen long olive cigars. "Mind if I smoke?"

"Not at all," Music said.

Vince lit one with obvious pleasure.

Good, Groton thought. *Halloran's not a smoker.*

"Care for one?"

"Yes, thanks."

My father, the chameleon, Reggie thought.

"Anybody else?"

"Thanks," Charlie said.

Reggie caught on. "They look like nice cigars; I don't mind trying one."

Though none of the Hallorans smoked, they sent their own clouds up, and Bobbie, who had lived with cigar smoke all her life, coughed softly. Music flicked on the ceiling fan. It spun lazily, moving the cloud around.

"Thank you."

"Not at all."

Groton looked at Vince and saw that Vince understood. Unless he'd brought a supply—and he probably hadn't—he'd given half his ammunition to the enemy. Groton saw with some satisfaction that the Hallorans quickly let their cigars go out in the ashtrays.

"Take the other fellow's play away from him," Groton's dad had been fond of saying. "Most everybody in the world gets by on very

71

few tricks. They never bother learning more than one or two, because learning new things is hard work." Groton guessed that Music Halloran had done the necessary labor and had learned them all.

Halloran raked up the discards and got the deck together by passing his hands over the debris. *Like God creating the world out of chaos*, Groton thought. *Fiat-something-or-other. Let there be order.*

"Seven," Music said, and dealt the two down cards. "The ante's light."

Groton threw in his five-dollar chip. "Sorry."

"Quite all right." Music dealt the up card.

This isn't a time to be daydreaming. But the old devil's hypnotic. His hands don't seem to move, but the cards pack themselves into a deck, then his hands don't move again, but the cards spin out in flat, hard trajectories and land with brakes. He deals left-handed.

"Ace."

"Sorry," Groton said again, and almost shook his head to clear it. Vince smiled tightly, and Groton assumed it was because he thought that Groton was trying to annoy Halloran. "Fifty," Groton said, without looking at his hole cards.

His only caller was Music, showing a ten of hearts. "Fifty better."

"Don't let a player raise an open ace unless he's an idiot you want along," Groton heard his father say so clearly that he could swear his dad was sitting behind him.

"A hundred back."

Music looked again at his hole cards as if he'd forgotten them. He put his hand into the table's pocket and threw out one maroon chip. "Five hundred more."

"Think I'll look."

Music smiled encouragement.

Ace, jack. A pair of aces. "Call."

Groton got Music's ten; Music caught a six of hearts. *Jesus, he's got four hearts, and he's dealing.* "Check."

Music raised an eyebrow. A dark green chip, a thousand dollars. "Call."

His aces got a six of clubs. Music got a four of hearts.

Groton checked.

"Twenty-five hundred."

Groton was being bullied, but didn't know how to stop it. Would Music raise an open ace with only three hearts? Did he have the flush, or had he started with a working straight that had fallen apart? Or did he just have a buried pair that couldn't beat Groton's aces? Had any hearts been folded? *One.*

"Call."

Jack of hearts. *Aces and jacks.* Music got a king of clubs. "Check."

"Five thousand."

They'd each started with stacks of ten thousand, for bookkeeping convenience. The game was no limit, with no limit on the number of raises, and not table stakes—a player out of money would have to buy more chips if he went broke in the middle of a hand. This pot wasn't yet finished and his first ten thousand was almost gone.

Groton felt that every passing millisecond of indecision was revealing what he held, as if some dark-haired woman had stepped from the shadows to peel his cards back one at a time to show them to Halloran.

"Don't think of the chips as money," his dad had said. "They're not money until you cash them. Of course, they never stop being money; you paid for them in the first place. Or promised to." The rules governing strategy were full of such contradictions, as if poker were a parallel reality you stepped into and out of at will, and in between, on the run, you had to somehow reconcile its paradoxes.

"Call," Groton said. The last card down for him was the nine of hearts. "I'll take out another ten thousand."

The chip trays slid out silently and Music pulled up the velvety insides and reached into a hollow underneath. He placed two flat, two-inch squares of brass on the table, then pushed one of them across to Groton. "Me, too," Music said, and kept the other. The chip trays slid back in.

"Check."

Music appeared to be thinking. He looked at Groton's ace, ten, six, jack, and the chip trays slid out again. Halloran brought up another of the ten-thousand-dollar squares. "Twenty thousand."

Music was saying he could beat the straight that Groton's hand promised, *but could he?* If so, he could certainly beat the aces and jacks Groton actually held. What had Halloran been holding when he raised the ace? Three hearts? If so, Music had the flush, and had got it in the first five cards. Three to a straight? With his king and another card—a nine, perhaps, like the one Groton had caught—he might have a straight, and that would win. Pair of kings? With that king up, Music had three of a kind and would win. Pair of aces? Then he had two pair, also, and would have needed to pair that king to win. Three tens, back-to-back-to-back? He might have filled by now—his bet said he had—but even without the full house, Music's three tens would win.

Groton would feel foolish folding this late. It wouldn't be the hand that beat him, but the player. But how could he have folded earlier? Dad, again: *"Don't follow one mistake with another. More money is lost to salvage hurt pride than for any other reason."*

Halloran could win too many ways; two pair was a lousy hand against this kind of money. Groton reached to turn his cards over and stopped. What was it worth—to him, to Bobbie, to Vince—to see how Halloran played? The information from this hand might make the difference in the session, might get Vince his boat. Would Vince pay another twenty thousand for that? If he lost this hand to Halloran—and he now thought he might—would Vince learn anything? And if Groton didn't lose, if Halloran was running a bluff, a call this early could gut him. The sad fact was that Groton would look a hero or a fool, whether he folded or called.

Here was the heart of the game. "Don't rationalize a decision," his father had told him over and over. "If you're doing that, you've already made the wrong one."

"Taking out another ten thousand and calling," Groton said, and in the same breath, "aces and jacks."

"Tens full of fours."

Music had the hand all along that his betting suggested. The anger in Vince's face might as well be spoken. *We've dealt two hands, I haven't played either of them, and I'm down thirty thousand.* Groton looked away from it. "Take out another ten."

"You couldn't have played it any other way," Music said. Groton knew he could have folded—*should* have folded—and probably would have if he'd been spending his own money. *But let's not waste it.* "It's nice to know you had the goods. I didn't think you'd raise my ace with three hearts, and it was hard to believe you had the three tens. *But you did.*" Groton looked at Vince and saw his scowl soften.

"Your cards," Music said.

They took a break at two o'clock for lunch, eating at the covered table, then going up on deck in pairs. Reggie and Bobbie ducked under a boom and staggered forward against the boat's roll to the bow. Vince followed Music aft, where they stood talking in the shadow of the second mast. Charlie and Groton leaned against the stern rail, watching the wake snake behind.

"Tough old bastard, that one," Groton said.

Charlie nodded.

"How do you come to be here, Mr. O'Donel?"

"Oh, you know. You hear things. I wanted some excitement so I asked around, and somebody put me in touch with somebody else, and that somebody else heard there might be a big game in Honolulu on a yacht, and still another somebody else made a couple of phone calls, and here I am."

"It's weird, isn't it?"

Charlie thought he knew what was meant, but he asked, "What?"

"The way things work. Phone calls. Flights halfway around the world. Time zones. Strangers meeting in"—he spread his hands to take in the ocean—"the middle of nowhere to take each other's money. That weird 'somebody else' who's not even involved helping them all do it as a favor." Groton watched the wake. "Do you know Music Halloran?"

Charlie shook his head. "I've heard of him."

"You're meeting him for the first time, then?"

"Yes."

"I met him once when I was a kid. My dad knew him. Let me tell you, you're in the middle of the toughest game you'll ever play."

"I'm holding my own," Charlie said, trying not to make it sound like, *You aren't.*

"Yeah, you can play." Groton looked at Charlie for a moment as if he meant to say something else, or something more, but then turned back to watching the wake unwind like silver thread from a blue spool.

"You, too," Charlie said. "Anybody'd get tangled up in that buzzsaw you did."

"You think so?" Groton laughed. "My dad would hang me by my ears if he saw me making that call. Too many ways to lose it."

"Some time in a man's life, he's got to push free from his dad. You don't know what he would have done. Or if he'd've been right when he did it. Your dad's playing for an employer and wants his boss to see the tough nut that needs cracking, maybe he makes the same play."

"Thanks." Then, "You don't miss a whole lot, do you, Mr. O'Donel?"

"As I said, I'm holding my own."

"How come it doesn't bother you that I'm playing Mr. Arthur's money?"

Charlie considered the question for a minute and thought about a rule of his own that was a distillation of all his father's teachings: *When you can, give 'em one more thing to worry about.* "Well, I look at it this way. Margaret's playing her old man's money, just as you are. That fellow Reggie, being the son, is probably playing Halloran's money one way or the other. If any of the three of you were any good, you'd be playing your own. And I don't think

Arthur made his money at the poker table so that leaves only one gambler any of us has to beat, and that's that 'tough old bastard.'" Charlie looked Groton in the eye. "I don't mind it at all. The money gets looser when there's too many different people making questionable decisions about it."

"Questionable decisions?"

"You make a twenty-thousand-dollar call on aces-up with your own money?" Charlie asked softly. "Of course not. And while it makes you more dangerous," Charlie smiled, "it frees up more of the money."

"I've got the feeling all of a sudden that you're the one to watch out for in this game."

Charlie shrugged.

"You've put me on my guard."

"If you weren't on your guard when you sat down, Mr. Groton, then you don't have the education Halloran—and you—thinks you have. I can beat Halloran. Can you?"

No, Groton couldn't. He'd need a good run of cards, and even then it would be scary. Halloran was in a different class, and maybe this O'Donel was, too.

"He knows how to manipulate a deck," Groton said.

Charlie laughed again. "So do you. That's why Arthur brought you along, isn't it? As long as the two of you are on opposite sides, I'm not going to worry."

"But you didn't know he was a card cheat, coming in, did you?"

"I knew it. I told you, I'd heard of Halloran. How do you hear of him and not hear that?"

"You came anyway?"

"Maybe that doesn't scare me." *Pride, Charlie.*

"*You* suddenly scare *me.*"

Charlie remembered Lia instead of Milo. "Good."

Reggie and Bobbie had their eyes closed. Reggie looked through slits beaded with spray and watched the sea shift in his vision like neon and oil.

"Just lucky, I guess," Bobbie said.

"How's that?"

"Isn't that how the line goes? 'Just lucky, I guess'? You were thinking, 'What's a girl like you doing in a place like this?' and I was giving you the answer."

"I wasn't wondering that at all. I was wondering what *I* was doing in a place like this."

"So salt water makes my radar crooked. Same answer?"

"I don't much like the ocean."

"What's the ocean got to do with it?" She rolled with the boat into his arm, then rolled away again.

"You play poker with your dad often?" Reggie asked.

"Hardly ever. This is a birthday present."

"For the girl who has everything."

"Not quite everything. I'm missing—Why don't you fill in the blank for me."

"Is this a quiz?"

"Of course."

"A purpose."

"A-plus." She brushed damp hair from her forehead and gave him a look of real admiration. "How'd you get it right the first time?"

"You wanted me to say, 'A man.'"

"Another A-plus. You see right through me."

"Uh huh."

"I've been coming on a little strong."

"Uh huh."

"Do you mind?"

"Nope."

"Is it working?"

"Yup."

"Good." She put her hands on the bow rail and stretched.

"Figurehead," Reggie said.

"Have you always been a straight-A student?"

"Let's see how you do."

"All right."

"Figureheads are:"

"Carved."

"And?"

"Wooden."

"And?"

"Beautiful."

"And?"

"Lucky."

"And?"

She faltered. "I don't know."

"Half-clothed. B-minus."

She smiled at him, a lit-up smile from inside, and reached for the buttons on her blouse. She lowered her eyes coyly.

Reggie, with an I-dare-you look, quietly said, "Call."

"I've got the goods," she said, and unbuttoned her blouse. She tucked it into the waistband of her slacks and unhooked her small bra. She pulled it out of an armhole and lifted it over her head with a flourish, then placed her hands back on the rail.

She was slim and hard, and he thought the slabs of her shoulder blades and the knobs of her spine *could* have been carved. Her nipples might have been knots. Reggie stared at them unabashedly. "I'll have to study your answer some, but I've got half a mind to change your grade."

◆

"Oh, Jesus," Vince said.

Music looked where Vince was looking and saw the man's daughter getting undressed up at the bow. "Does she do this often?"

"There's some chemistry between our kids, Halloran."

It looked more like biology, but Music said, "I doubt it."

"She'll be naked in a minute."

"I doubt that, too."

"What the hell's she doing, then?"

"If I had to guess, I'd say she's turning my son's brain to putty. I've got to admit that I've never seen it done this well, though. With such *elan*. She could be a great player, with some training. She's not afraid of anything."

Vince took his eyes off his daughter, finally, shaking his head. Music kept looking.

"What do you want for the boat, Halloran?"

"A million dollars."

"She's not worth a tenth of that."

"To you, she's worth all of that. Value's the most relative concept man's ever devised. You ever play with a bug?"

"A joker? Sure."

"What's a good lowball hand with the bug working?"

"Seven, I guess. Or an eight."

"Six," Music said. "Eighty-five or eighty-six will break even normally, but it loses more often than not with a bug in the deck. On the high side, flushes are more common, and straights, which makes full houses worth that much more, because more often they'll have good hands to beat. Poor players don't adjust to the new circumstances and bet those flushes, straights, and medium eights the same. But hand values change, Arthur. Look at your daughter."

Vince didn't. "So?"

"She knows all that instinctively. She just slipped a joker into the deck. And it's one hell of a card because she's the only one who knows what it's worth." He admired her a little longer. "I wish she were a Halloran."

"Right now, I do, too." Vince was glad that Halloran thought it was a ploy, but at the same time he hated to admit that he didn't know if it was or not. And Halloran's admiration of her would only serve to make him more careful. *I've lost another ace*, he thought. *Like those damned cigars.*

Vince looked at her again, and now she was facing him. She waved her brassiere gaily. "Oh, Jesus," he said again.

His view was cut off as a sail fell between them. The crew jibed the boat badly, and it came around in a clumsy, lumbering turn.

Walston padded up behind Music. He pointed at the girl. "That's not a good idea. Not with this crew."

"Tell her that, Captain."

"Aye, aye, sir." Walston gave Vince a look, then hurried forward.

"He's got daughters, too," Music said.

"Poor man."

They went below again and sat at their places. Clockwise from Music was Groton, Charlie, Vincent, Reggie, Bobbie. The deck lay in front of Charlie.

"Your deal, Mr. O'Donel," Music said.

"Low draw. The wheel's perfect."

"It's strange," Groton said, "that so many right-handed people on this boat deal southpaw."

So Groton had noticed that Charlie, too, dealt left-handed and thought it was time Vince knew it. "How can you be sure I'm right-handed?" Charlie asked.

"I've watched."

Charlie grinned and switched the deck to his other hand in the middle of the deal. The cards still spun perfectly to their targets.

Music, once more, was proud of his son, in spite of the immediate, silent admonition about pride that came as a reflex. Music had learned to deal, of course, from his father—who *was* a southpaw—and Charlie and Reggie had learned from him so they dealt left-handed too, though Reggie, like his grandfather, came by his left-handedness honestly. Music wondered at the circumstances that had made his son learn to deal ambidextrously. He thought of his own grandfather—the boys' great-grandfather—and the story of his mangled hands. Had he missed noticing scars on his son's? He'd certainly missed noticing something in Groton.

Music looked at his cards idly, disliking low draw unless he were in the last betting position, and although he had only two players behind him, neither would give up the position to him easily. He had a rough hand, a pat hard nine, and let it go.

Vince pushed a handful of brown chips into the center, and Charlie called.

"I'll play these."

Charlie hesitated, then drew one. Music thought he heard a second slide out, but that made no sense unless Charlie had arranged two top cold cards and didn't want the first. Was he good enough to do that?

Vince dropped a dark green chip on the table, then a maroon one. "Fifteen hundred."

"Fifteen hundred better."

"All right."

"Eight," Charlie said, and Music wanted to wince.

"Seven." Vince spread his cards and took the pot.

Charlie threw his hand in without showing it and shoved the cards to Arthur. "Nice hand."

What are you up to, Son?

Music watched Charlie take money from everybody in the next four hours, then turn it over to Vince in one way or another, once by whipsawing his own brother unmercifully. Vince began to sit taller, as if he'd been filled with air.

"Dinner?" Music finally asked.

"What time is it?"

"A little after six. And we should decide whether to go back to port."

"Or?"

Music shrugged. "Anchor somewhere, I suppose."

"I'll play all night," Vince said. "What about you, Bobbie?"

Bobbie?

"I'd like to see the inside of the hotel. How far from Honolulu are we, Mr. Halloran?"

"I'll ask the captain."

They stood and stretched, and while Vince poured a drink, Music went on deck to find Walston. When he came down again, Margaret had a drink, too.

"The captain says he can put us in just after sunset, between nine-thirty and ten."

"Oh, that's great."

Vince didn't look pleased. Music wasn't, either. They'd played for nine hours, and the Hallorans only had about ten thousand of Arthur's money, because for some reason Charlie had decided to give it all back. He looked at his son, and Charlie gave his dad the sign for *stand pat*.

"Let's eat a little something and play our way back into port," Charlie said. "I'm tired, too."

Music took him aside in the galley. "For someone who wants a stake, you're making a mess of it."

"Am I? You were about to lose Arthur for good a couple of hours ago. Now he thinks his luck's turned."

"And has it?"

"It's about to." Charlie put his hand on his dad's arm. "I can see the whole deck, Dad."

"Your cards, O'Donel."

Charlie studied them, spread across the table in the throes of the finished hand, then gathered the deck together face-up. He took in the positions of every card, and then, with his eyes closed, studied his memory and shuffled the deck. On the fourth riffle, the five of diamonds fell where he wanted and he offered the cards to Vince for cutting.

He got them back. "Draw. Jacks."

He dealt a pat straight to Groton. Three kings to his father. Four to a flush to Bobbie-cum-Margaret. Three sixes to his brother. Three queens to Vince. And the ace, deuce, trey, four of diamonds to himself.

What was this? Forget the skill in his fingers from all the long years of study; what about the synapses in his brain that fired like tiny pistons and sorted each card, remembered it, and found a place for it in the deck? Wasn't that magic?

Reggie folded his trip sixes when it was his turn, giving his brother a look as he did it, and so the five of diamonds wouldn't be on top, but three cards down. Charlie seemed to be watching himself as if through water, making the appropriate bets, dealing the necessary cards. When it came time to fill his own hand, he dealt, for the first time in his life—or maybe in anybody's—a *third*, and it slid out without a sound.

Charlie looked at the straight flush in his hand—even with the cards disordered—four, ace, three, two, five, it was a beautiful thing—pure, symmetrical—and when Vince's four queens raised Groton's straight and his father's full house, he folded the winning hand. He knew if he chose (or rather, *when* he chose) he could see each hand as the player saw it, from inside that player's own eyes, and could even work the muscles in their fingers that called, raised, folded. Give *this* up? Give up being God?

"I'm going to beat you like a redheaded stepchild, Halloran," Vince said, pulling in the pot his four queens had won. "I'm going to hit you so hard, when you wake up your clothes will be out of style."

"Four queens is a nice hand," Music said. "I won a boat with it once."

Charlie got a glimpse of the bottom card as Groton made the deck—so quickly it was intuition as much as vision—and he cut it into the top, ten cards down. It was dealt to him, and it never helped, but it was the last bit of proof he needed that he could do whatever he wanted. That long genetic Halloran history had finally flowered. He smiled and waited for the deck to come around again.

He went after Arthur seriously by beating up on his daughter and Groton. His brother and dad did the same, whether they were dealing or not, and before the cards had gone around twice, Bobbie retired from the table after losing thirty thousand of her father's money.

Music gave Reggie a signal, and Reggie was only too happy to lose a small fortune to Charlie and follow Bobbie out on deck.

"Four of us," Charlie said, and gave the deck to Vince to cut.

"Three," Groton said. "I'll just watch."

"Play," Vince told him.

"All right, I'll play." Groton was in forty thousand of Arthur's money. Vince was up about ten, which meant with Bobbie's losses, Vince was really losing sixty. Halloran had the thirty Bobbie had dropped, and about ten of Groton's forty; Vince had ten of that same forty, which meant O'Donel was up about thirty with the ten Halloran's son had lost.

Vince needed Groton to play in order to get some of it back, but Groton didn't like the shift the game had taken. Vince was getting gutted through his proxies, but winning big hands of his own, and Groton didn't give Vince credit enough to be cautious.

"Five stud," Charlie said. He'd shuffled the king of diamonds into the top of the deck. He had a king as a hole card and one up— paired, with a four kicking.

Groton had an ace and a queen showing, and he drove it like aces.

Vince showed a nine, ten, not suited.

Music had a six and seven of hearts. To stay in at this point, Charlie knew his dad must have another heart in the hole, one that worked twice in the straight and the flush. Music had been making hesitant calls because he was unsure of his son's play, and he wanted to throw some confusion into Groton.

Groton, unconfused, bet ten thousand. Music stayed. Vince stayed. Charlie raised twenty thousand.

Groton called, but with a hitch in the throw that might mean queens. Music hesitated for a long time, then called too. Vince folded.

Groton's ace, queen got another queen, for two pair or three of a kind. Music caught a heart, the two, that took the straight and the straight flush away from him, but had to be four hearts. Charlie didn't know their hole cards, because he hadn't wanted to. He caught a worthless card, a jack.

Groton bet the open pair of queens. "Take out fifty thousand and bet it."

"Just a minute." Vince looked a little embarrassed. "It's my money."

"That's not news," Music said.

"I want to look at the hand."

"No."

"It's my money," he said again.

"Mr. O'Donel?" Music asked.

"I know he's not playing his own money, and that's all right with me—where the money comes from isn't my concern—but I don't much like the idea of playing against partner decisions." He looked at Vince. "You stake a player, you stake his actions, his judgment."

Groton was embarrassed, too, looking like a kid who'd been caught trying to be an adult. Vince sat back and glowered at Groton, but gave up because he had to. *You'd better win this monster.*

"Take out fifty and bet it," Groton said again.

Music called.

Charlie, showing a king, four, jack, raised fifty thousand.

Groton's embarrassment turned to anger. "The best you've got is a pair of kings."

"I guess that's right."

"It's a dumb raise."

"I want the hearts out."

"It's too late to get the hearts out," Music said.

"Then I want the queens out."

"These queens will knock you into next week. Take out a hundred thousand."

"No!"

Music ignored Vince. He brought up a pile of the two-inch-square brass chips and stacked them in front of him. "It looks as if we're going to need these." He gave ten of them to Groton. He did some figuring on the note pad beside him and gave Vince a twisted smile.

Groton put them all in the pot, then pulled half of them back. "Just call."

"You want to raise."

"My employer's heart's about to fail."

"Some time in a man's life, he's got to push free from his dad," Charlie said again. "Or his employer. You know enough to play the hand like it's worth."

"I'd be easier in my mind about it if you weren't dealing."

"Who do I give the deck to?" Charlie asked softly.

Groton shrugged.

"Do I give it to *you*? To Mr. Halloran? To *your* boss? Tell me, Mr. Groton, do you have any reason to suspect my honesty?"

"Just that dumb bet."

"I think you're seeing ghosts. I don't think you're comfortable with large sums, and it's affecting your judgment. I think if I make this same play in a limit game, to shove those hearts out, you don't think about it twice. And I think, Mr. Groton, that's why you're working for people who have the money."

Charlie put the deck down and leaned forward. "Maybe I don't have you beat right now—I think I do, even if it doesn't look it— but I know enough about the game to know that *the money* can beat a player as easily as the cards. You don't know that, but you should."

"Deal the cards."

"No."

"No?"

"If I win the hand now, you'll accuse me of cheating."

"What *do* you do for a living, Mr. O'Donel?"

"I'm a mathematician."

"These are high stakes."

Charlie nodded. "I'm a *very wealthy* mathematician."

"For Christsake, Groton, I brought you along to tell me this. Is he or isn't he?"

Groton couldn't put a picture to his worry. Finally he had to shake his head.

"Then play, damn it," Vince said. "Deal the cards."

"No," Charlie said. "He's afraid to play the hand the way he should, and he's afraid of my dealing. I want somebody else's fingers on this deck, and I want that raise."

"All right, damn it, my daughter will deal it. Bobbie!"

"I thought her name was Margaret?"

Vince didn't say anything.

"I'll let Halloran's son deal it," Charlie said.

My God, it's brilliant, Music thought, *he'd saved a heart on top and would get his brother to give it to his dad.*

Bobbie came down with Reggie. "What do you want, Dad?"

"Nothing."

"Do you mind dealing the last card?" Charlie asked Reggie, who'd followed her. His little finger flashed out, *top, mine,* and Music sighed to himself.

"All right."

"There's a raise pending," Charlie said. "Fifty thousand. Otherwise, I deal."

"How about a house?"

Charlie looked at Groton's cards, misunderstanding.

"I don't have the money to make *my* raise, but I own a house."

Charlie considered it. Two things could go wrong. Groton's two pair or three queens could turn into a full house on the last card, an eleven-to-one shot most likely. His dad's hand could fill in, too, but then the house would be in the family and Charlie could take it for his split. Both hands were out of his control. All he could do was get Reggie to give him the third king and hope he could do it quietly. Cheating came down to luck, too, sometimes.

"Where is it? This house?"

"Kailua."

"That's—where?"

Groton looked at him strangely. "Other side of the island. Over the Pali. Near Kaneohe."

"*This* island? Hawaii?"

"Oahu, yes."

"How much are you putting against it?"

"The rest of the hand."

Yes! Charlie wanted to say. "No. The hand might go a couple hundred thousand yet." Charlie looked at his dad. "And the hearts might not want it."

"Put it up as a side bet between the two of you," Music said. "Put money in the pot. We'll know in a minute if I'm staying longer."

"All right with you?"

"Okay," Charlie said. "If you raise that fifty."

Groton did. Reggie dealt the last cards. Groton got a ten, Music's heart. Music got a spade. When Reggie dealt Charlie the king of diamonds, he did it quietly.

What a pair of boys, Music thought. We could own the world in a year.

Groton now looked at an open pair of kings and swallowed visibly.

Charlie's glance swept across Groton's stricken face, but didn't stop there; he asked, "How much money *do* you have, Mr. Arthur?"

6
♣

Lia's colleagues wanted to see the jellyfish welts.

John Czurki, a nervous, pasty-complected colleague in math, had been predictably lewd. "Where'd it get you?"

"On the legs."

"Wrap its tentacles around your thighs?"

"Yes, I guess so, John."

"You guess so?" He waggled his fingers. "Any self-respecting jellyfish would make sure you knew it."

"I don't know any self-respecting jellyfish. The ones I work with think the same things about themselves that I do."

John Czurki was hard to daunt. "Portuguese man-of-war?"

"I don't know, Czurki. Slimy, soft, white, repulsive. It had some unspellable name."

And then she'd been free of him but had had to answer questions from those who did care. She'd invented a whole phylum of sea life before noon, then had to talk about it as she was, of course, the world's only expert. *Damn you, Halloran, you've made me a liar. And it's* hard.

She'd been glad to get to her class, having given up attending any more of the conference. Lia stood facing the board, holding a pencil of blue chalk. Her mind had been emptied by what she liked to call a brain cramp.

"They're starting to call it fractal geometry," one of her students said.

"I know that."

When she still didn't move, help came from all sides behind her. "Dr. O'Donel." "University of Hawaii." "Nineteen seventy-one."

"Don't be a wise ass," she said, without any heat. "If any of you manage to pass this course, then graduate, then by some act of God or physics we don't yet understand, go on to become working mathematicians, you'll come to realize that the mind is too fine a machine to be wasting on students. It rebels, once in a while."

"Lorenz," one of her students said.

"Ah, yes. Thank you, Morgan. Lorenz. And Shaw." She began to write. "Right now, this is the province of physics and aeronautical engineering, but in a couple of years it's going to belong to mathematics. It's beginning to look as if we'll refute Einstein's famous statement of faith—that God doesn't play dice with the universe." She turned and mirrored the shock she saw in their faces. "This is an exciting time. The rules are changing. Maybe God does play dice with the universe, but if He does, they're loaded."

And that, of course, had made her think of Halloran, and he'd caused her brain to seize up. "We just need to figure out how."

She scrawled a heading on the board in her big, looping, childish hand, and said, lowering her voice and making it weird— "*Strange attractors.*" The class giggled, and she moved easily into the second half of her lecture.

Lia looked at her watch and put the chalk down, wondering as she did how her students managed to follow the maze she always ended up drawing on the blackboard.

"You've probably forgotten, but you all have papers due next week, and I haven't yet seen a draft from anybody. I don't even know what you're writing on." She looked at their mock-serious, comically horrified faces. "But then, you probably don't either. See me in my office before the weekend."

"It's Thursday, Dr. O'Donel."

"That's a good start, Brian. It's always nice to have a grasp of the calendar. And the alphabet."

She turned them loose. "I mean it. My office. Today or tomorrow."

"Whatever caused you to cancel classes earlier this week has turned you mean," Brian said.

"Be glad the conference wasn't in Minneapolis. Minneapolis in the spring can make murderers."

Her office was still the comfortably cluttered closet that always reminded her how much of her own work she wasn't finishing. Students thought they had it tough, but they had only the one career. "And an easy one at that," she said aloud. She settled back into her swivel chair, more at home than she would be at home.

She dragged her briefcase onto her lap and began unpacking it. The scent of crushed plumeria and orchids that spilled out made her think suddenly of the bottle of her mother's perfume Liam had poured into her hair. It had taken weeks to scrub the scent out, and Lia always missed it a little bit, afterward. She lifted out a lei that Charlie must have tucked between her folders and held it to her lips.

An exciting time, she'd told her students. Science always had been. She imagined the universe to be a cosmic casino where the players walked around and gambled in the fog. Once in a while, the fog lifted for a second and they all got a glimpse of the game.

Do that enough times, and you could hazard guesses at its rules, but you never knew for sure. Physics is like this, she discovered. We get glimpses of the board and impose the rules we think govern it. Somewhere out there, in the world of physics, was a rule like *en passant* in chess that she thought might change everything.

In an odd way, her briefcase was just another example. Reach in to pull out notes and get flowers instead. What would it be like to be married to a master of sleight-of-hand? What might she discover in knowing Charlie that might otherwise forever remain a mystery?

The first of her students knocked and came in.

Lia got home very late, past midnight. She still felt unsettled, as if she were somewhere between fantasy and the world. She wished the house were a mess so she could clean it, put things away in their places, but it didn't need it. And she really didn't have the energy, anyway.

She poured a bath scented with oils, tossed in Charlie's lei, and climbed in after it.

♦

"He didn't take it from me. He got it all from you and my addled daughter."

"He could have, Vince."

"That O'Donel character, maybe. He cut you up. But Halloran doesn't frighten me."

"O'Donel isn't what he seems."

"What do you mean?" When Groton didn't say anything, Vince said, "Do you think he put some moves on you?"

"I don't know. I thought about it all night. I replayed every hand he was in, especially the ones he dealt, and I've got a big uneasiness about him. He made more than a few bad plays that shouldn't have made him money."

"So he's lucky."

Groton shook his head and pushed his breakfast away. He looked out at the water from Vince's lanai. "It's more than that. You can't count on luck the way he did."

"You can if you're lucky."

"Lucky? Those three kings?"

"You don't know that he had three kings."

"We both know he had them. You really want me to call a quarter of a million to show you something you already know?"

"He didn't deal the last card."

Groton nodded. "I'm still working on that."

Vince looked as if he were working on it, too—as he well ought to, Groton thought—but Vince wasn't replaying the hand in his memory. He stared vaguely out in the direction of the yacht harbor, picturing the bare, graceful masts, the teak deck and polished brass, and even seeing, as if in the flicker of an oncoming accident, his nude daughter as a figurehead under the bowsprit.

"O'Donel was right about you and money," Vince finally said. "It's a part of the game you're not comfortable with—your jugu-

lar—and he went for it." He almost laughed. "And tore it open."
Still not looking at Groton, he said, "And luck. You've never had
any, I think, and so you don't understand it as I do. O'Donel was
lucky and unafraid, and those two things beat you. Those two
things will beat almost anybody."

"It's your money, Vince. You believe what you want. But I'm
telling you that his play was wrong too often, and no matter how
much money he says he has, he couldn't live to be as old as he is
playing that badly and still have any of it left."

"How did he do it, then?"

"I don't know."

"Well, I'll see if I can't put your mind at ease, Bill. I owe it to
my bank account to spend some more money finding out for sure.
If there's an O'Donel in Wichita, I'll know it by this afternoon."

"Good."

"And I've never met a boat's crew that won't tell you everything
they know, and some things they don't, for a little cash. Go down
to the gate and ask everybody coming out if they're off the *Music
Hall*."

"I've got to be in Kailua."

"On Monday. This is Friday. I might want another game with
Halloran, and if I do, I want to know what's what." He finally took
his gaze off the harbor and turned it on Groton. "I brought you out
here for your advice, and now I'm taking it. The least you can offer
now is to stay here and see it through."

"And if you find out O'Donel cheated me?"

"Cheated *me*."

"I lost my house."

"I'll buy it back for you, if I have to. I've got the money to exact
revenge, and I'll have enough left for justice. Now you go down
there and send the crew up to me."

Bobbie came out onto the lanai as soon as the door closed behind Groton. She was still in her nightdress, and Vince had to turn
away as the breeze molded it to her. "I wish you had more mod-
esty."

She waved a hand, dismissing the thought as silly. She took her father's coffee. "I waited till Groton left."

"Thanks for small favors."

"What's the matter, Dad?"

"You naked at the bow is what's the matter. You frittering away my money because you got yourself addled, when you should be doing the addling, that's what's the matter."

"*Half* naked," she said. "Good coffee."

"I ought to send you back to San Diego this morning."

"I won't go."

"I know that. You're too much like your mother."

"I'm too much like you. If Mother had been anything like either of us, you never would have married her."

He had to admit she was right. "How serious is this thing with the young Halloran likely to get?"

"Thing?"

"You know what I mean."

"It depends on how lucky I am." She smiled and held the coffee cup under her nose. "It could get pretty serious, Dad. I don't take my clothes off for everybody."

"That's really good to know."

"I like him."

"Great. An heiress—"

"I'm hardly an heiress, Father."

"The unmarried daughter of a rich man is an heiress."

"The unmarried, unbrothered daughter of a *very* rich *old* man is an heiress."

Vince flapped a hand up and down, meaning, *Whatever.* "I want better for you than a drifting card sharp."

"Is that what he is?"

"That's what his old man is. What did he tell you he does for a living?"

"I didn't ask."

"What did you talk about up on deck for two and a half hours?"

"Talk? We didn't *talk*, *Father.* We screwed like weasels in the sail locker."

Vince closed his eyes. "Don't do this to me, Bobbie."

She poured some more coffee and put a warm hand on his. "Sorry. And sorry I didn't play better."

"I didn't see much wrong with your play."

"It *was* hard to concentrate," she admitted.

"For him, too. It's a wash."

Bobbie inspected a fingernail. "I want to see him again."

Vince nodded.

"He'll probably call."

"He probably will."

"I don't want you to scare him off."

"If he's got any sense, he's a lot more scared of you than he is of me."

Bobbie laughed and got up and kissed him on the neck. "I'm going to get dressed and go out."

"You mean you're not going outside like that?"

"*Pbbtht.*"

"Charming."

"It's my upbringing," she said, and walked to her bedroom.

"So what am I supposed to tell him if he telephones?" Vince called after her.

"*When* he telephones, you tell him to telephone again. Jeez, dads don't know anything."

"Dads know everything," Vince said, but only he heard it. "They just don't like to admit any of it to themselves."

◆

"Any of *Music Hall*'s crew gone ashore yet?"

"Don't know."

"Captain? Owner? Guests?"

"Still don't know. I just come on. They don't log out, except the guests."

"Can you tell me the guests that logged out last night?"

"Could."

Groton put his hand in his pocket. "What will it take?"

"Please and thank you and twenty dollars."

"Please take this money, thank you," Groton said, handing him the bill.

"Let's see. *Music Hall, Music Hall.* Three guests signed out at 9:52. Arthur, Arthur, and Groton."

"Should be another, named O'Donel. Maybe a few minutes later."

"Nope."

"Maybe this morning."

The man checked. "Nope." He turned back to the previous page in his log. "Only three guests come aboard, and all three went ashore again."

"How many on the boat?"

"How come nobody says please and thank you anymore?"

Groton handed over another twenty.

"*Music Hall*'s got the captain and three, an' the owner and his two sons. That's seven."

"*Two* sons?"

"That's right."

Groton gave the man a third twenty. "Thank you. I'll wait around for the crew. Do you know them when you see them?"

"The captain, I do. The owner, and his sons. Not the crew."

Groton nodded and went to wait in the shade of a tree.

◆

Bruman had no desire to leave the *Music Hall* until it tied up again in San Diego, and maybe not even then. She was the finest boat he'd ever sailed in, and although the rest of this lot, the new-hires, were green, the captain knew his business. The new owner kept to himself. Bruman could do a lot worse, and he knew it.

His chores done, the crew going ashore, he turned up the radio and rubbed the cat's belly. The cat purred, a sound like a little diesel, then caught Bruman's hand when it got too near a wrong spot.

"Hear that, cat?" Bruman said, nodding to the song. "Watch those claws of yours, you old bugger, or *you'll* be skippin' over the ocean."

He rubbed Cracker Jack again, harder, the fine scars on his hands glinting in the light, and Cracker Jack drew blood and then was gone, hissing.

"Damn things can transport themselves. First here, then somewheres else." He snapped his fingers. *Like that.*

◆

Groton phoned Vince and told him that O'Donel was Halloran's son and said he was sending two men up.

Ten minutes later, the two crewmen, curious about Groton's promise of easy money, knocked on the door of Vince's suite in the Ilikai. Vince gave them a couple of cold beers and asked them to sit.

"Captain Walston seems a fine man."

They nodded warily.

"And the owner, Mr. Halloran."

They nodded again. They'd seen Vince the day before and knew this had to do with the game.

"And his sons."

Another nod from each of them. Their beers were nearly empty already so Vince got them two more.

"How long have his sons been aboard?"

"These beers are good, Mr. Arthur," one of them said. "But it's Mr. Halloran pays our wages."

"I'm not wanting to cross him, either," the other one said.

Vince sat opposite and tried to look friendly. "I'm not asking you to cross him. If a hand or two had gone the other way—you know his business is poker, and the *Music Hall* is a floating gambling game, don't you?"

Curt nods.

"If a hand or two had been different, the *Music Hall* would be mine, and you'd be my crew, and I sure wouldn't want a crew that would cross *me*." He smiled. "But Mr. Halloran's a gambler, and I'm a gambler, and gamblers look for an edge. That's our nature; it's expected on both sides and completely above-board."

The crewmen exchanged glances and drank their second beers.

"Mr. Halloran had a big edge yesterday—almost an unfair one—and I just want to whittle it down a little so the game's more even. Just so it's fair."

They said nothing. Vince decided that friendly was wrong; that sailors were uncomfortable with it. He put on his CEO look and said, "And another fact about gambling is that the players pay for the information they get. Nothing comes free, right?"

One of them grinned. "Right."

"You learn about an opponent—a corporation or a gambler or the guy you're fighting in a bar—one move at a time, and every move you get to see costs you something."

"Right! Usually. There's some you don't see but one move with."

"You know somebody like that?"

"You have another beer?"

Vince gestured to the refrigerator. "Help yourselves."

"Bruman's fast like that. Says he doesn't think the Cap'n likes him much, but."

"But?"

"But he's a damned good sailor'n so he'll have a job as long as he wants it."

"Good navigator, too," the other one said.

"Good at everything," the first one agreed.

"He's not ashore with you?"

He shook his head. "Stays to himself, and stays on the boat. Wouldn't want to go ashore with him, anyway."

Vince pulled a handful of folded hundreds out of his slacks and riffled their edges idly. "Why not?"

"Like you said, every move costs you something."

Vince misunderstood and peeled a hundred off for each of them.

"Thanks. What I mean is, everything about him is scary quick. Just isn't normal, that's all."

"Where's he from?"

"Australia, someplace."

"Why does the captain keep him if he doesn't like him?"

"He was hired by the last owner, he says, the one before Mr. Halloran." The man finished his third beer, and burped. "Good sailor, though, like I said."

"You haven't been on the *Music Hall* very long, have you? Don't know the skipper or the owner very well? Or this Bruman?"

The sailor nodded, agreeing. "Skipper hired us the day after Mr. Halloran's second son showed up. He was still finding his sealegs, and we was *anchored*."

"That would be Reggie?" Vince asked, guessing.

"That's right."

"And the name of the other one?"

"You played cards against him, didn't you?"

Vince peeled off another hundred.

"Charlie," the man said.

Charlie Halloran. So he gave the deck to his brother to deal that third king. "How would I get to talk to this Bruman?"

"Come aboard the boat."

Vince took another layer from his roll of hundreds. "Thank you, gentlemen. Is this enough to make sure this conversation stays private?"

"We got no reason to tell Mr. Halloran any of this."

And good reasons not to, Vince thought.

"An' besides, we didn't say nothin' you didn't already know."

◆

One thing Charlie could do with his new freedom was introduce himself to his mother. *Maybe she remarried. I'll wait to find her when the stink of the slaughterhouse is gone.* Just now, it was still with him.

"One hundred and fifty-three thousand four hundred and ninety dollars," Music had said.

"And my house."

"Fifty one, one sixty-three, each," Reggie said. "Unless we're going to have the house appraised and split it."

"The house was a side bet. But you're welcome to visit once in a very long while."

"You've forgotten the overhead." Music tapped the deck with his foot. "We split a hundred and forty."

Reggie counted on his fingers. "Forty-six thousand, six. That's still a good session."

"You think so?" Music left no doubt he didn't. "You had the fattest fish you'll ever gaff and you threw him back over the side." He frowned. "Some of the scales came off in your hands, is all." He turned his eye on Charlie. "You could have gutted him."

"Maybe."

"Not maybe. I didn't know on your deal if you were giving me winners or second-bests. Imagine what that felt like to *me*. I don't think more than five or six thousand dollars changed hands all night without you arranging it, and I couldn't catch you."

"But you're sure I did?"

"Your eyes still light up, Son. Maybe that's God's way of warning the innocent."

"Predators only eat what they need, Dad."

"Wait a minute," Reggie said. "Do you mean you would have taken more, but you didn't want it?"

"That's right."

"We all could have retired."

"Dad never taught us to hunt in packs. You retire the same as anybody in this business, when your hand slows, or your eye gets cloudy." He touched his face with a hand. "Or when somebody catches you."

"You'll regret it, Charlie," Music said. "You'll go out to your house and find that forty-six thousand dollars will fix the roof and pave the driveway and pay the taxes Groton hasn't, but in a year you'll be hunting around in back alleys for grocery money."

He turned to his other son. "You, Reggie, have good hands. I hardly heard that second, and I was listening for it."

"Groton missed it, anyway."

Charlie blew a breath out. "Some people you can't kill, and some people you can't save. Groton's one of the last kind."

"That pride of yours will get you hanged," his father said.

"No, but shame might. We're all born with the rope in our hands, Dad. The trick is to stay in the open, out from under the trees."

Reggie pointed. "Hawaii's full of trees."

"And ocean. I'll leave the marks to you and Dad. You like the work. To me, it's got a stink I can't stomach anymore."

"You're a self-righteous ass, Charlie," Music said. "I watched you work them. Nobody can get a taste of that and then stop. You're looking for an excuse to chase that young lady. You're proud of yourself for admitting to her who and what you are, but you still haven't admitted it to yourself. Go chase her. Chase yourself, too, and when everybody catches up to everybody, leave word for the rest of us in Kansas City."

Charlie had looked out at the water with the morning lying on it, then at the city that seemed to swim in cloud. "You won't see me again, Dad, unless you're passing through my town." *My town.* He waved a hand at the blurry outlines of Honolulu, as if it were all potential places. "And if you do come through, I'll tell the gamblers who you are." He stood up. "Now let's get to the bank and cash that check so I can have my split and go."

Music stood up, too. "You'd really tell the fish who I am?"

Charlie nodded.

"Then I guess that means you'll have looked around and figured out who they are, doesn't it?"

He'd worked his dad over, but he knew where the blame had lain all along. He'd never *asked*. And Mom had never *looked*. His dad understood both of those things as well as he—better—and his old childish admiration for his father came back to him now, warring with a renewal of his shame, and he heard again in his mind's ear Groton's statement, *tough old bastard.*

Charlie, too, was a tough bastard when he was around the old man. All the Hallorans were tough bastards when they smelled the blood near cards. Lia had seen that and had run. As Charlie's mother must have. As Charlie did. A smart girl, Lia; a rocket scientist. His mother? A down card. Himself?

Charlie's appointment with Groton was at the bank in Kailua on Monday morning. His mind was easy about this end of things; sharps would cheat like middle-aged husbands when they had a hand in front of them, but they wouldn't welch on a bet afterwards. How had his dad put it to Lia? *When the con's up, you say, 'Aw, shucks.'*

He carried a signed note, anyway, duly witnessed by a million-aire, just to be on the right side of the law.

He wondered which poor chump had paid for the house when the Grotons got it. He didn't consider for a second that anybody in that family, any more than in his own, had done any honest work or collected honest wages or signed a check each month for the mortgage. Groton's dad or granddad or uncle had swindled some Hawaiian, maybe taking the house in kind because he was forced to, or maybe, like Charlie, he'd just wanted a place to call home.

He'd have to ask Groton.

Charlie felt a kinship with the man even though he didn't much like him. He knew that if Music had been a poorer teacher, or if his genealogy had left him with less quick in his hands, he might have ended up the same, ill-suited to his work and unfit for any other. *It's all such an accident.* Then he smiled at the enormity of the heresy that thought was to a Halloran.

He tossed restlessly, tired and wired and still wide awake, unac-countably missing the harbor's gentle movement underneath him, remembering Lia in another bed and unable to keep those memo-ries, like photographs, out of his mind.

He regretted, a little, leaving the *Music Hall* so quickly and renting this cheap room. It had such heat in it that he got up and opened the windows to the traffic noise. Somewhere out there on the mainland, behind a cascade of blinds like these, his mother waited. Lia and his mother merged like a double exposure, and as he didn't know what his mother looked like, Lia's face became less distinct.

Standing naked at the window, he held onto the hope that she—both shes—couldn't dislike him any more than he disliked himself.

7
♣

Reggie didn't call Friday afternoon, or Friday night. By Saturday morning, Bobbie was cranky.

"He knows where we're staying, doesn't he?"

"Yes."

"You didn't warn him off or anything, did you?"

"Threaten to have his hands broken? No. I haven't talked to any of them since the game." Vince pulled a piece of paper from his pocket and unfolded it. "I got a call from San Diego; there's no Liam O'Donnell in Wichita. They checked professional organizations and found a Lia O'Donel, one *n*, one *l*, who teaches mathematics, but she's a woman here in Hawaii, and I'm trying to figure *that* out. Maybe a typo."

"He said his name was Liam, Daddy, not Lia."

Vince looked at his notes. This says 'Lia.'"

"Exactly."

"What sort of name is Lia?"

"I don't know. It's an alias. And, anyway, it's not his brother that interests me."

"*Maybe his* brother."

"Most certainly his brother," Bobbie said. "Why do you refuse to believe you've been swindled?"

"Why do *you*?" he asked softly, then immediately regretted it. *Why is it so damned hard to just love each other?* Her mother—his first wife—had waited for those same moments, certain in her heart that he didn't love her and that with time he'd prove it. So he had. "I'm sorry, honey."

new dark-blue slacks. Pink was a good color on him, even with the new burn that made his face shiny.

"Where are we going?"

"Dinner."

"Dinner, where?"

"I've chartered one of those harbor cruises," Reggie said.

"Not really?"

"Not really." His grin said he wasn't quite sorry for reminding her of what she already knew. "I thought maybe you'd had enough of boats for a while."

"I have."

"Me, too. I've got a reservation at a place on top of a mountain where we can look down on the ocean."

"That sounds nice. But let's take a table away from the window."

"Whatever you like. Maybe they have one in the basement."

When they had their drinks, at a table away from the windows, Bobbie leapt into that first new silence, partly because she owed her father something—an apology, perhaps, or maybe still another defense—and partly to prove to them both that this was a good match. "We know that Liam is really your brother Charlie."

She waited expectantly. *Come on, come on. Don't you see that I haven't trapped you? Just nod.*

Reggie was thinking of Lia, how Charlie had told her right up front. How had that turned out? He was thinking of his father, and of Vince Arthur, and of the money they'd taken from him. Did Bobbie have a small caliber pistol in her handbag? Was she wired, with the HPD listening? The hell with it. Reggie nodded.

Bobbie let her breath out. If she asked the next question—*Did you cheat us?*—she was afraid everything would fall apart; and if he volunteered it, it would fall apart, too. "Thursday was such a long time ago it seems to be part of another life. Where have you been since then?"

She saw with relief that he understood and sat back comfortably as he launched into a series of explanations, hour by hour and sometimes minute-by-minute, of his doings since Thursday night.

Reggie had an easier manner than his brother; he was relaxed and funny, and the skin around his eyes crinkled in a way that told her he laughed often. Or maybe he squinted a lot in harsh light. Maybe his brother was funny and relaxed, too, when he wasn't being Liam O'Donel.

"The first thing I had to explain to my father was why you were getting undressed up at the bow," Reggie said.

"Funny. My father asked me the same thing. What'd you tell yours?"

"Told him I was just lucky, I guess."

Bobbie didn't tell him what she'd told Vince.

"Then they wanted to know what we did on deck all night."

"Like a high school date," she said.

"That's what I told them."

"That's not what I meant."

"Kissing. Groping around in the dark. Couldn't get the fasteners unfastened."

"You didn't tell them that?"

"No." He grinned. "Told them I *could.*"

"It's not Thursday night I want to hear about. A girl expects to get a call the next day."

"The next day was a family parting." Reggie looked down at the silverware. "Charlie's getting out." He spun his fork idly. "It didn't go well."

"Families are a difficult business," Bobbie said.

"Especially ours. As you saw, none of us are quite sure who the others are."

"Did you cheat us?" she asked, then both hands flew up to cover her face. "No. Never mind. Don't answer that."

"I'll answer it."

"I don't want you to." *Please, don't.*

"Which?" Although he would have lied easily a couple of seconds before, he wasn't sure now what his answer would be.

"No. Please."

"That question jumped out of somewhere. I don't want it hiding, poisoning us."

"Can I ask it later?"

"If you still need to."

"Let's leave it like that then."

He winked at her. "Friday. Let's see. Friday, I mooned around on the boat after Charlie left and wondered why you didn't call me."

"Ha!"

"It's true. No, it isn't. I mooned around about my brother, Bobbie. And about my mother."

"Margaret?"

"You knew."

"Groton made me do it."

Reggie nodded. "It didn't work. It might have, if we hadn't been talking about her the night before. She's buried business for too many years."

"What happened?"

"The same thing that always happens in this family: somebody doing something he shouldn't and getting caught at it."

"Your father."

"And an ugly blonde."

"Ooh."

"It's the ugly part, apparently, that Mom couldn't forgive."

"No."

"No?"

"I mean yes. Maybe she wouldn't forgive any of it, even if the other one had been Liz Taylor, but that . . . well."

"Charlie put the old man on the ropes until he told us."

"That was the first you heard of it?"

"Yes."

"Why?"

"We never asked before." *We never asked about anything.*

And there she'd been, up at the bow, taking off her clothes. *Jesus.* "I see what you mean about your family."

"Everybody's got secrets," Reggie said. "But we have more than most."

"Part of what all of you do, I imagine." Even though she wanted to avoid the issue, her mouth wouldn't let her. This was her own guilt, her own way of absolving her father of blame.

"Yes. I'm a card sharp, Bobbie."

"I know."

"I'm sorry."

"Me, too."

"I'll give my share back."

She shook her head and began to cry.

◆

"Arthur."

"Yes."

"Bruman."

"Yes, Mr. Bruman."

"My mates say you're payin' for information."

Vince held the phone away for a moment, as if he were about to sneeze. "I'd hoped they had closer mouths."

"No worry. There's things said below decks the air don't hear."

"And you want some of this easy money?"

"That's what all of us want, isn't it, Mr. Arthur? The easy money?" Bruman chuckled. "Isn't that your worry, mate, that somebody's after a lot more of it than me?"

No dumb deckhand, this one. "Maybe. What can you tell me I don't already know?"

"Talkin' ain't what I do best. My mates said you showed an interest in me, which gives me an interest in you."

"Let's meet, then," Vince said.

"Somewhere in town."

"My hotel?"

"Somewhere in town, I said."

"This is my first time here."

"Used to be a bar on King Street," Bruman said, "called Pojo's. If it ain't there, another one is. Ask a cabbie."

"That's not my sort of place."

"Good."

Hard customer. "How will I know you?"

Bruman laughed. "We spent a day on the same boat, mate; I know *you*." He made a sound into the phone like gum popping. "Don't be more than an hour," he said, and hung up.

Most cities were a collision of the ugly and the beautiful, but in Hawaii Vince had assumed the ugly would be less so, or better hidden, anyway. It surprised him that King Street, just a block behind marvelous Kalakaua, smelled like sweat in the gentle heat, and he had to push through a litter of paper and fruit to get to Pojo's.

Inside wasn't any better and smelled worse. He bought two beers and waited. He felt, not heard, the man behind him. "Bruman?" Not liking his own voice, Vince reached for one of the warm beers.

"That's right."

"Let's make this quick."

"All right. You're the businessman. What's on your mind?"

Vince had been thinking for nearly an hour about that. "Do you play poker?"

"Not like you do."

"But you've played?"

"Sure."

"Ever play with a bug?"

"The joker? Sure. I don't like it."

"Good gamblers don't. But very good gamblers do. The very good gambler wants to complicate things whenever he can."

"Throw what his opponents know out of whack."

"Yes."

"You want me to be this bug."

I think I wish he were dumber. "Maybe."

"You do, or you don't, cobber."

"Get one thing straight. I said maybe, and I mean maybe. Halloran knows more about the game than I do, but he's got something I want."

"The *Music Hall*."

"Yes. I don't want to slip a joker into the deck and then have it surprise me. I want to put it where I know I can use it, when I want to use it, *if* I want to use it."

"Barristers call that a retainer, I think," Bruman said.

"Yes."

"You want to be sure of me."

"Yes."

"You want to know I'll run when you call."

"And not earlier."

"Jokers fill in flushes and straights, right? And they're aces?"

"In lowball," Vince said, "they're wild."

"Ah."

The two men drank for a minute, and Vince wished his were cold, but even as rich as he was he wasn't going to pay another five dollars.

"You don't worry that I'm too wild. 'Is he wild *enough?*' is what you're thinking, isn't it?"

Vince nodded.

Bruman leaned back and looked Vince in the eye. "I hold the belief that enough money can buy anything."

"How much for *almost* anything?"

"What, for instance?"

"Sinking a boat, maybe."

"In the harbor, you mean."

"I don't see you as the kind of man who'd pull the plug on himself out in the Pacific."

"Just so we're straight," Bruman said. "In Honolulu?"

"Is the price higher in Honolulu?"

"You bet. It's a damned hard place to run from."

"Is that why you stay aboard the boat, Mr. Bruman?"

Bruman's face got ugly in an instant, which gave Vince a couple of answers. He remembered what the crewmen had said about Bruman's quickness, and he leaned back a little, scared for the first time. Oddly, that fear felt good.

"Boat's my work. Cap'n says we go with the tide, what's he going to do? Look around in the inns and pubs for sailors to yank on the halyards?"

"Sure," Vince said, answering the first part of the question and the unspoken part too.

Bruman picked it up, as Vince knew he would. "All right. How much to sink the *Music Hall*? Here in Honolulu, let's say, oh, a hundred thousand. In San Diego, when we get back, or maybe a week or so after we get back, I'll do it for half that. Both cases, I have the money first."

"Can you ground her on a reef?"

"Not in San Diego." He looked idly at a half-naked girl serving drinks while he thought about it. "Maybe. Depends on the reef and the weather. I'd need charts."

"Do you think you can ground her and make it look like an accident?"

"I guess you don't want anybody killed?"

"That's right."

"People die in shipwrecks, Mr. Arthur."

"Shallow water."

"They don't all of them drown. Some get wood shrapnel in their throats or lungs. Some are pinned by a mast, maybe, and drown when they shouldn't. Maybe the tide pushes a man into the coral and flays the skin off him. Think of that and the salt. Maybe the coral just cuts him, an' leaves the sharks to pull him apart." Bruman raised his hands. "You can't plan how a shipwreck comes out."

"In the harbor, then."

"No way to make that look accidental. If you got diesels aboard, you could do it, 'cause boats blow up now and then. But sailboats don't blow up by themselves too often."

"Fire?"

"Sure. Maybe take half a dozen boats with it. Maybe some more lives, too." Bruman shook his head. "Get me some charts and I'll look at the reefs around here. An' bring with 'em a couple thousand dollars. What do you call that in business? Consulting fees?"

"Yes."

"Tomorrow night."

"All right."

"I'll let you know then if it can be done with any surety. But here's something you probably haven't thought of, Mr. Arthur. Before that boat moves from her slip to go to any place but San Diego, you might be aboard her again."

"What's your point?"

"You've thought of that, have you?"

Vince had.

"Can you swim?"

♦

Charlie called at noon to ask if he could see her, and he sounded so casual about it that Lia almost said, "Sure," without thinking. The ease in his voice suggested that he might live right down the block or had been a childhood friend. *Or that he's the lover you met a week ago.* She'd had to make an effort to remember that she'd left angry, without saying goodbye, *and none of that's apparent in his manner over the phone.*

"When?"

"Lunch?" he asked.

"What makes you think I want to see you?"

"Seven hours in your bedroom. And a couple of nice dinners, and some good talks, and this hole in my heart."

"I'm angry at you."

"And the hole in *your* heart," he said, as if he hadn't heard her.

"You sound pretty sure of yourself, mister."

"I am."

Lia wondered if she could ever get used to Charlie knowing what he shouldn't. "I think . . . I think . . . I think I need to think . . . about all this," she said, and cursed herself for getting tangled up like a schoolgirl.

"Shall I call back?"

"Please."

"Okay.

He hung up without a goodbye and called back before she'd moved away from the phone.

"I'd like to see you. I'd like to explain how I am around my family. Or used to be."

"Used to be?"

"I'm finished with them."

"Oh, Charlie."

"It's not a loss, Lia. It's not as if I picked them in the first place."

"You can't 'finish' with a family. That's why it *is* a family."

"Then maybe we need a new word for what the three of us were. The law probably has a couple. *Nest, den.*"

"I don't like telephones."

"Good. Let me come over."

"You're not letting me think."

"That's always to my advantage."

"Still looking for those, huh? Won't you always be looking for advantages, Charlie, no matter what you say?"

In that same moment of elation, when he'd asked himself with some surprise, *Give this up?* another voice inside him had yawned, and he'd understood. If there's no sport at all, if the game bird or animal is tied to the tree, why hunt? He'd played out the rest of the session with a quiet satisfaction, knowing that his suspicions were true, that the top of his profession was nothing more than boredom.

He said as much to her now, that he'd won the game he'd been looking for all his life.

"I know that," Lia said. "You've won a house."

"*What?*"

"I had a dream about you."

"A good one?"

"No. I was in the bath—"

"That sounds like a good one."

"I was in the bath," she repeated, "and I fell asleep, and I saw you drowning." *You, Liam, one or both of you.* More than that, *I'd drowned with you, with you both,* but she didn't tell Charlie that now.

116

She should have awakened from a dream like that in terror, slouching as she was up to her lips in cold bath water, but instead she had come awake with a calmness she'd been craving for years.

Lia's brother, Liam, had vanished a day before his thirtieth birthday and was presumed drowned. It was her father, surprisingly, who refused to accept his son's death and chose to believe, instead, that he must be a prisoner somewhere in the Yucatan, or that he was an amnesiac, or something, anything, else.

Lia's mother had received the news with a boil of grief that had finally subsided into determination. The chance for great joy had left her, and she acquired a serious face even performing the smallest tasks, as if by carefully cutting a potato or peeling an onion she could balance her loss.

But Lia got the guilt. She assumed, being a twin, that she would be privileged with inside information, that a crack would open in her heart if he were dead, or a conviction that he was alive would follow her. Neither happened. He might, for all she knew, be living happily in one of the Mexican desert states, or in Puerto Rico, or his bones might be sliding up and down the continental shelf; she had no *knowledge* one way or the other. No dreams, either. But how could he be alive?

Liam had been an anthropology student, studying family relationships in a small village on the Pacific coast of Mexico, but when it came time to come home he'd decided to travel a bit. She knew from his letters home that he had stayed a while in Villahermosa and then had gone into Campeche and the neighboring state of Quintana Roo. Then, apparently, he had found his way into Corozal, in Belize, where he'd gotten onto an old gulf freighter.

The flat, green shore of the Yucatan seemed an unlikely place for a shipwreck, but the *Entregar* had broken up off the tiny port of Champoton in calm weather. All of the crew and passengers—and even three horses—all but Liam, had made it ashore.

The hollowness of her brother's absence returned to Lia elliptically, like an unsecured moon settling into a wrong orbit, and she'd felt it again in the bathtub, pulling at her and raising tides. In the dream, she fantasized that he was still with her, or still on the

planet somewhere that had a phone number she could find with as-
sistance, and she could call him up into a visual memory and hold
conversations with him.

He'd come then.

Easy, Li.

"Oh, Liam."

He sat on the toilet seat with his feet crossed at the ankles and
his arms straight at his sides for support. His thick hair was more
yellow than red, but his short beard (one she didn't remember) was
almost orange. His jeans looked wet and very blue. His most dis-
tinguishing feature had always been the long, curling eyelashes that
he—unfairly, instead of she—had been given by their mother; he
batted them at her now until she smiled.

"Oh, Liam," she said again. "Where are you?"

Right here, Li. Turn off the faucets, sunshine. There's enough
water around here without your adding to it.

"I'm not even sure why I'm crying."

You're in love, honey. You've got your hormones in a stir.
You're thinking about marrying a man Papa wouldn't much like,
and—he hiked a thumb over his shoulder—he lives on a boat.

"I'm not thinking of marrying anybody."

Uh huh. Tell that to someone else. We shared a room till we
were seven, and I didn't get my first good night's sleep until they
put a bed up in the attic for me. And it was *hot* up there.

"What's that supposed to mean?"

That you're not a casual sleeper, Li. You've never been any
good at sharing space.

"That's not it."

That's most of it. The rest is sitting up to your ears in water,
thinking about me. You shouldn't; I'm fine.

"I don't know where you *are!*"

I'm right here.

Liam held his arms out, and she sloshed up to hold him, but he
smiled and toppled as if he'd lost his balance. He was turning in a
slow, back somersault the two feet to the ground.

Pike position, he said, crossing his arms and straightening his legs. Look, kiddo, don't be afraid of anything. There's not much in this life—well, that life—that you can choose, and nothing at all that I'll let hurt you. I promise. *Trust me.*

Then he broke into little colored squares and dropped into her bath water like petals.

That had been the beginning of the dream; he took her down with her into the rest of it.

Liam hadn't died alone. He wouldn't have drowned at all if it hadn't been for the Portuguese kid with all the whites of his doe eyes showing, who had pushed down on his shoulders and climbed on top, as if by doing that Liam's feet would somehow reach the bottom. Even while it was happening, Liam had thought, *I'll drown, and what will the Portuguese kid do then?* Strap Liam onto his legs like stilts and pull a few wires and walk ashore?

He'd struggled, of course. He'd thrashed in a panic, finally, and he knew that his killer—but maybe that was too strong a word—would carry for life the scores Liam's fingers had left in his calves.

Lia remembered sinking with him into the ink-dark blackness and growing colder and hearing the *whump!* as the remaining air was forced from the dying freighter—or was it from her lungs?—and then the two of them were spiraling down together with the ship to bump against the bare bottom. A strange, slow rain of objects, some square and some not, thudded down after for what seemed like hours. Lia had turned slowly to look at him, her dead reflection, and saw Charlie, not Liam, looking back. "I have a house," the dream-Charlie had said. "I've just won it in a poker game."

If Liam had jumped from the starboard rail or from the fantail or from the bow—or anywhere at all but from where he had, next to the Portuguese kid—or if he'd jumped five minutes earlier or five minutes later, he'd have bobbed along with the rest of them in the oily water, catching a plank or a Styrofoam-filled box as they had, and he'd have come ashore with the crew and the horses. If the Portuguese kid had been a year or two older, or a better swimmer, or hadn't been on watch all night and awakened so abruptly to such a horror, he might have thought twice before he tried standing on Liam's head.

Lia was crying into the phone, now, telling Charlie of her dream and her brother.

"I'm not going to drown, Lia. I'm not going back aboard the boat. I'm not leaving the island."

"You did win a house then?"

"Yes."

"You surprise me."

"How?"

"I expected you to laugh, or something. Tell me dreams are silly. I thought you'd be more . . . rational."

"I'm always rational," Charlie said.

Perhaps it was the flatness in his voice, each word careful to carry no inflection, that brought her another thought. "Are you *calling* me?"

"What?"

"Are you seeing a bet? A bluff? Is that what you think this is?"

"No."

"Because it's not."

"No. Lia, I believe you. Let me come over."

"No."

"Don't hang up!"

The urgency in his voice stopped her. How had he known she was about to do just that? Had her intentions crept into that small word? Could he, could anybody, hear inflection at that level?

"When I won the house," Charlie said, hurrying, "it was like collecting wages for a show. The best mechanic in the business, my own father, didn't know a thing. I could do anything I wanted. I have, or *had*, no explanation for the way the cards behaved, until now."

"My dead brother?"

"Your dead brother."

She wanted to say, "Come over, then; I love you." She wanted to say, "Goodbye, Charlie; I hate you." The two canceled each other neatly, like Xs in an equation, and she saw her hand replacing the receiver and pulling the phone's plug.

The knock came just as Lia put her hand on the doorknob to go out. Almost too late, she thought, and opened it, and jumped into Charlie's arms.

He steered her back inside until they fell into the furniture. Charlie got up and sat on the arm of her chair, and she twisted around so he could hold her, then slid down the arm and into the seat, and she twisted around some more until the two of them were comfortably jammed together, mouth to mouth, chest to chest. Then the chair's catch broke and they fell back, horizontal, laughing. After a while, with Lia's permission, Charlie slowly undid her buttons.

"We're going to break this chair."

"We already did." The recliner was as flat as an examination table. "It's listing a bit to one side and going down at the bow."

"Get up. It's the only good chair I've got."

"Had," he said, but he allowed himself to be pulled out of it and led into the bedroom.

She fell back onto the bed, only half in her clothing. "Now finish what you started."

"Yes, ma'am." He tugged on her opened blouse, freeing it from underneath her, then bent her arm at the elbow so he could pull it loose by its sleeve. "Aren't you going to help?"

"Uh uh."

Her bra was undone in the front. He worked it off her like a shoulder holster. "I'm sorry about the morning on the boat."

"Shh."

"I took you for granted." Her bra dangled from his hand. "I embarrassed you."

"Shh!"

He wondered if another Halloran had ever been told twice to be quiet.

Outside her window were the sounds that neighborhoods generated: doors closing, children running, cars coming and going. The afternoon sun was on the other side of the building, and the light on this shaded side, through her jade-green curtains, washed the room in underwater colors. He sank down in that green light, the world outside receding, and moved his hands in the slow strokes of swimming.

"Are you really going to move into that house?"

"Yep."

"And then what?"

"I don't know. I have to find what I'm good at."

She reached down and tugged on him.

"Not much of a future there," he said.

"I know you're not impotent. Are you sterile?"

He ignored that. "What'll you pay?"

"I've got some money in savings."

"But what about when that runs out? I need a career, not the part-time work you're thinking of. You'd hire me the way you would somebody to come over and turn your flower beds."

"An apt image," Lia said. "Maybe you can find three or four women with good jobs who'd pool enough of their resources to provide you with a salary. To turn their beds."

"Rich women."

"Old women. Very old women."

"Retirement benefits."

"Vacation pay."

Life insurance, Liam said.

"Income taxes."

She laughed, finding a pun he hadn't intended. "But that's too much like your old work, isn't it? What are you going to do? Really?"

"I don't know. I've never looked past the game I'm sitting in, much less the next one. It's funny, but I've taken paychecks from people working just about every job you can name, and I've never wished to be any of them, and I've wanted to be all of them."

"That's some of why I left as I did, I think," Lia said. "I thought that your work excited me—and it did, for a little while—but I had trouble with the real knowledge of it."

"Me, too."

"Most careers take an education," she said.

"I haven't any. None past high school, anyway."

"Enroll at the University."

"In what?"

"Mathematics. You're a natural. And you'd probably get good grades if you took the right professor."

"I think I've already taken the right professor."

"And you're about to take her again."

"See that it gets on my transcript," he said.

◆

The noise in the harbor wouldn't let Music sleep. He'd grown used to the sounds of boats—their rattlings and clankings, their coughing, growling engines, and even the ballpeen hammering of shod feet on fiberglass decks—but on Saturday nights all the boats threw parties. A dozen different radio stations bounced off the water and didn't blend. Lights and laughter and even the click of ice against glasses carried to the *Music Hall* and kept him awake.

Music finally gave up and dressed in a shirt and slacks and prowled his dark boat barefoot. The black water moved in a slow, oily dance of shifting colors that rode the small chop like living creatures, like dark neon jellyfish.

He glanced up at the cylindrical tower of the Ilikai and wondered if Vince Arthur were standing on his lanai staring back, trying to pick out the ketch from the clutter. *It's this one, Arthur.* That a boat named *Music Hall* would be the only one in port without a party was an irony Music appreciated.

Music. His boys in their whole lives hadn't asked where he'd got the name. Then, when they'd been pushed into it by Charlie's girl, they'd failed to ask his real one, the name he kept underneath it. *It's Kenneth*, he said silently. The shape of it was vague and uncomfortable in his mind's ear.

Walston had known this unease, this regret. There comes a time when a man looks up at the stars and wonders if he's done anything right, and Music knew he was at that moment now. He hated the self-pity, had hidden it, and tried on a lie to see how it would fit. *You're just counting a deck, Music, to see if all the cards are in it.*

He looked at the lie and decided that it fit all right.

His eye. Shouldn't it have been revealed to them once in all the years they'd spent together? As a young father, he'd been strangely pleased by the fear he saw in them when he turned it their way, but shouldn't he have eventually outgrown the need to be terrible? Why hadn't he used it as a lesson once or twice? He should have plucked it out at the table in the middle of a drill and tossed it into the pot. He could have lectured them on—what?—surprise? And why hadn't he been honest about it the other night when Charlie had asked?

It's raising boys, Music decided. You daren't go soft, ever. That poor devil up there, he thought, thinking of Vince, has got to raise a daughter, which probably has its own evils. But boys. He shook his head.

Their mother. Margaret. He'd been happy, married to her. He wished again that he'd taken her by the wrist before she'd walked out of that hotel room, had turned her so she'd face him while he confessed his stupidity, his crimes. He should have tried to explain to her that the women he chose—prostitutes, most of them—were always the ugliest in town, as different from her as he could imagine. It had all made sense, once, but he had to admit now that it no longer did.

Did the boys need to know that she'd never come back for them because she'd understood what they were, what they would become, and that she couldn't change it, that they'd be better cheats without her?

Who could possibly know how good a mother she'd been? "No use fighting what we're made of," she'd said on one of his later visits when he'd come to brag about their sons, and she made it plain that she meant him, too. Margaret had always seen the world clearly; she didn't deserve to be a civilian.

Music had to admit that Charlie had caused him some doubt, and some small guilt, for a day or two, there. Who can be accused by his child of criminal behavior and not feel frail? And how could

Charlie know that his father meant to spend the rest of his life making up for that?

But then he'd seen his boy at work. *He has to be psychic.*

Cracker Jack rose from the scuppers and rubbed against Music's leg.

"Cat."

Whose voice was that? It wasn't Walston's. "He's here," Music said. He lifted him onto his lap.

"Mr. Halloran."

Because of his one eye, Music had lousy night vision, no depth perception, and had trouble separating the figure from the mast. "You're the Australian?"

"Right-o."

"Have a seat, if you like."

"That's all right, sir."

"Never knew 'sir' to sit right with an Australian. You don't need to use it. 'Mr. Halloran' will do just fine."

"You're all right, mate. Mr. Halloran."

"Sit down, Bruman. Pet the cat." He felt Cracker Jack stir against him and grow heavy, and then the cat's neck hair came up stiffly against his hand. "Second thought, just sit down."

"I'll go back for'd. Didn't mean to disturb you." Bruman touched his forehead with his fist and went.

Music let him go. Cracker Jack relaxed. "Are *you* psychic, old fellow?" he asked softly. "Like my boy? You see something, too, in that Aussie that I need to watch?" He already knew the answer.

He'd met more Brumans than most men do. Every town had a collection of them, and they all gambled because it was easier than working. Sooner or later, odds dictated that they had to run across a man whose work—whose *labor*—gambling was, and then the odds insisted that they get beat silly.

That's when trouble started. Music had carried a derringer for years and had fired it twice before he got wise enough to take a little less than he could out of the game, and to take it with him out a bathroom window sometimes, before the game was finished.

He'd spent his sons' lives warning them of Brumans. (When he'd seen Charlie's cut cheek and learned he'd got it from diving out a window, he'd felt—all at the same time—failure and anger and relief. *Don't you notice all your relatives dying violently? Don't you understand that you and your brother are alive? Don't you know why?*) And now maybe he had one of them on his boat.

Cracker Jack got some purchase on Music's knee, then hung his head over the side of his leg and went to sleep.

The moon, a sun-sized white hole in the clouds, uncovered at times to shine like a spotlight. The yacht basin seethed with boats and people, the city with neon and noise, the island with fire and life. And yet, Music knew, climb high enough, and you wouldn't see a glimmer coming from either the vast, black Pacific or the whole dark side of the world.

8 ♣

Cracker Jack's hind legs kicked sporadically as he leapt or crouched in a dream field or deck, and Music's fingers trembled with dealt cards. The parties in the yacht basin burned themselves out until only one or two of the boats showed lights. The city bars closed; the only cars on the road belonged to cops. Hawaii's different in that no trucks hurtled through to someplace else, no tourists or travelers hurried to get a jump on the morning. Bruman and his two mates slept in their bunks without snoring.

Walston woke at four-thirty as always, walked the boat once, then went back to bed. He hated this time. At four-thirty, he seemed to be the only man alive. In a way, he was, for the two little girls were lashed into their bunks below, he had his arms to his elbows in the spokes of the wheel, and his wife was skating across the deck as if it were ice, her mouth open in surprise. He'd lost a sail once, years later, that had skittered over the side in the same loose way, billowing into the same shape for a moment and just as quickly gone, and his heart had jumped because he didn't believe in coincidence.

He woke at the same hour more often than not and relived for five minutes those last five minutes as if he needed their reminder. The pain was still sharp, though the grief and guilt had largely left him, and each morning was a little like laying flowers on a grave. There'd never been a moment he could have circled back for her. She was lost as soon as she fell, back first into the wave trough. He hoped she'd sunk like a stone.

The rain started. It pattered into the sea, then bounced off the deck, and Walston heard Music's footsteps come down into the salon. When he didn't hear the stateroom door open, he got up.

Music stood in the middle of the room, dripping, looking as if he didn't know where he was.

"I should have woke you," Walston said. "It almost always rains before dawn."

"Cat tried to get me up, then quit. What time is it?"

"Nearly five."

"How about some coffee?"

They sat at the poker table with cups in their hands and listened to the rain on the canvas awnings and the teak deck and the sound of it hissing like coals into the sea.

"Your boy get back in from his date?"

"No." Music smiled, but without humor. "Arthur's got to be going crazy up at the hotel."

"Hallorans took him twice."

"Yes. It will seem that way to him."

Walston didn't press. He wanted to avoid for a little longer what he had to say, so he looked around for a safe subject. He always only had one. "You haven't told me your plans, Mr. Halloran."

"I don't know them yet, Captain. I might try to put another game together, I might not. Arthur might want another, and I might give it to him. Or no. I thought I'd wait and see what happens with Reggie before I go on." *And who knows? Maybe Charlie would come back, or call.*

Walston poured a second cup for them both. "I wouldn't play again with Mr. Arthur."

Now Music was awake. He put his cup down. "Why not?"

Walston shifted uncomfortably. "Something the crew said."

"Bruman?"

Walston looked surprised. "No, Jackson. The one who talks too much." Then he didn't say anything.

"You want me to pull it out, one question at a time?"

"No. Sorry. I heard something late last night—just a snip of conversation—and asked a question or two of my own, and it turns out that Mr. Arthur invited the boys up to his suite and gave them each a lot of money."

Music waited.

"You were asleep on deck, and I let you be."

Music let him twist.

"They ended up telling Arthur you had two sons aboard."

Music thought back and decided Walston couldn't know that one of them had pretended to be a stranger. "Why does that worry you?"

Walston again looked surprised. "I know you like a close-mouthed crew. And I guess you're used to large money in a way that I'm not."

"How's that?"

"Four, five hundred dollars, whatever it was, seems like a lot to pay for something you already know."

"I've said before, Captain, you could be a player."

"What do we do now?"

"Wait for Arthur." Music picked up his cup again. "Thanks."

"You want me to fire 'em?"

"I'd like to talk to them."

"They'd rather be fired, Mr. Halloran. Jackson's scared to death you'll—"

"I'll what?" Music asked, but he knew.

"Turn the evil eye on him."

Music rubbed his eye, then opened it wide and tapped on it with a thumbnail. "It's an old routine, Captain. I've got it pat. I can stop the needle on the evilmeter anywhere I like. It's someone else on board that worries me."

"Bruman?"

Music nodded. He liked this captain very much. "He worries Cracker Jack too."

"I'll get rid of him."

Music thought about it, then shook his head and gave Walston one of his cold smiles. "Just tell him I'd like to talk to him."

♦

Lia was surprised to see the bed empty when she got up Sunday morning. She smelled coffee and smiled to herself as she belted her robe. *What a love; he's making breakfast.*

But Charlie-love had made his own breakfast hours ago and now sat at the kitchen table dealing cards in the empty space he'd made by pushing a bowl of cold cereal and a carton of milk aside. A picture of an abducted child on the milk carton stared back at her.

"Hey," she said from the door.

"Hey," he said back, frowning.

"What's the matter?"

Charlie held the deck out to her and flicked his wrist as a dowager might, opening a fan. "Take one."

"I thought you'd finished with all this."

"Just take a card."

Lia drew one hesitantly and held it against her chest without looking at it, afraid that she might make an innocent mistake, a wrong choice, and would confuse—or worse, wreck—the balance between them that had once again grown delicate. "How long have you been up?"

"It's the seven of spades, right?"

She peeked at a corner. Nine of hearts. She felt as if the card had a fortune attached to it, and she wished she knew it. "Right. How about I make us breakfast?"

"Let me see it."

"Why?"

"Because I haven't been right yet."

"Okay, it's not the seven of spades."

He frowned again—or maybe more deeply—and tried to remember the deck's order. "Jack of spades."

"No."

"Nine of diamonds."

130

"Close enough." She showed it to him.

"Not close enough. There isn't any 'close enough' in this business." He held the cards up again facing her so she could look at the blurred destinies. "Take another."

"Charlie."

"Please."

She closed her eyes and chose.

"King of clubs."

She looked and shook her head.

"Look at the fan. Is the king of clubs anywhere close?"

"I don't know where I pulled it from."

"Right here." He flicked the deck's invisible notch with a thumbnail. "Look on either side."

She had to spread some cards apart to find it at the far edge. It seemed that the deck he held softly in his hand was something living, and hurt, and that she was attempting a delicate surgery without even a textbook.

"It's gone," Charlie said. "The magic."

"Good."

"*Good?*"

"I told you I'm having some trouble with all of that. You said you were, too."

Charlie pushed the chair back and turned in it. "If I could have sat down this morning—or last night, or whenever it was—and found every card in the deck the way I did on the boat, then I think I'd be done forever. But I can't; it's gone. It's left me, if I ever had it."

"Isn't that a good thing? To get out at the top?"

"I'm not sure that *was* me at the top. If I could do that again, there'd be no way to ever lose, the risk we tell ourselves we work for. But it wasn't me, Lia." He waved a hand at the cards. "It was your brother."

"You wanted to quit before all this happened, though."

"Yes."

"And now you don't?"

"Yes."

"You do or you don't?"

"I don't know. Does it make a difference to us?"

She thought probably yes. "I don't know, either. I have to work on some papers."

Charlie had chores of his own. He sat at the table, listening to the shower run, and watched the cards as if they'd get up at any minute and go.

◆

It amused Reggie that Bobbie snored. No cute little grunt-and-whistle, this, but a steam-driven engine. He put a hand under her shoulders and another under her bottom and turned her over. The snoring stopped but she began to talk in her sleep.

"*Gezurndi annem alkili.*"

"Uh huh."

"*Tazzik. Herrum!*"

"What?"

He'd never met anyone like her. So unlike a Halloran, he thought. Neither her body nor her mind knew how to keep a secret.

"*Gorffelcue.*"

"Love you, too," Reggie said.

He got up and stood by the window, cranking the louvers open. It was a cheap hotel on the highway near the airport, and the room was hot. He'd argued for someplace better—the suite next to her father's at the Ilikai even, if she wanted to twist the knife—but she'd wanted to slum it. "I want to feel like a cheap date," Bobbie said. "Prove to me you're worthless."

"Don't we have enough trouble with your father as it is?"

"I'm over twenty-one. Are you?"

Sometimes it didn't feel like it.

Watching her take off her bra and wave it at her father then sit at the table five minutes later and lose lots of his money, he was struck by the difference in parents and offspring. She was entirely her own person, which shamed him. Had he gone a week in his life without wondering what his father would do or think? He guessed not.

She'd been no less in charge making love. She'd unbuckled his belt and pulled it from its loops so that it snapped like a whip.

"Oh, Lord, you're one of those."

"Yee-*haw*," Bobbie said, and then she was on him.

Reggie didn't know what to make of her, even now. He turned from the window and looked at her. Her bottom was as brown as the backs of her hands. At first she'd been—not demanding but insistent—and Reggie hadn't been able to shake the idea that she saw this as a punishment for them both. But the second round had been slower and quieter—at least, nobody had knocked on the wall—and she'd cried through part of it, but had finished laughing and happy.

Reggie went along with whatever mood she found herself in, feeling as if he were sitting through a film's coming attractions. Chase scene, love scene, moment of sentimentality, long, overworked moment of melodrama and tragedy in bad light. She kept nothing back.

"Well, mister," she'd said, cuddling just before they slept.

"Uh huh."

"Is that an answer?"

"I don't know. Did you ask a question?"

"Do you suppose sailors in the old days used to diddle the figurehead?"

"What?"

"You know, do you suppose they held onto the bowsprit and—" she pumped her fist in the air as kids do when they want truckers to pull the air horn.

"I guess I'd have to take a good, close look at one," Reggie said. "It sounds risky."

"Love is."

"I'm not sure I'd call that love."

"Sex, then."

"I'm not sure I'd call it that, either."

"All right, masturbation."

"Yep. That's it."

"Isn't that risky, too?"

"Make you blind," he agreed, sleepily. "Splinters. That's how Dad lost his eye."

He'd drifted into sleep with her breasts warm against his ribs, his legs over hers, and he half-imagined that she'd said, "No, it wasn't that."

Reggie dreamed of machine sex (something that had never occurred to him before) and he knew, on waking, that it was because of that conversation and the air conditioner in their room that rattled and coughed and blew hot air all night. He couldn't remember much of what he dreamed and decided that was a small favor. Then a clear picture came to him of round, hard, steel shapes and greasy, moving parts—pistons—and machinery noises and steam, and all-in-all he was pretty sure it had been a nightmare he had no wish to recall. Somewhere in it there'd been bicycle spokes. He tried to push it away, but got the rest.

Bobbie had been the machine, of course. Gleaming with sweat or light oil, her eyes glowing like dials, she'd reached out with telescoping arms to pin him while she sat on him like a metal punch. He'd finally, desperately, reached around blindly for a plug and pulled it.

Then he'd watched as a thick pair of female hands had carved Bobbie's shape from a living tree, the grain in the dark wood like a map's contours, swelling at her breasts and hips and shrinking at waist and wrists and ankles. He'd been given a cloth and a squeeze bottle of oil and, as he rubbed, her skin began to shine with warm light.

Those hands swam into his vision again, but now the nails were brightly painted, and the fingers held paintbrushes and pots of paint and a blueprint like a coloring book. He'd bumped the hands away, spilling the paints, fearful as he did it.

Dreams. Like snoring, or talking in your sleep, they made a person terribly vulnerable.

Reggie was impatient to be outside where it was cooler, where they had a chance of finding breakfast, but it looked as if she'd sleep all day. He got back into bed and moved around until he had her in a hug. In spite of himself and the vague uneasiness that had come with his dream, he fell back asleep.

"That was a *date*," Bobbie said.

"That was more like a thirty-mile hike." Stretching, he sat up. "Why don't you call your father and tell him you're all right?"

"I'm—"

"I know. You sure are. But it's—my God, it's *noon*—time to let him off the hook."

"Shower, first. Then hook-removing. Then lunch somewhere very nice, with wine and shady trees. Then, if you behave yourself, you can take me to dinner."

"You said you were a cheap date."

"I said I wanted to *feel* like a cheap date; I never said it wouldn't be expensive." She turned on the water in the shower and stepped in. "There's not much room in here."

"I'll wait."

"What I meant was, you'll have to stand scrunched against the tile away from the water until I'm finished."

"I'll wait," Reggie said again. He watched her blur behind the frosted plastic panes of the shower door, then a hand appeared as if from another dimension, followed by a wet, real arm. "Or maybe not."

"Not," Bobbie agreed.

She managed somehow to get a lather from the thin motel soap, and she worked it expertly until he wanted her again.

"I learned this in college, living on a coed floor," she said.

"Uh huh."

"Bowsprit."

"Uh huh."

She soaped her breasts. "Figurehead."

♦

"How much of Vince Arthur's money did you take?" Music asked.

"I ain't taken any. Man says I did, he's a liar."

"You met with him."

What did he know, and what was he guessing? Bruman matched Halloran's dead-eyed look and said nothing.

Music sat at the table, his hands quiet in front of him as if waiting for cards. "You don't want to work on this boat any longer."

"I do, yes."

"You've an interesting way of hanging onto a job. What did you talk to Arthur about?"

"Who says I did?"

"The man who pays you. Me."

"The other two might have went up to his hotel."

"He gave them their severance pay. What'd he give you?"

"He ain't give me nothin'. I told you that." Bruman took a seat uninvited. "But if he were to call and offer me a job, I'd be your insurance, Mr. Halloran. If he thinks he's got somebody aboard then he don't need to hire another. And let me tell you, mate, he could hire a dozen to do what he wants without walking a block from his hotel."

"Do what?"

"Do almost anything." Bruman had to fight the urge to look down at his own hands. "Sink the *Music Hall*, maybe."

"Is that the deal?"

Bruman shrugged. "How would I know?"

"Why don't I believe you, Mr. Bruman?"

Bruman shrugged again. "You the sort of man believes anybody, ever?"

Halloran stood, and Bruman stood with him. "No," Music said. "I'm not. Remember this: bluff once."

"You think I'm not being straight?"

Halloran ignored the question. "A gambler doesn't bluff to win, Mr. Bruman, he bluffs to get caught bluffing. He wants to lose that time so when he's got the goods later the players remember that he bluffed, and call. All of us have a good memory for weaknesses, or what we think are weaknesses."

Bruman went forward wondering which of them Halloran had told him about. He climbed into his rack and watched the other two stow their gear in their duffels in a humid silence.

"You on the beach, too?"

"Nope," Bruman said.

The other one nodded, expecting nothing else. "Show Halloran your knife?"

Bruman levered himself up on an elbow. "He's not the mice you are. An' you don't want to make my knife your business."

The man hesitated, then jammed the rest of his clothes in and closed up the top of his seabag by easing three grommets over the brass staple so it made a square.

"Well?"

"No."

"You're on the beach because you can't keep your mouths shut. You keep them shut about me, or I'll have you both out of your skins without any more warning."

Bruman caught a flicker of himself from outside, like a glimpse of something foreign. Then in that same blink he was back again, but a little uneasy in his own skin. *Weaknesses.* Halloran had cursed him, somehow.

"It's going to come undone," Bruman said into the phone.

"Why?"

"'Cause Mr. Halloran's a smart ol' badger, that's why. And you're not. Those two morons you talked to told him, and he guessed the rest. He'll replace 'em with real sailors."

"It's the greed," Vince said. "It's got an odor Halloran doesn't miss."

"The difference 'tween a T-bone and a Porterhouse is just a quarter-inch."

"What the hell's that supposed to mean?"

"Porterhouse is there all along, it just depends where you slice it. Mr. Halloran knows it."

"I'm still not following you."

"This owner's suspicious of everybody, all the time, like breathing. The greed's in all of us."

Vince noted the *Mr.* in front of Halloran and didn't know anymore where Bruman stood. His worry for Bobbie had kept him from making a decision, but now the right one came. "I'm going to play him again, for the boat."

"I think we ought to meet as we planned. You win the boat back, I want to keep my job aboard her."

"I'll think about it."

"You'll do more than that, mate. It's your line I'm standin' tangled in, and you put the bight in it. Somebody pulls on it, I'm danglin' by my heels."

"I'll consider all the options."

"I'll do the same, mate. Sunk boats don't care who owns 'em."

◆

Bobbie banged the hotel door open against its stops, throwing her arms up as if inviting a hug. "I'm home."

Vince stared at her for a moment before turning back to the window.

"Uh oh." She moved to the bar. "How about I pour us both a drink?"

When he didn't answer, she offered him a cold beer the way he liked it, with tomato juice leaking down through it like blood.

He ignored it. "I wish you'd go back to San Diego."

Bobbie left his beer on the windowsill and mixed a vodka-and-bitters for herself. She sat on the sofa and drew her legs up. "In case you've missed it, I'm grown up."

"I know."

"Have been for a while, now."

He nodded.

"I meant to call you. Last night and again this morning."

"It's four o'clock, Bobbie." He looked at her and made himself believe she looked just a little apologetic. No, she's just tired. "I don't want to know what kept you from calling."

"The details are always the same, aren't they, Father? I know there've been times when you've put everything on hold—even shipped *me* off somewhere barren and desolate—so you could be with a woman. That trip to Europe you took when I was ten."

"That was business."

She grinned at him. "I never believed that. And I found the photographs you took of—what was her name?"

"Lila," Vince said, after a minute. *Jesus.* "I was a lot younger then."

"About my age, now, if I have the math right. Did she have anything to do with the divorce from Mother?"

Vince shook his head. "I should have burned those snapshots. I should never have brought them home. Or taken them in the first place, or something."

She grinned at him again. "The last time I looked, they were still there."

Vince had to smile, too, even though he didn't feel like it. "Has anything in my life been private from you?"

"Not if I could help it. When you wondered the other night how you'd ever raised a daughter who could take off her clothes and wave them at her dad, I was thinking of that paper sack of Polaroids and the home movies you keep in the library."

"So you found those, too."

"Come sit down with me, Dad." She patted the sofa cushions.

Vince picked up his sweating beer glass but it slid through his fingers and bounced. The red foam soaked into the carpet pile. "Oh, damn."

"I'll make you another."

"Make it bourbon."

When he had his new drink solidly in both hands, Bobbie said, "Don't you see that your secret life taught me something you never would have been able to if I hadn't been so—"

"Curious?"

"Sneaky. Parents teach their kids how to behave—oh, at a cocktail party, let's say—but they never teach them how to behave *after* the cocktail party, if you follow me. There's no way they can, really, is there? And yet it's something all of us need to know. I wasn't horrified when I saw you on film—"

"I am."

"Wasn't horrified," Bobbie said again, "but happy to know that sex is fun, is—" She looked up at him from under her lashes, and when he returned her look to see why she'd paused, said, "Imaginative. That's no small gift."

"Something you take without asking isn't a gift." But Vince's anger was gone, and she knew it. "How old were you when you found that stuff?"

"Thirteen."

"Oh, Lord."

"Just the right age, Dad. It made that whole confusion more sensible."

"And did it—"

"Did it, what?"

"Christ, Bobbie, I don't know how to talk about this."

"Give me more of a hint."

"Sooner."

"Ah. Did it make me curious sooner?"

He nodded.

"Maybe. I don't know. I lost it about the same time as my friends."

"I don't want to know."

"In high school."

"I said I didn't want to know." Vince swallowed half his whiskey, then said, "Who with?"

She smiled. "Bobby Rawlins."

"Christ."

"Bobbie and Bobby. It seemed like fate at the time."

It always does, Vince thought. *We have the capacity to convince ourselves of anything.* "All this has a point?" he asked.

"That I've been grown up for a long time. That you've given me—whether you knew it or not—the means to be happy."

"A sex manual for my daughter."

"You still don't get it. You never did anything shameful. You were loving and kind and funny. And the women you were with were loving and kind and funny, back. I'll admit you jump-started one or two of my own affairs, but there's nothing in any of that stuff that I wouldn't have learned on my own or seen someplace else. That sex manual, as you call it, was more of an emotional roadmap, Father."

"California would have me in jail."

"We're in the middle of a sexual revolution, Dad."

"Rebels, by definition, are criminals. Ah, well. Ah, *shit.*" He finished his drink and gave her the glass for refilling.

"And we're not in California either."

"What difference does that make?"

Bobbie handed him his new drink. "You don't know?"

He shook his head.

"This is Paradise. The rules don't fit. Don't you feel—I don't know—the *hum* of it all around you?"

He didn't.

"Hawaii's this huge engine. There's a place on the other side of the mountain, a Marine Corps base, *Kane'ohe*, where breath was breathed into man for the first time. Don't you feel that breath, Dad? I don't ever want to go back to San Diego."

"Young Halloran—"

"Reggie."

"Reggie Halloran's a drifter, like his father."

"Drifting lands you on a beach, sooner or later," Bobbie said. *Washed up*, came to Vince's mind.

Bobbie disappeared into her room for so long that Vince was beginning to worry again, this time that she'd taken the vodka into the bath and drowned. He called room service and ordered dinner for two, *mahi-mahi*, with a bottle of California's best white wine, and he'd only just hung up when Bobbie came out, dressed for dinner.

"I have another date," she said, when she saw his look.

"With Reggie?"

"Of course with Reggie."

"I don't think this is another date, sweetheart. It sounds like it's still the same date with an intermission."

"You won't wait up?"

"I don't think I can stay awake that long twice."

"You won't worry?"

"Of course I'll worry."

"Good."

The door closed behind her.

"I'm going to play Halloran again," Vince said to the empty place where she'd stood. "Dinner's on its way up." He sighed. "Be careful."

Vince didn't hear Hawaii's hum on Kalakaua Avenue, only car noises and the sliding-skidding sounds of amateur feet in flip flops on root-buckled pavement and pieces of banal conversations from Iowa or Illinois or Indiana. "—Lion's Club next Tuesday, and—" "—don't you think Ruth would—" "—and oh, honey! look—" "—feed the dog?"

He thought perhaps there was a hum where she was, on a beach under the palm trees looking out at the glowing white lines of breakers, or at the top of one of these paper-sharp mountains, or on a rocky headland staring back at the red and purple lights of the city. Maybe there's a hum if you're twenty-nine and in love in a place a long way from home, when you're a woman who had been given with her first breath a hum of her own, when it feels as if the whole world has been waiting patiently like a package for you to arrive and open.

He'd probably forgotten.

Vince turned up a narrow side street—an alley, really—to get to King and passed the open door of a tattoo parlor. His steps slowed for a second, as if his feet wanted to take him inside. The window was covered with neat squares of paper and the tracings in different-colored inks of skulls, knives, dragons, and (oddly, he thought) flowers. Vince bent his head around the door and looked in.

The shop was empty except for the tattooist, a kid with long, greasy hair who looked up over the top of his comic book for a second and then went back to his reading. Or looking at the pictures.

"Help you?" An older man stood beside him on the sidewalk, a man older than Vince. The only hair on his head was a pair of white muttonchops from the ear to the chin. "I can draw anything."

Vince looked back at the kid with the comic book.

"He's my apprentice. He's got a good eye, believe it or not, but for now I only let him work on the kids and the drunks. He's good at drawing the cartoons and skulls that children want after they've been drinking. They think it's a philosophical statement. Maybe it is, Vietnam been going on so long."

"I don't want a tattoo. I just—" Vince waved at the lit door to explain.

"Tattoo parlor, I know. Magic place. The boy in every man wants one, and he doesn't want one both at the same time." He made an odd, grasping gesture with his hand as if to say, *You figure it out.*

"I guess that's right."

"I know it is. Girls got charm bracelets to tell 'em where they've been; men got tattoos. At least, that's the way it was. Girls're gettin' 'em, now, too."

"The flowers," Vince said.

"Flowers. Spiders in webs. *Mushrooms*, for God's sake. Things from *life*, you know?" the man said, meaning nature. "An' they put 'em in the damn'est places."

Vince smelled whiskey on the man's breath and knew the tattooist could probably smell it on his.

"Man's got a slab of meat on his shoulder, or his bicep, and that's where we sink the needle. It hurts, you know? That's its attraction. Girls come in and want me to do their tits, or their navel, or work in the fine hairs at their crotch, at the root of things. Sometimes I think I'm a gynecologist." He shook his head. "They're tougher by miles than these squids and jarheads I get.

Send the ladies over to the VC and wrap up the war in a couple weeks."

Remembering his conversation with Bobbie, Vince thought the man might have a point. He looked at his watch. Eight forty-five. "How long's it take?"

The man smiled, like he'd just sold a set of encyclopedias. "'Pends on what you want. Come on inside."

Something simple, Vince thought. *Loose lips sink ships* slipped into his head from another war. Those Polaroids of sex with Lila. The ketch, that engine of his. That engine of Bobbie's, whatever it was. *This is nuts.*

Bruman was waiting when he got to the bar. "Thought you'd run out," he said.

"I've got to hang around and put out all the little fires I've started."

"Is that what I am, mate? A fire?"

Vince paid for a beer, sliding two dollars onto the tray and grazing the nearly naked breasts of the waitress. He gave her another five for a tip and she moved into it so he did graze them. The hidden mechanisms of the universe started to clank and rattle. *What a simple, effective piece of advertising that is, hugging the tray in that spot.*

Vince's gaze shifted to Bruman. "I don't know. Once in a while, in the factory, we brew up a batch of perfume that we all would have bet money on. That I *have* bet money on. Then we put it in the glass bottle we've paid a fortune to design and produce, but when you take the expensive little top off, the stuff stinks. It smells like an alligator fart or something. I don't know why. Maybe it's the chemistry with the glass, or maybe what we've mixed just doesn't like the bottle, but either way, it isn't perfume anymore, it isn't even aftershave."

"First I'm a fire. Now I'm a bad smell."

"You just don't fit in the bottle. I'm going to pour you out."

"An' how you going to do that, mate?"

"You tell me. I'm not going to carry you around."

"I want to work that ketch."

Vince shook his head. "I understand that. You're not more in love with her than I am. But Halloran won't keep you much longer, and you're not crewing for me. Think of something else."

"You get cut?"

"What?"

Bruman pointed to a spot of blood on Vince's shirt just below the shoulder.

"Stabbed."

"Stabbed?"

"Couple thousand times."

"Let me see it."

"No." Vince flexed his shoulder, feeling the bandage pull. "We don't know each other that well." He realized as he said it that the thing was more intimate than he'd imagined.

"I got two," Bruman said.

Of course.

The waitress, bent over at the next table, had an ink stain at the curve of her bottom under her fishnet stockings. *Whole damn world.*

"That thousand we agreed on."

"All right."

"And an airplane ticket to another port."

"Which one?"

"I ain't decided."

"Decide. I'm not flying you to Singapore."

"Suva."

"Where's that?"

"The Fijis. Man lose himself in 'bout half a thousand islands. When I get tired of that, I can work myself back home from there easy."

"Suva, then. And a thousand dollars in cash. And we're done with each other."

"Quit," Bruman agreed. He finished his second beer and took one of Vince's. He looked at the blood spot on Vince's shoulder, then at the waitress. "Mr. Halloran picked a good one."

"How's that?"

"You're the easiest money on the island."

9
♣

Groton's house seemed like somebody else's dream. What if there were no escaping any of it? Perhaps Music had been right, and Reggie, too, that choices had been made long before he was allowed to question them; that the deck was cut, the hand dealt, and he could no more throw it in than he could avoid making love with Lia one more exhausting time.

Charlie pulled up in front of the bank in Kailua at five to ten, not remembering any part of getting there and not knowing what he would do when he got inside. Put the house under a wrong name? He half-hoped that Groton would welch on the bet.

Groton didn't. He tapped on the driver's window Charlie had up, even though the top was down. "You ready, Halloran?"

Halloran. All right. "Vince's daughter had my mother's name. Was that your idea?"

Groton nodded.

"You don't understand my dad. A play like that could only backfire."

"I thought it might unsettle him. Or you—as it turns out."

"It didn't. What are you going to do now?"

"Me?" Groton shrugged. "Sign the house over. I didn't go in blind. I got a little blind in the middle of it, or at the end of it, but—" He shrugged again. "I'll get it back."

"How?"

"Any way it takes." Groton smiled, and turned, and went inside.

♦

Music longed for the unbearable weight of the Midwest's sticky heat, the kind that rubbed against the skin like balloons and built into spectacular evening storms, for Missouri's unshaded dirt streets humped with wheel ruts, for a small town's sullen players drinking in smoky back rooms. He missed the smell of horses in the farming towns, the peace that came over him when he walked into the one saloon or grange hall where a game was going, and he missed seeing the slim boys who always got past the bartender somehow to slink into corners to sit with their chins on their knees, their bare, brown feet flat on the cool earthen floors, their arms and hands a knot that ended in laced fingers. Boys in those days could while away long afternoons in the stink of cigar butts, sit in the damp of spilled beer, and dream of growing up to be card sharps. *What has become of an America like that?*

Maybe it needed a Depression. Music and his dad had played their first game together in 1931 when Music was fifteen, when the whole world, it seemed, was out of work. The two of them would drive into a town in his father's '29 Durand, look around and rent the best rooms available—sometimes in a hotel, but more often in a house that had a private parlor and a phonograph—and stay ten days or a week before they'd taken what nickels and dimes there were in those back rooms. He'd understood even then that the desperate squalor they moved through like a wind was an unusual time in history, even though it seemed as if it would never end, and that the people whose houses they shared would rather not share them.

"Money's so hard to come by, Son, Miss Liberty still has their fingerprints," his father said, showing him a dime as if it were true. "It's a better time than any I could invent for you to learn all this. You can take a dollar out of these games, you'll always feed yourself."

Look at me now, Dad. You never could shed yourself of that thinking; you never stopped gambling for quarters. You died in a refitting yard, and your last son sits on his own yacht in Honolulu. I've got a fish on a string who can't see straight for wanting it, who's going to put up a quarter of a million dollars in a two-man freeze-out in the hope of getting it. Against me! And you know, Dad, I'm half tempted to lose it to him.

"You come in and sit down in a half-hour," his father had said, "and don't give any sign that you know me."

How often, Music wondered, had Hallorans pretended not to know each other?

"Morning, Mr. Halloran."

"Hello, Captain."

"I've been thinking about the problem you gave me."

Music nodded.

"You want to sail this morning, but you've fired my crew."

"Two-thirds of it," Music agreed.

"Two-thirds of it. I can sail her short one hand, not two."

"There must be a seaman's union."

"Heading there, now, Mr. Halloran, but I don't hold out a lot of hope."

"Do what you can, Captain. I'd like to be clear of the harbor by nine."

He watched Walston go ashore, walking with that strange limp sailors acquired, able to see the man's frustration in his shoulders. Walston would have to do his best; Music had promised Arthur a game, but he sure didn't want to play it this close to civilization.

Bruman padded barefoot onto the deck with a bottle of brass polish and a rag. He glanced at Music and went forward.

Music slipped below to rouse his son and kick him off the boat. Reggie had come in very early, very quietly, but the sound of the door clicking shut had awakened Music just the same. He wondered now what sort of sleeper his son was. He collected the cat on the way, scooping him up still asleep from the stairs, knocked softly on Reggie's stateroom door, and with Cracker Jack hanging limp in the crook of his elbow, went in.

"Jesus, Dad."

"Hi, Mr. Halloran." Bobbie nonchalantly pulled the sheet up to cover herself.

Music turned quickly and strode out before she'd finished, but couldn't lose the still-vivid picture of her long brown legs.

"Come in, now, damn it."

"I thought you'd be asleep. And alone."

"Not either," Bobbie said. "Not for a couple of days."

"Your father's coming aboard in," he looked at his watch, "about an hour and a half. I think both of you should be gone by then."

"Another game?" Reggie asked.

"Just the two of us."

"You're taking the *Music Hall* out?"

"Yes."

"That's fine," Bobbie said. She reached a long arm under the sheet and Music watched it travel like a burrowing animal toward his son, the sheet humping behind it like a wake. "That means the suite at the Ilikai's empty."

Vince came aboard punctually at nine. At Music's invitation, he sat under the striped awning on the afterdeck.

"Coffee?"

"Thanks."

Music poured a cup for Vince and refilled his own. "The captain's away, hiring a crew. Our late start is your fault."

"I'm in no hurry." Vince pulled out a long cigar and lit it.

"Patience is a fine quality in a gambler."

Vince nodded. "Not patience as much as pace. How long do you figure it will take to bust one of us?"

"Two-man game, with two and a half on a side, it could take a good long while. Then again, it might only take a dozen hands. Or only one." Music shrugged. "No way of telling, really."

"Change your mind, Halloran. Sell me the damn boat. I've been twisting on this hook too many years."

"Your hook, not mine. What would you name her?"

Vince rubbed his shoulder absently. "What do you care? This boat's only four queens to you."

"You have a name ready for her," Music said. "What is it?"

"The *Divine Scent.*"

Music laughed. "We think alike."

"Maybe."

"You've camouflaged it with your perfume factory, but *De Vincent? Vincent's?* It's as clear as the *Music Hall.*"

"To you, perhaps. You're pretty good at camouflage yourself."

"I never pretend to be anything but what I am."

"The father of Liam O'Donel?"

Music put his coffee cup down in its ring on the table and looked at it instead of at Vince. "But what I am is a liar," he said softly, *when I have cards in my hands*, "and I don't pretend otherwise. You knew that when you sat down."

"It wouldn't do any good, then, to expect an honest game?"

"You'd be foolish to, considering how I make my living."

"You stole it from Stace." It wasn't a question.

"No, I didn't."

"There's no way I can know, is there?"

Music shook his head. "I'll tell you right now that I'll play you straight up, but you'd still be foolish to believe me."

"That's your edge, isn't it?"

"I don't need an edge. You're a fine card player, Mr. Arthur, for a civilian. But you're not as good as I am and you never will be. You never *can* be." Music lifted his hands an inch from his thighs in a gesture Vince couldn't see, almost an apology. "That's the truth."

"But the outcome of a game between players of nearly equal skill can be determined by the cards."

"Sure. Luck comes to us all equally *over a lifetime*. And you've no right to assume levels of nearly equal skill."

"How much skill is there, really?"

Music considered it. "Maybe I just take whatever edge is available, however it reveals itself. I plant the seed of hesitation in an opponent without thinking. And *that's* probably the most important difference between us. Thinking's tiring work. You'll tire before I will."

"Sell me the boat," Vince said again.

"I might."

"You might?"

"It depends how the game goes. Let's say you have me in a corner—or believe you do—and you're about to run me through with what you think is an immortal hand. Let's say, at that point, I offer you the boat for two hundred and fifty thousand dollars. What do you do? Do you play out the hand and try to get it for nothing, or do you buy the *Divine Scent* when you have the chance? In other words, Mr. Arthur, if I offer the boat, am I bluffing, or am I trying to lure your monster hand into a showdown with a bigger one?"

"I buy the boat if you offer it."

"Do you? *You* have that full house with aces this time, and on the board I have four unconnected cards. If I'm lucky, one of them is even a queen. Do you give up that much money then when you might not have to?"

"I see."

Music nodded. "The *Music Hall*'s my ace. More than that, my joker. But she's your kill card." At Vince's look, Music said, "The card that kills a hand. Your worst nightmare, if I play her right." His expression said, *And of course I will*. "I don't *need* to cheat."

"I'll play anyway."

"I know."

That conversation done, they waited silently for the captain to return. Vince's eye wandered across the hulls nearby and settled on a cabin cruiser two slips down. A blonde in only the bright handkerchief-sized bottom piece of a bikini lay sunbathing on her stomach.

Vince cleared his throat and looked away. "My daughter's been seeing a lot of your son."

I've been seeing a lot of your daughter, Music wanted to say. "Biology. No matter what you try to do, there's no stopping it."

"We might end up in-laws."

"I've thought of that."

"See each other on holidays."

"I don't see why. See in-laws once, at the wedding, or maybe twice, if you live longer." But he gave Vince a nod of appreciation for being an apt student. "You don't quite have the hang of it, but it's good that you're trying."

"It wasn't that; I just wondered what you thought about the possibility."

"It's different for fathers of sons."

"I guess so."

Was it? Maybe it's just different for fathers who take an interest in their children's lives. Music had a stake in his kids—the investment he'd put in—but he wasn't sure how much deeper it went, or how to put it into language for himself. He'd be angrier, he decided, if they played badly than married badly.

"My sons aren't much like me," Music said, out of sympathy for what Vince must be feeling. Unaccustomed to sympathy, he was surprised at himself.

"Bobbie's too much like me."

"They can't be perfect, can they?"

"No."

"They have to take a seat and get their cards and make their own mistakes."

"Yes."

"We ought to do the same."

"Yes."

"Two hundred and fifty thousand against the *Music Hall.*"

"Yes." Vince rubbed his shoulder where the unfinished tattoo, a fan of five blank cards, still itched.

"Ought to hire a kid to sit in the corner and be quiet," Music said. He might have told Vince why, if Vince had asked.

"Call."

"Aces up."

"Three twos," Music said.

"A narrow margin."

"Do you think so?" Music collected the cards and put them together. "I've always thought of the dividing line between two pairs and trips to be a canyon, like four of a kind or a straight flush to the rest of the hands."

"It's just the next hand up."

"You held aces and fives," Music said, shuffling. "Three deuces are—let's see—nine hands more than I needed. Aces and sixes would have beaten you as easily."

"Maybe aces and sixes don't call."

"And maybe, knowing you can't have three of them, they raise you into next week." He placed the deck in front of the empty seat between them for cutting. "Trips, early, is the best start you can get, but trips, late, is the hand I like most to be sitting across from at the showdown. Three of a kind, especially if the player has struggled to get them and feels he's earned something, will call even if he's convinced that he's looking down the barrel at a straight or a small flush." Music took the cards back. "Usually, to show that he had a good hand and that life's unfair."

"It sounds as if you've done it, too."

"Sure. Seven stud." He dealt the two down cards and flipped the third up. "But not since I was nine. Unless my opponent has the common habit of over-representing his hand and plays every board that might be a straight as if he had it. Your bet. What I'm telling you is that I understand the *psychology* of threes." *And do you understand the psychology of yourself? This need to undo what you've done?*

"A hundred."

Music looked at his hole cards by flicking them with his thumbnail. "Call."

"You're telling me that I lost less money on the last hand because you were holding three of a kind instead of two pairs."

"You can look at it that way. I respected the three aces you *might* have had." *The full house you* should *have had*, Music thought, *the way you were betting.* "I knew you'd paired the fives."

"Two pair's a hell of a hand in five stud."

"It's a decent hand. Threes are a good hand in that game. A flush is a hell of a hand, but stupid to play. You ever lose against a flush in that game, you ought to deal it every chance you get because that player's going to go down. Five stud's an odd game."

"You don't like it?"

"It's the best game there is," Music said simply. "It's the distillation of poker. And average players," he smiled wryly, "tend to overestimate their hands. It's your bet again."

"Five hundred."

"Call."

"Then why are you dealing seven?"

"More action. There's a better chance for the monster to come in. More importantly, a better chance for two good hands to happen in the same deal." Music dealt the fifth card. "You're paired."

"Two thousand."

"Call."

Vince looked at Music's cards. Jack, eight, seven, the jack and seven suited. "You're building a flush."

"Maybe. That's never the first assumption I make."

"You're sandbagging a straight you've already made."

"Maybe. But some wouldn't consider a two-thousand-dollar call this early to be sandbagging. You've missed the obvious."

"Which is?"

"Threes. Isn't that what we're talking about? In seven stud, every player is possibly tripled from the opening bet."

"Unlikely."

"Very. Unless he calls large, expensive pairs."

"You just had trips."

"Ah, ha." Music dealt the last up card. "It's still your bet. You know, science has found that lightning *does* strike twice. It does it all the time, in fact. The next bolt of lightning doesn't know where the last bolt has gone, and probably goes, like the last one did, to the place that's most attractive to it." As if talking to a child, or somebody he wanted to keep offbalance, Music said, "This hand doesn't know what the last hand did."

Vince hesitated, then bet two thousand again.

"Raise ten."

Music's hand hadn't improved; he'd caught a two off-suit.

"Call," Vince said.

Music dealt the last card down. "Your bet."

"Check."

"Here's where threes—or just the possibility of threes—does its work," Music said. "You've spent a lot of money on a decent beginning, kings and somethings. Tens, probably. That makes you feel safe because you look at my hand and know I need a ten for the straight I'm showing. Maybe you even have a fistful of spades underneath and think I haven't flushed.

"But threes. You'd have to have too many of my cards to feel comfortable about my hand, and of course you can't have them and still have any sort of hand of your own.

"We go through life paired, Mr. Arthur. Most of us, anyway. Noah made it his business, at God's direction. *Straight* and *flush* mean *honest* and *wealthy*, but *threes? Trips?* It's odd. It's an accident. It's *queer.*" Music looked down at his chips as if counting them. "But it's not, you know. It's the opposite. How does it go? 'I tell you once, I tell you twice, what I tell you three times is true.' Or something like that. The first time is happenstance; the second, coincidence. But the third time, that's fate. Fairy tales know this. *Children* know this. There's magic and order in threes."

"Make a bet, Halloran."

"A hundred and twenty-five thousand," Music said, but didn't count it out.

Vince had kings and tens, as Music had guessed; Music was showing a jack, eight, seven, two. What must he have to make a bet that size? Halloran could have anything, Vince realized, from seven unconnected cards up to—assuming the nine, ten, queen (or seven) of spades—a straight flush. He could have a full house, completely hidden. Anything in between. He'd just put half the boat on this hand, as he'd threatened to. He'd spent this deal lecturing about threes.

Did that mean he had them and was ready to theatrically turn them over? He could almost hear Music saying, as he showed his hand, "Do you see what I mean?"

"Fold."

"Good move."

"You had them, then?"

"It doesn't matter," Music said. "You can't call that much money with anything less than kings full. All I needed to make that bet was a king and a ten of my own." He watched Vince slowly collect the cards and knew he itched to turn Music's hand up. "Sometimes the best hand is just a bunch of cards the other guy wants."

Bobbie.

If Music had known what Vince was thinking, he would have added, *Charlie.*

"Your son Reggie knows this."

"Of course."

"I think my daughter does, too."

"Your daughter's a player."

"She's been driving me out of pots since she was thirteen. Half the time she doesn't show the hand she's playing. She's held a secret against me like a buried bug for nearly twenty years."

"How do you know?"

"She just told me."

"Why?"

"It was a showdown."

Music nodded. "We forget the cards our kids have been saving. Charlie's doing the same thing. It's a deliberate, devastating blackmail, and you can't call the cops." He smiled. "And you can't shoot 'em."

"We had to have screwed up, somehow."

"No. It's poker. Or rather, poker's life. You hold the truth back from whoever wants it and sell it for whatever it's worth."

"Not with your own kids."

"You must have kept something from her or she wouldn't have had a hand to play against you." Music looked deliberately at the deck, and Vince began to shuffle. "You look at nature and you find that every living thing manages to survive through one deception or another. It makes you wonder about the genius behind it all, doesn't it? I've always suspected that the snake in the garden was some poor mark God dragged in off the street to take the fall for Him."

"If it's a con, it's held up for a long time."

"He's God," Music said. "He's got tricks we haven't seen yet. Deal the cards."

"You mind a break?"

Music didn't.

"Mind if I pour a drink?"

"Help yourself. Bring it up on deck."

When Vince came up a few minutes later with a weak whiskey-and-water, Music was standing with the captain. "The *Music Hall* has a crew again," Music told Vince. "We're debating what to do."

"Let's get out of the harbor."

"Day's half gone."

"You think we're going to finish this game anytime soon?"

Music shook his head.

"Neither do I. I left a note for Bobbie not to expect me back tonight."

"Easy sail to Molokai," Walston said. "Or we can sail a long reach to Kauai."

"Pick one, then," Music told him. "Take us whichever way the wind's going."

"Molokai. Or put into Lahaina, on Maui, if you like. I've always wanted to sail into Lahaina."

"Fine."

"You want to meet the crew?"

"Not really."

"He's worn himself out teaching," Vince said.

Music nodded at the truth in that. Perhaps, like Charlie, he wanted an opponent on equal footing for some reason. Perhaps it was something else, but similar, an act of contrition. *Jesus*, he thought, startled, *what if whatever my son has is contagious?*

"Tell 'em I'm an evil old bastard who'd just as soon split 'em in half as look at 'em."

"I already have. And I guess Bruman would have told them the same by now."

"Keep an eye on that one."

"I thought you'd made yourself easy about him."

Music shook his head.

"I thought you'd fire him," Vince said.

Music shook his head again. "Fired the other two you got to."

"*I* fired him," Vince said.

Music looked at Vince, then up at the bow where Bruman was leaning on the rail. "I wonder if he knows that."

♦

Teaching, Lia thought, was one of those things that was supposed to get easier with practice. The end of a semester, too, should be a reward, something so easy she could phone it in, but in lots of ways it was more hectic than the beginning of the term.

First, she was behind. Every year she was left with an impossible amount of material she somehow hadn't yet gotten to, and only a week left to cram it into their heads. Second, her students needed to review for the final. How had they managed to forget *everything* she'd said? Third—and by far the worst—were the papers she had to deal with, from a brainstorming session at their inception (even the thinking machinery in her good students seemed to shut down when they were required to develop a ten-page thought), to helping pick a little coherence out of a helpless muddle of a draft, to the exhausting and humbling task of grading.

And of course the registrar would want her final grades before she'd even worked up the courage to look through the leaning white stack of pages that always ended up crouching on her desk.

And now, in the middle of all this, her mind was clouded with Charlie. She unlocked her office door and sat at her desk with a dread that approached terror.

Her first student that day was a timid girl whose name she always forgot. The student didn't knock, exactly, but laid the tips of her fingers against the wood and stroked it. "Dr. O'Donel?"

"Come in—" *Damn, what was her name?* "Come in." Lia fixed a smile. "Having trouble with the paper?"

The girl's head bobbed shyly several times, then stopped at the bottom of a nod as if a plug had been pulled.

"What do you have?"

"Nothing."

"*Nothing?*"

"I don't have a title."

"A *title?*"

"I like to start with that."

"Well, the title can wait, don't you think? Until after you see what you've said?"

The student nodded, still not looking at Lia.

"What would you like to write about?"

"Don't know."

"What has interested you in the course?"

A shrug.

And so it went. It was all so completely hopeless. Lia began every year determined to do a better job with these papers, find some way to help the students get a running leap at them earlier, but every year she found herself sitting in her office shaking at such encounters. Perhaps it was because she, too, had trouble getting words onto the page and didn't feel expert enough to offer any honest advice.

Then again, she always told herself, perhaps the most important part of their college experience was the deadline that is put off until too late (hadn't she told them the deadline was last Friday? she was sure she had) and the fear that goes along with that mistake.

"Tell me the name of somebody whose theories we've talked about in class."

"Lorenzo?"

"Lor-*enz,*" Lia said.

"Lorenz," the student said.

Jesus, how would this girl ever manage to pass the final exam? Was this the fault of her teaching? It couldn't be. Ask her what she liked for breakfast, and she'd say she didn't know. And she might not.

"And what do you remember about him?"

Another shrug.

"He'll be on the exam—Claire?" Damn.

"Kathy."

"Thank you. He'll be on the exam, Kathy."

What if the students gave *her* an exam? *What's my name?* It's easy; I've known it for years. You've graded my work all semester, Dr. O'Donel. *What's my name?*

"I know."

Lia saw a shadow in the hall. Another student circling. She sighed. "Who is it?"

"Morgan," he said, putting his head in.

"Do *you* have a paper topic?"

"No. Well, maybe. I don't know."

"Come in."

By five o'clock she had taught two classes (poorly), had seen all the students who had papers due, and was exhausted. She wanted a hot bathtub and a cold drink.

Maybe if Charlie finds an exit from his life, he can help me find one, too. But you have a summer stretching out in front of you, girl. "Hang on to that," Lia said aloud, pulling open her car door. *You've papers of your own to write,* another voice said, and she groaned. *You should have stayed at that conference.* She nearly screamed.

Her house suddenly seemed too tiny to live in for another minute. The kitchen, always small, long a disappointment, now seemed no larger than the vegetable bin in the refrigerator. The bathroom barely held the tub and toilet and sink, and she felt whenever she was in there that she had to crouch. In fact, she felt as if she were crouching all the time in a nook off the kitchen where she'd squeezed in a dinette and four plastic chairs, in a rectangle of bedroom, in a square of living room. Even the parking space at the curb in front of her house, between two pickups that never moved, was too much like her slot at school, a closet of an office made even smaller by file cabinets and books. The thought of Charlie waiting inside made it smaller still.

But he wasn't there. Lia undressed (with her bra looped around her wrist by one of its straps, even her body looked too small) and, ignoring the bathroom mirror, she swallowed her growing claustrophobia and stepped into the tub. She added bubble bath on a whim, but too late, and had to sit in a puddle of thin foam and oil.

Liza wished to have the chance once again to be tossed into the air by her grandfather and whirled around again in the safety of those big hands. She wanted to go back home and walk through the dozen rooms of that old house, stand in the light of its tall windows, lie down in its openness, put her fingers on that ruined piano and plink its keys.

◆

After the *Music Hall* cleared the harbor, Music and Vince returned to the salon and played without saying anything more than "Call" or "Raise" for nearly four hours, except Vince sometimes pointed out possible flushes and straights when he had the deal.

Music must have finally talked himself out. Vince was still uneasy at Bruman's presence on deck, the way he would be if a hitch-hiker had taken the wheel of his own car. He forced the man from his thoughts whenever he reappeared at irregular moments so that he could concentrate on the cards.

He played cautiously and lost very little. This isn't any fun, he thought, and it was only when Music said, "No, head-to-head games are hard work," that Vince realized he'd spoken.

I must be getting tired. He expected Music to answer that too. Music dealt.

Vince got fives, three of them back-to-back-to-back, an embryonic monster. Music checked the nine he was showing, then folded at the first bet. Vince put them up silently and took the ante. But after two more hands, those fives, and what they might have become, still haunted him. "How much do you think you've," he considered the word *won* and dismissed it, "taken out of poker games in your life?"

Music saw his two sons, ten thousand hot hotel rooms, his wife saying, "She's *ugly*," and shrugged. "I make a living."

162

"Have you played for this much before?"

"I've never *risked* this much before," Music said. "But I've never had better odds while I was looking at this kind of money."

"It always comes down to that for you, doesn't it?"

Music took the cards and moved them around in his hands as if they were unfamiliar. He surprised Vince by saying, "No. Odds are a big part of the picture, certainly, but that's not what the game is about. It's not what life's about."

Vince waited out the spell Music was in.

Music was thinking of Charlie. "Let's say we both play the same number of hours—tens of thousands of hours—of poker in our lifetimes." He looked at Vince as if he'd asked a question, so Vince nodded. "Luck is going to give us hands in the same proportions: x number of winners, x number of losers, x number of the ones in between." He looked again, and Vince nodded again.

"The winning hands are going to win, unless you're stupid. The losing hands are going to lose, unless your opponents are very stupid. The simple secret here is to win the most you can with the ones that are sure of winning and lose the least you can with the ones that are sure of losing, and that means learning to recognize which is which as quickly as you can."

Vince nodded without Music looking for it.

"That's some of the game," Music said. "But *most* of the game is how you play the middles: the two pairs, the trips, the weak straights, the small flushes. Can you adjust their relative values to match the game's environment?"

Vince nodded.

"Well, can you?"

"Sure. I think."

"What's three of a kind worth in this game, between the two of us? More, or less, than normal?"

"More."

"Why?"

"Because there's just the two of us."

"Fewer hands?"

Vince nodded.

"I think you're wrong," Music said. "I think three of a kind isn't as good a hand. The cards don't know how many players there are, and with fewer of *us*, there's more of *them*, so a smart player might try for more monsters. Fewer showdowns, but more spectacular ones. More full houses." He smiled at Vince. "Maybe. I might be wrong."

Full houses. Full boats. It occurred to Vince that Music might be talking about something besides poker. "Are you thinking of your sons?"

Music's face showed a look as close as he ever got to surprise. "Yes."

"You're wondering how you've played your middle hands."

"Yes."

"I wonder, too, with Bobbie."

The cards lay still, in a heap, but Music's hand surrounded them like parentheses as if he suspected they might escape. "There's four courses of action for hands like those. One is to give up on them, even if they might be winners. That's for the faint of heart, but a good play, sometimes. Second is to follow along and not kick up any dust and hope for the other hands to fall apart." Music stared at Vince, who thought he was looking somewhere else. "Third is to drive it unmercifully, goring everybody with your horns, and push out those hands that have better odds than yours of improving."

Vince waited. After a long while, when Music didn't move or blink, Vince asked, "What's the fourth?"

"The fourth requires my particular kind of knowledge. To deliberately make another hand better, then lose to it."

"Why would you do that?"

"Lots of reasons," Music said. "Especially if you're a father."

Vince got up and made a drink, and when he saw that Music still hadn't touched the ruins of the last hand, took it up on deck to leave Music alone at the table. The *Music Hall* was driving east at about eight knots under a red-bellied spinnaker. A man he didn't know was at the wheel.

Bruman, under the foremast, beckoned.

"The deal was, you use that ticket to Suva I bought you," Vince said, when he'd wandered forward.

"It's still at the airport, mate. I'll get on."

"I wanted you off this boat. Off this island."

"I'll get off both."

"Halloran knows I bought you. This is your last trip."

"Maybe everybody's," Bruman said.

"What does that mean?"

"It means maybe I sink the *Music Hall* before I go."

"Why?"

Bruman grinned. "Jus' cussed meanness. Don't fancy either of you gents."

"If you can't sail her, no one can?"

"That's it."

"I'm busting my brains out down below to win her."

Bruman shrugged.

"You'll stay on as crew."

"You said not. I don't believe you now."

"You want more, is that it?"

"I'm always willin' to listen to an offer."

"I've got to win the boat, first."

"You've got a hope." Bruman swung around the mast and moved up to the bow.

Vince looked out at the sea. Everywhere it looked like a nice afternoon.

"You have a gun aboard?" Vince asked Music when he went back to the salon.

"Why?"

"Bruman."

Music stood up from the table and stretched. "It's about time you told me what you've done."

"The boat's at hazard," Walston said. "And maybe our lives."

"Yes. My fault, Captain." Music offered him a seat at the table, then stood over him.

"What do we do about it?" Vince asked the captain.

"Steer around reefs. Put him ashore on Molokai."

"When's that?"

"With the last of the light. Three more hours."

Vince shook his head. "I don't trust him for three more hours. Or three more minutes."

"Sailor doesn't take his own boat out from under him, not in these waters." Walston made a swimming motion with his hand, the thumb sticking up, that all of them knew meant *sharks*.

"This one's crazy."

"He wants more money," Music said. "Give it to him."

"I don't think so. I think this is more like I'm-going-to-take-my-ball-and-go-home."

"Let's ask him."

"*Ask* him?"

Music nodded. "Bluff's over. Let's look at the cards."

"Do we have any?"

Music smiled. "I've always got cards."

The captain called Bruman down, and they all took seats.

"Arthur tells me you're going to sink my boat," Music said without any preamble. "Is that right?"

Bruman looked over at Vince, then back to Music. "Me?"

"You. I've got a bad feeling about you, Bruman. Even the cat doesn't like you."

"Fuck the cat."

"Yes or no?"

"You believe me if I say no?"

"I'll want an explanation for what you told Arthur, and I'll lock you up for the rest of the trip."

"Lock me up where?"

Music looked at Walston.

"Put him in a stateroom, I suppose," the captain said.

Bruman said, "I stay on deck."

"It might be dark before we get in," Walston told Music. "And this is a crossing I haven't made. I don't want him on deck."

"There's your answer to that, Bruman."

Bruman stood up. "I'll go ashore at Molokai, but I'm staying on deck, doing my job until we get there. And there's not a thing any of you can do about it. The first man gets close to me loses his fingers, and worse."

Walston got up and started to move to the stairs.

"You goin' for the shark rifle?" Bruman asked.

"It's the right weapon."

"Look at it recently? It's missin' its bolt."

"I've had enough of this." Music reached a hand toward Bruman's head.

A knife appeared, but Music had a derringer in his fist, leveled at Bruman's ear. "I've played against your kind since I was a boy, and until you came on board, that was the last time I felt a need to carry this. But I still remember how to use it, and I've got hands like stone." He pushed it an inch closer. "This is a four-shot pepperbox, and I'll put at least three of them in your eye."

Bruman moved back that inch. "Now what?"

"Twitch."

"I put the knife down, and go sit in a stateroom, you still let me off on Molokai?"

"Rather see you go over the side, right now," Walston said.

"Shoot him," Vince said.

"Yes," Music said, seeming to answer all of them, but he was looking at Bruman.

Bruman smiled at all of them. "All right, then."

But when they had him locked up, Walston said, "That's a mistake."

Music shrugged. "It's one I can live with." He winked at Walston. "I don't have any bullets for this gun. I don't even remember the caliber."

10
♣

Bobbie pulled the heavy drapes closed against the morning in her half of the suite on the Ilikai's thirty-second floor and snuggled down naked in the near dark beside Reggie.

Her father wouldn't approve, but that didn't bother Bobbie; in fact, she was tempted to send a bellhop out to buy her a camera so she could leave her father a lumpy brown paper bag of her own Polaroid prints. Maybe then he'd see her the way she'd seen him, grinning at the camera as he mounted a woman—Lila, he said her name was—from one direction or another, gripping this or that in his hand. Lila's lipstick had been smeared along her cheek, and in every photograph she'd had her mouth open (talking, sometimes, from the look of it; panting, sometimes, apparently), and so it was easy, almost imperative, for Bobbie and her two very best girl-friends to write captions to go along with the photographs.

They'd giggle and shriek up in her room, and even (with di-minishing innocence) try to imitate the sexual positions they were looking at, trying with their limited knowledge but terrific imagi-nations to make the pictures come alive.

The best of the captions they invented had been one for a pho-tograph of Lila crouching on the bed, with her head half-turned from the camera to look back at her own rear. Her mouth, of course, had been open. Bobbie's dad, behind her, had a fistful of cheek in each hand. The caption they'd come up with had been, "It looks like a *what?*"

Like weasels, she thought. Zoo creatures, her father and Lila. She slid a hand between Reggie's warm thighs and slept.

Reggie woke first. The bed, the room, the short-haired blonde woman who lay nude beside him were all as irretrievable as his dreams for a moment. *Bobbie. Honolulu.*

He got up carefully so the rolling motion of the mattress wouldn't wake her, hunted around for his shorts, pulled them up, went into her bathroom, and softly closed the door. The face he saw in the mirror didn't seem entirely his.

Bobbie, too, came out of her dreams disoriented. Her first thought was that something was missing, and it took a minute to name that something *Reggie*. She lay listening, but the suite was quiet. She turned her head and saw his clothing beside the bed. Only then did she smile, stretch, and let her breath out with a happy sigh.

She, too, got up to go to the bathroom, and she, too, looked at herself in the mirror, and although she couldn't see her own face superimposed like a double negative over the ghost of the one he'd left behind, that's what happened, and her heart knew it.

Bobbie put on a robe, suddenly demure, and went looking for him. Reggie sat on the lanai with a beer in his hand, still in his boxer shorts. She put her hands on his shoulders and bent down to kiss his forehead. It was burning.

"Hot."

He nodded. "I slept badly."

"Me too. Why, do you suppose? Aren't we having a wonderful time?"

"I got dreams I didn't want."

"Me too." Bobbie searched for what she could tell him. "I dreamt of my father."

"You're lucky," Reggie said. "I dreamt of *mine.*"

She moved around and stood in front of him, putting herself between him and the sea so that her shadow fell across his face. She leaned back against the railing and it looked to Reggie from his angle as if she were balanced there.

"Careful."

Bobbie nodded. "Is he that awful?"

"Dad? No, I guess not. He was only part of the dream, anyway;, I got the whole family, or most of them. All of them but me." He grinned at her. "Our family's not pretty."

"At least you're not in cages."

"Oh, yes." He pulled on his cheek until his face stretched. "We're trapped in this." He held up his hands. "And in these. In my dream, our cages were cards, but it's our skins that imprison us.

"Hallorans aren't like the rest of you, Bobbie. Dad used to say that we were wolves in wolves' clothing, but he was wrong."

"I was trapped on a card, too," she said quietly. "In part of the dream, anyway. In the rest, it was real cages."

"He was wrong," Reggie said, as if he hadn't heard her, "because we're animals taking the shape of people."

"Weasels, in my case," she said.

"What?"

"Nothing."

Reggie stood with her at the lanai's rail, and they turned together to look out at Kalakaua Avenue. His hand touched hers. "My brother laid it all out in front of his girl."

"Careful," she said.

He nodded.

♦

Charlie parked his rented Firebird at the curb and looked at Groton's house. *My house. Then why not pull into the driveway?* He turned the engine off instead and stood on the sidewalk.

Groton had recovered the deed from his safe deposit box that morning and had transferred it to Charlie in the presence of the city clerk, even offering to pay the small registration fee. He gave Charlie a key to the house, said the movers were due to arrive that afternoon, and shook hands. But Groton's moving truck wasn't at the curb, and Charlie's key didn't fit.

He walked around the house twice, ducking under brown papery banana leaves, alert for those huge, hairy spiders he'd been told Hawaii had, and waded through knee-high, flowering weeds.

He tried the neighbor's doorbell (not knowing what he'd ask), then sat on the steps and waited. There weren't any kids in any of the yards, no cars driving down the street, no mothers in plastic chairs sipping iced tea in the shade of their porches. Between their roofs, Charlie had a view of Kaneohe Bay and the Marine Corps base that stuck out into it like a finger. A woodpecker drilled hollowly at the top of a palm; a cricket under the steps chirped twice, timidly, then even the cricket went silent.

The houses across from him moved like mirages, like grass underwater, and he doubted for a moment that any of it—the game, the hand, the result—had happened. Perhaps he was sitting on a stranger's front steps, those of a man who would come home from work in a few hours, pick up the afternoon paper from the front lawn, and give him a questioning look as he unlocked his own front door. Or, worse, maybe that stranger would walk by him—*or through him*—without a glance. Charlie would find (in that same afternoon paper that he picked up from the yard) that he wasn't in Kailua at all, but in Stillwell, Oklahoma, or Little Rock, Arkansas, or somewhere in Idaho, and he'd have to figure out how he'd come to be here, what he was supposed to be doing. *Waiting for what, Charlie, waiting for whom?*

It was a bit like the certainty of seeing the seven of diamonds folded just before it turns up in your hand. Maybe it *is* only a mirage. *All of it. Lia too.*

At the end of that thought a screen door squealed open, banged shut, and he looked up to see a neighbor woman frowning at him from her porch.

"Mr. Groton isn't home."

"He's supposed to be. He's supposed to be moving."

"He didn't say nothing to me."

"You've seen him, today, then?"

She hesitated, giving herself away. "No. Only the locksmith this morning." She eyed him. "To see that you don't trespass the man's property, no doubt."

"Actually, I'm trying to get into my own house. Mr. Groton transferred the deed this morning. Remind him of that when you see him."

"I'm watching you."

"Watch this." Charlie hunted through the ruined garden and came up with a brick. He showed it to the woman, then tossed it through the window with an easy, underhanded arc.

"I'm calling the police."

"Of course you are."

He carefully picked triangles of glass from the glazing and climbed into the hole while she did it. He picked up more glass shards inside, and the brick, then threw them all back into the yard.

Groton's house was a small one of concrete block, painted white and topped with a shake roof. It had a neat, simple floor plan, one level, what they'd call a ranch in California, a rambler in the Midwest. The windows were deep-set and louvered with frosted glass. It looked as if Groton might be back any minute; not so much as a kitchen drawer had been overturned and emptied. There should be packing boxes, shouldn't there? *What sort of man transfers a deed but changes the locks? What sort of man wants a thing but walks off and leaves it?* "What sort of man," Charlie said out loud, "breaks out his own front window with a brick?"

He heard his father's voice next. *In six months you'll be hunting in back alleys for grocery money.* He heard, too, something his father hadn't said: *What is it with you and windows?*

The police didn't come. Charlie had bet with himself that they wouldn't, that the neighbor was in on the play, which worried him more than a little. No matter how good, you couldn't fight a whole table that had taken one side against you. Would neighbors do that? *Depends on the neighbor,* he thought.

Charlie patched the window with the side of a sagging cardboard box from the back porch and took the front door off its hinges. He dragged the couch outside, intending to pile all of

Groton's stuff along the sidewalk and the steps, but changed his mind. It was too much work and got him nothing, and who wanted to live in an empty house? As he was getting a grip on the couch to drag it back, a shower thundered down, the water in a wall, and Charlie took cover from it on the porch, watching Groton's furniture run with water.

"Ruin it," the neighbor woman called through the downpour.

Charlie smiled and waved, and she went back inside. After the rain, he had to turn away three people who wanted to buy it, not quite sure why he didn't sell it to them.

When the daylight failed, somebody knocked at the hole where the door had been, and Charlie, on his way to answer it, sent a pane fragment skidding with his toe. He was a bit surprised to find that Groton filled the hole.

"Hello, neighbor."

"Neighbor?"

"I've taken rooms." Groton waved at the house next door.

"You forgot to leave me a key that fits."

"I see you found a way around that."

Charlie nodded. "Finding a way around things was my whole education."

"You're not going to win, you know, not even with all the patience you Hallorans are famous for, not even with the skill you Hallorans have in your fingers."

"Why didn't you just welch? Why go through this silly game?"

"I don't know what you're talking about. I'm new, here, just trying to be friendly." Groton fixed Charlie with a look that Charlie knew well. "I plan to be so fucking friendly you won't be able to stand it."

"Interesting strategy, sandbagging."

"Soft play was my dad's style," Groton said.

"Not mine."

"No."

"My dad's, I mean."

"No. Your dad's as hard as they come. Cold as snakes."

Charlie shrugged. "It's necessary."

"Being a mechanic, you mean? But he takes the word at its word, so to speak. He fixes *things*. To you and me, marks or not, they're still people."

"To you, not me. We're all machines. We're engines and switches and wires and greasy bearings. Music, too."

"You don't really believe that. He hasn't done that to you."

"Yes."

Groton sat on the porch rail, fidgeting. "You told me, when you were pretending to be somebody else, that sometime in a man's life he's got to get free from his father." His hand stilled. "But you haven't yet, Halloran. And it's a crying shame, because you can play cards." He worked up a smile. "And probably nothing else."

"I've never liked it."

"Never liked what?"

"The life."

"Which? The good, honest games in nice places, with all the action a man can stand, where the drop of every card is another challenge to his skill? Or the Halloran sort of games, where everything's known except how you're going to avoid getting caught, always wondering if this time you'll get killed?"

"That one."

"Then don't live it." Groton stood. "You've never needed to. The game is pure, Halloran, and worth playing on its own terms." He patted the cardboard over the empty space that had been a window. "Look at the corner you've got into in your first day as a civilian."

♦

Bruman began a hammering that echoed in the boat's bowels, shook the bulkheads, and drove Music and the others up on deck and into the open.

"He'll ruin that cabin," Walston said.

Music shrugged, then nodded, then watched the sea. It still had shards of red in it, although the ball of the sun was down. Molokai, alongside, was a black hump like a whale; the horizon behind them where Oahu had disappeared hours ago looked like a scratch. He turned to Vince. "I'll sell her to you right now, as she is."

"Done. How much?"

"What's the fair market value?"

"Fifty thousand."

"Is that all? I risked more, myself, when I got her from Woods."

"I know."

"You had five times that against her."

"Yes."

Music cocked his head, as if listening for something under the hammering. "Write me a check with five zeroes and pay the slip fees when we get back."

Vince opened his checkbook and patted his pockets until he found a pen.

"*If* we get back," Walston said.

Music's good eye winked, but Vince didn't know whether it was deliberate.

"He can't sink her, Captain, by beating on the bulkheads," Vince said.

Walston took his pipe out. "Maybe." He looked down into its bowl and dug his finger around in it, then changed his mind and put the pipe back. "That's a lunatic who's locked up down there, Mr. Arthur, and the definition of a lunatic is that you never know what it is that he can't do."

Bruman's idea was simply to make as much noise as possible. Nothing too bad could come of it. They'd either let him out—or anyway do something stupid and give him an opening to get by them— or they'd figure if he was hammering he couldn't be scheming, and they'd want to get out of the noisy salon and leave him alone.

It worked on the nerves, he well knew. Whenever Bruman wanted a fight later, when the boat docked, or after he was done drinking, he kept talking, goading the man. It got him jangled. But if the fight was soon, he'd say nothing. Lots of noise, or no noise at that's what puts a man on edge and throws his timing off.

Bruman paced the small room, sizing it up with his hands, feeling every object as a blind man might. The staterooms and the salon were fitted with hanging kerosene lanterns, a return to the original decor. He hadn't any matches to light them, but Bruman thought he could probably set fires in the rain with two damp sticks. He took the hurricane lamp down and shook it. Part full. The smell was white gas, not kerosene. *Better still.*

Bruman turned off the overhead, unscrewed the light bulb, and laid it on the bed to cool while he hammered on the bulkheads in the dark with a bookend. They'd got his big fighting blade, but not the clasp knife in his dungarees pocket that all sailors carry. He opened it now and picked out the awl.

When he was convinced the light bulb was cold, he drilled into its aluminum base. He poured a little gas from the lamp into the hole, then screwed the bulb back into the overhead.

Now the tricky part. Bruman tore a narrow strip from a bed sheet, soaked it in gas, then wound that around the light bulb a couple of times and hung it like a party streamer to the open porthole. He wadded the rest of the sheet up and dragged everything else flammable to that side of the cabin. He stripped clothes from the dowel in the closet, hefted it like a hockey stick, and hid in the bathroom.

Reach through the door crack with the clothes pole and flick the light switch on. There ought to be one hell of an explosion.

The hammering had driven Cracker Jack out of his nest in the sail locker and up on deck with the people. He raced from one end to the other, his tail standing up like a brush, his yellow eyes like wild lamps. A keening howl followed seconds behind him like a sonic boom.

"Cat's nuts, too," Vince said.

"It's the noise," Music said. "I hope. How long before we make port?"

"I'm not sure it is the noise," Walston said. "He slept straight through the refitting of the salon you had done in San Diego."

Music guessed what Walston was thinking and asked again, "How long before we reach port?"

"Not long. We're just abeam of Ilio Point." Walston pointed. "Those lights ahead should be Hoolehua. There's an airport there."

"Distance and night are my enemies." Music stroked his cheek absently. "The one eye."

"Six or seven miles," Walston said. "Inside an hour."

"How far offshore are we?"

"Just outside the reef. Half a mile. Why?"

"Break out life vests. See if you can't get the cat into something."

"I could unship the dinghy and tow it."

"Who's paying the captain's salary?" Vince asked.

Music looked at Walston, then at Vince, then patted his pocket with the check in it. "I guess you are."

"Why all this panic?" Vince asked Walston.

"It's the cat," Walston said after a minute. "I've never seen him like this."

"So?"

Walston looked at Music for help, but Music said nothing.

"He's a strange beast," Walston said. "He sometimes knows things before he should."

"That's nuts. *You're* nuts."

"Rats leave ships before they sink," the captain said.

"Rats live below the water line. They know trouble first."

"There's stories of them fleeing a ship in the harbor before it sails."

"Same thing. They still know it first."

"Cats aren't rats," Music said levelly, as if that should end the argument. "And I've got a bad feeling too."

"That's why you sold her to me?"

Music nodded.

"On a hunch?"

"Call it that."

The three of them watched as the cat skidded around them in a wide turn and headed back toward the bow.

"What about the dinghy?" Walston asked.

The pole didn't quite reach. Bruman supposed at first that he'd have to risk exposing a little more of his arm than he would like, but then he thought of coat hangers. He twisted one around the end of the dowel, keeping its hook on the end, and scuttled back into the small head with the gaff he'd made. He flicked the switch on the exhaust fan, glad to hear its steady purr, then reached out with his gaff and flicked the other switch.

Music clearly heard glass breaking before the *crump* of an explosion that knocked him off his feet. The sea to port glowed white for a minute like ice, then yellow with flame. Even above the noise of the fire and the panic of the crew, he could hear Cracker Jack howl.

"Bruman!" a voice yelled. He thought it must be Walston's. "Bruman!" it said again. "Bruman!" like an echo, like an engine.

He was down there, a prisoner, perhaps trapped in the fire, and would have to be pulled free. Music tried to stand, but couldn't. He watched as the two crewmen were released from the rail like arrows, and in perfect racing dives disappeared into the black water.

Hands shoved yellow canvas into his face. "Put this on." It bounced off, fat with air.

"The cat," Music said.

"Don't see him."

"I *hear* him."

"Don't have time to worry about a damned cat," Vince said.

"Bruman?"

"Below."

"Walston?"

"Below. To get Bruman. Get that on."

"Tear up your check."

"What?"

"If the cat survives."

"Jesus, Halloran, you're a piece of work."

"Hundred-thousand-dollar cat," Music said. "I can't get my feet under me."

Vince bent to look at Halloran's ankle. "I don't think it's broken. Christ, I hate fire."

"I hate water."

Bruman had hoped the explosion would blow the stateroom door off, but instead the door to the head slammed closed, bounced open again, and Bruman caught the flash and glass in his eyes.

The doorknob was already hot when Walston got to it. He wrapped his hand in his shirt tail and unlocked the door, but when he pulled, it wouldn't open. *Heat-buckled.* He hammered on it with the flat of one hand until that burned, then with the other, and hollered for Bruman.

Bruman heard his name, or thought he did; it was hard to sort out from the rest of the noise in his ears—the fire and a thrumming in his head. "I'm blind!" he called back.

"The door's stuck."

"I'm blind!"

"You'll have to kick it out."

"I'm *blind!*"

"You don't find the door, you're going to cook."

Bruman crossed his forearms in front of his face, bellowed, ran out into the middle of the cabin, and then, counting on his memory, spun and kicked at what he hoped was the door. It slammed open, and he was free.

The door hit Walston in the forehead. He went down like a beef under the knacker's hammer, without anything resembling a thought.

◆

Vince finally got the life vest over Music's arms, dragged him to the starboard rail, and rolled him underneath it into the sea.

"Hundred-thousand-dollar cat," Music said, then took a mouthful of water.

The sails were on fire now. The aft mast burned like a candle. The *Music Hall* was listing away from him, showing more and more of her round, weed-streaked bottom.

Bruman stumbled into the salon, knocking against the chairs and grabbing hold of each one like ponies on a merry-go-round until he realized that the table was *round*, or nearly, and that he couldn't find his way out doing that.

She was listing about three degrees, Bruman judged, and he knew he was in trouble unless he found the stairs quickly. She'd be sinking on her port side, which made the companionway *this* direction, unless he'd turned himself around completely by now and was heading back up the passageway to the staterooms. Take three steps, he told himself, then turn around if you don't find them.

The pain in his eyes was awful. He tried not to think of what the salt water would do, but concentrated instead on his chances of jumping blind into a night sea without any idea of the distance or direction to shore.

What are the currents, here? Where are the reefs? Was he bleeding badly enough to attract sharks? Surely the boat was burning brightly enough to bring help; he'd call out every four or five minutes and hope it arrived.

Vince couldn't keep his footing and get below. He finally gave it up and hoped the other two were out. Nothing, not even a cat, could find purchase on that tilting deck.

Cracker Jack had stopped howling and was panting fiercely, his ears flat. His claws ached. The ruff at his neck was beginning to smoke. And he was as heavy as a stone.

Bruman reached the deck and let himself roll into the sea. *No burning oil on sailboats, just wood and canvas that smoked and hissed and went out when it hit water.*

The cat saw his last chance and took it, not deciding anything, but simply moving with the catlogic and catspeed he'd been born with. He sank nineteen claws into Bruman's neck and shoulder as the two of them fell. When Bruman howled and turned, Cracker Jack howled back and turned with him, rolling him over the way a lumberjack works a log. And when he opened Bruman's carotid and Bruman began to sink, Cracker Jack climbed to the top and began to swim.

Music watched without expression as his boat—Vince's boat, he reminded himself—went down, but Vince watched it sink with an ache.

"See anybody?" he asked Vince. "Anything?"

"No. I don't think Walston got off. Or Bruman. I don't see the other two, either." *Or the cat,* but he didn't say it.

"Crew probably swims like eels. I watched them go over the side."

"Breakers," Vince said.

"What's that?"

"Behind you. Breakers."

Music paddled awkwardly in a circle, fighting the life vest, and saw the white line of breaking water. "It's a little soon for that, isn't it?"

"Yes."

"Reef?"

"I think so."

"Is that good or bad, do you suppose?"

"I don't know," Vince said. "This is my first shipwreck."

"Cut us up, I'll bet."

"Like glass."

Music thought of his son and the trouble he'd given him not yet a week ago. "Sharks."

"We'll bleed to death, first, skinned alive in salt water."

"A relative of mine died that way more than a century ago," Music said. "Skinned by a pair of trappers and hung up on a hook like a side of beef."

"You're joking."

Music tried to shrug but the life vest wouldn't let him. "So the story goes. They got cheated at cards by my great-grandfather's uncle. It's never been anything but a dangerous business."

"Why do you do it?"

"Maybe because it *is* a dangerous business." He laughed softly. "Or maybe it's because it's all I know."

"Reef. Now."

"Yes."

The current pushed them onto it almost gently. Vince cut his hands climbing up it, but Music simply walked on as if the coral had been carved into steps.

"I'll be damned; there's your cat."

Music had to strain to see, but he finally made out the black lump balanced precariously in the ocean on what turned out to be a spar. When Music leaned down to gather him up, Cracker Jack came up all claws, but Music held him.

"You owe me that hundred thousand dollars after all," Vince said.

"Why? Did *you* save him?"

A fisherman found them at sunrise, standing on the water like holy men. The tall, gray-haired half of the pair stared at his rescuer as if he were expected (but late). He held up his hands in acknowledgment to the fisherman's wave, and the fisherman saw he was holding something—a cat, it turned out—but from this distance the man looked as if he were manacled.

Charlie woke that next morning in the middle of a calculation, as if finishing the math a dream had started: the time difference between Hawaii and Kansas City. He looked at his watch and checked it against the dark windows—just before dawn—and wondered where the *Music Hall* was. *What are you up to, Dad? Why did I come awake thinking of you?*

He'd spent his childhood sleeping fitfully through endless dreaming hours while part of him figured the odds, played invisible hands, counted cards, opening his eyes only to wonder what his dad would think of it all before he had come awake enough to understand that his father wouldn't—couldn't—think anything of it.

He put a hand on a cold wall. This house had in it the same lack of welcome that he remembered from all the other places he'd lived in, as if houses knew that Hallorans were only boarders who'd be staying a week or two, a month at most. He'd grown up with the normal childhood fears of the dark, but in *his* dark it was the closet itself that menaced him, or the stairs, not something in or under it. Although he had tried, Charlie had never been able to figure out how to hide from the thing he was hiding in.

He sat where he'd fallen asleep, even though he ached with a too-soon, old-man's stiffness. He concentrated on the shapes in the room, on the walls, as helpless as he'd been as a child, unable to avoid turning them all into faces, hands, and more vague, more sinister threats. Houses didn't like Hallorans.

Just move. Charlie levered his weight out of the chair, and swayed when he was vertical. The whole family had knees that insisted on locking up like rusted parts. He stared out the black windows at the strange black neighborhood.

Something might crawl in the hole.

In six months you'll be . . .

Back in back alleys.

Charlie looked into the kitchen, at its unfamiliar shapes, at the white metal of the refrigerator and the stove that seemed to give off their own eerie light.

He negotiated the living room clumsily, banging his shins against the shins of chairs, stumbling over objects that he would have sworn hadn't been strewn there in daylight.

The other half of the house was lit by the neighbor's porch light and a lamp in one of her downstairs rooms. As he watched, another light came on upstairs and he had to check his watch again to see that it was only four-thirty. Groton.

What was Charlie supposed to do? Call a cop? Buy a gun?

All the rules he'd ever lived by said you played the hand you were dealt despite your misgivings, paid your debts however suspicious, and kept your mouth shut. Nobody said you couldn't fold and walk away.

Milo couldn't get his hands out, Charlie. He was eaten by wolves.

The backyard might be his, or any black square of ground planted with night-dark trees. What was history but an endless series of sieges, of arrayed armies or ideas—or piled cash and the Hallorans' brand of luck—battering the walls of another closed town? The lights next door silvered the leaves like moonlight, a light that was, after all, only borrowed.

Every hand dictated a time for the player to decide how much he was willing to pay for more cards. Good players decided it early.

"What's your investment?" his father had asked him again and again. "What's the pot worth now? What's it worth later? *How much more* is it going to cost?"

♦

"Mom?"

"Lia? Where are—"

"Here, home—"

"—you?"

"—Hawaii."

They both laughed, as they always did when readjusting to the pauses made necessary by a conversation of this distance. *Like here to the moon.*

"It must be early; is it light there yet? We've just finished lunch. What's the matter, honey?"

"Oh—" Nothing much, Mom. What do you do when you love a man you don't understand? Love a man you shouldn't? "—Nothing."

Dad would have believed the lie, or not disbelieved it so quickly, and it was Dad she had thought would pick up the phone at this hour. She could see her mom standing in the kitchen, her hip against the refrigerator, her eyebrow arched the way it did when she didn't like an answer, a hand out to her husband to stop him from taking the phone. She heard another connection open.

"Lia?"

"*Daddy.*"

"What time is it, there? Five?"

"Almost."

"Are you all right?"

"I'm fine. I knew at this hour you'd both be home." She heard her father grunt, satisfied.

"Lia?" her mother asked. "What is it?"

"I've met somebody," she said, uncertain how to approach it. The second open line shut off like an ear clearing itself—her dad hanging up gently.

"That's nice."

"Do you have a minute? Are you going out?"

"Your father is. I have all the time in the world, sweetheart."

"Is the piano still a wreck?"

"The piano?"

"The one in the living room," Lia said stupidly.

"Uh, oh. Let me sit down."

Lia, half an ocean and half a continent from the house, could hear a chair being pulled across the linoleum, could even hear, she imagined, the front door closing softly, sticking a little, behind her father.

"What is it, honey?"

"Is it? Still a wreck?"

"Yes."

"Tell me why, please. You loved that piano."

"But I loved your father more, dear."

"I—don't—un—der—*stand*." Lia now was gulping as if there weren't any air, honking at the end of each syllable the way she did when she laughed.

"I'm not sure there's anything *to* understand, honey. Do you remember it getting broken?"

"Yes."

"That fight with Grandpa?"

"Yes."

"You must have been young, seven or eight. I wanted it left that way, at first, to embarrass him, your grandfather. To let him know whose house he was fighting in and to remind him that childishness of that sort hurts others."

"They never hurt each other," Lia said, mishearing.

"Others," her mother repeated. "No, they never hurt each other. And Grandpa never laid a hand on your father when he was a boy, at least not that I've ever heard of. It was only when they were both men that they started behaving like that."

"Why, do you suppose?"

"This man of yours isn't violent, is he?"

Lia paused in the pause, getting herself under control, and her mother, even so far away, heard it.

"*Is* he?"

"No, Mom. But he's in a violent life. And I'm afraid that violence will come into mine—into ours."

"Tell me." And then, after Lia had, her mother said, "A gambler? Really? People can make their living that way?"

"Charlie does. His whole family does. Has, he says, for generations."

"Charlie?"

"Charles Halloran. I'm in love with him, Mom." *And shouldn't be!*

It was her mother's turn to sit silently in the pause. "Math," she said finally. "Tornadoes."

"That's part of it, but not all of it. And now I need to know—I think I do, anyway—why you left that reminder of violence in your house. I still don't understand."

"I was angry at your father, too, of course, and wanted to hurt him with it. *Look what you've done*, that sort of thing. And I wanted, I guess, to give him a warning of some sort."

"How's that?"

"We—you and I, all women—carry our futures with us," her mother said, "but men are different. I thought your dad needed a reminder that todays cause tomorrows."

"Did it work?"

"When Liam—went missing," her mother said quietly, "your father sat on the piano bench, his hands as steady as stone in the air above its keys, for hours it seemed. But he wouldn't—couldn't—touch it."

"Mom—"

"I don't know if it worked the way I meant it to or not. But it helped him through his grief somehow." Her voice took on an edge of tears. "Beautiful things get broken." Lia heard her mother's long inhalation, like a wind. "Beautiful things get lost."

Neither of them spoke after that for several long minutes, minutes made longer by the open line that hummed with sea currents, gathered in the cable stretching under the Pacific. "I don't know what to do," Lia finally said.

"It's all such a gamble, honey," her mother told her. "All of it. Love, life . . . children, *everything.*" Her voice seemed to grow distant. "There's danger all around us. If you love him, it might not be all that bad an idea to choose a man who knows more than a little about risk."

◆

When Vince came in, Bobbie was dressed and sitting beside Reggie on the couch, watching an afternoon movie on television.

"Bobbie?"

"Hi, Dad," she said, without looking up. "You skin that old goat, my future father-in-law?"

"That old goat's fine," Music said. "The other old goat's pretty skinned though."

Bobbie twisted around, and Vince lifted his bandaged hands. Stumbling, she rushed between them into a hug.

She and Reggie asked at the same time, "What happened, Dad?"

"The boat's gone," both fathers said.

"Gone?" Reggie asked.

"Sunk." Music dropped Cracker Jack onto the carpet, where he crouched, sniffing. "Four missing, presumed drowned. I think you're looking at the only survivors."

"Jesus, Dad."

It seemed as if Music were looking at his son, but he was watching Vince and Bobbie from the corner of his good eye. *No hug. No 'Are you all right, Dad?' No—*

"Are you all right, Dad?"

Music forced down a smile that wanted to come. "Not a scratch, except from the cat." He looked over at Vince, who still held his daughter. "The *Music Hall* wasn't mine when she burned."

"*Burned?*" Bobbie cried.

"Burned first, then sunk," Vince said. "These aren't burns, but the coral, a reef, when we needed one. Halloran, there, just walked ashore."

"I don't like the ocean," Music said.

"So he got it away from you?" Reggie asked, not believing it.

"It was his. Which reminds me," Music said, turning to Vince, "that means it was uninsured."

"The papers weren't signed, and anyway they're gone with the witness down with the boat," Vince said. "Far as anyone knows, it's still yours."

Music fingered the still-damp check in the pocket of his new slacks. "Walston was a good man," he said, which isn't what he meant to say.

"You could collect the insurance and give it to me."

"Fraud."

"I could stop the check."

Music saw understanding come to Reggie and was saddened by it. He'd wanted just once to seem vulnerable to his son, and now that was lost.

"Well, Halloran?"

"The honest thing," Music said, picking up the cat, who hadn't moved from where he'd been put, "is to honor your check and take the loss, a good hand busted. But failing that, I'll have to report her sunk and collect the insurance. I make a little less that way, and you lose a lot less that way, and you make us both worse than we are. But I guess it's your play."

"I don't understand your qualms, Halloran. You'll cheat some poor joe out of his paycheck, but not an insurance company?"

Music opened the door, the cat settled peacefully in the crook of his arm. "I haven't cheated an honest man since the boys were in school," he said, and went out.

Reggie just missed him at the elevator, saw the doors slide closed, but took the next one and caught up with his father in the lobby bar.

"What did you mean by that?"

"By what?"

"That you haven't cheated since we were small."

"It's the truth. As a matter of fact, I haven't cheated since your mother left. Unless the victim was a sharp, then I'd beat him half to death." Music put Cracker Jack down on a chair and ordered two ginger ales from the waiter.

"Animals aren't allowed in here, sir."

"I'm blind in this eye," Music said, tapping it with a fingernail. "This is a seeing-eye cat." Music looked at him with such a dead expression for so long that the waiter went to get the drinks.

"But you taught *us*. Charlie and me," Reggie said when the man had gone, as if his father had forgotten who his children were.

"You had to have a trade, and that's the trade the Hallorans have."

"But you don't practice it? You had Charlie cheating the whole table. That's just you, cheating at a distance." *Cheating at a generation's distance*, Reggie realized.

"That's Charlie's business. He said he wanted out of the life, but he took the first opportunity that came his way to step back into it, didn't he?"

"Why didn't you help him, Dad?"

"I did. He just hasn't realized it yet." The drinks came, and Music paid for them. "If he goes straight, it's because of me, in *spite* of me, to show me that he's better. He doesn't want to be as good as I am; he wants to be the opposite of what he thinks I am."

"You're still shucking your sons."

"I guess so."

"And what about me, Dad?"

Music looked at his elder son sadly. "You're not a good enough player to be honest. Most of this screwed up family isn't."

◆

The confusion Charlie was feeling only got worse when he saw his father coming down the street. Music stopped half a dozen houses away, checked a piece of paper, then looked up the street and counted the houses. His eye, of course, fell on Charlie, and Music smiled.

His father stood at the join between the sidewalk and the driveway, much as Charlie had the day before, and looked the house over from the roof vent to the steps Charlie sat on. He leaned to the side to take in the jungle growing there. "Not a bad-looking place for ill-gotten gains."

"Ill," Charlie said, "but not quite gotten yet. Come on in."

"Oh?"

Charlie pointed next door with his thumb. "Groton."

"Ah. He wants it back."

"He wants it back all right. And I'm not sure I won't give it to him."

"Never give a man anything, Charlie. Make him win it if he wants it."

"Come on in," Charlie repeated.

Music, as if to frustrate his son further, turned his back and stared out at the bay. The water was dark, flecked with red.

"You could have sailed in," Charlie told him. "Just climbed the hill and looked back at home."

"The *Music Hall*'s at the bottom of the ocean."

Charlie was quiet for a moment. "*You* sink her?"

His father turned back. "Me? Why would I do that?"

Charlie shrugged. "Maybe to keep from getting beat."

Music looked at him strangely, then walked past him and into the house. He pivoted slowly, as if he were thinking of buying the furniture, and said, "You break that window out to get in?"

Charlie heard, *You break that window in to get out?* and nodded.

"You really think I'd do that?" Music asked.

"What? Break a window?"

"Set fire to my own boat and take her out from underneath me in the middle of the ocean."

"Is that what happened?"

Music nodded.

"My God. I thought you meant she'd sprung a leak in the harbor."

"No. Off Molokai."

"Are you all right?"

"I'm glad you both asked. I wasn't sure you would."

"I'm sorry about all that, Dad. I've been rethinking what I said."

"Don't."

"What happened? With the *Music Hall*?"

193

"It was Arthur's doing. He hired a man to sink her if the need arose. Now he wants me to hand over the insurance check."

"Why does he—Oh. You'd sold her first."

Music smiled again. "You're really as sharp as they come, Charlie. Your brother thought Arthur had won her."

"Impossible."

"Thank you. How about without cheating?"

"Still impossible." Charlie pointed to the kitchen. "Get you something?"

"Cold water."

"You haven't had enough of that, huh?"

When Music had his drink and a seat, he held the glass with both hands and stared into it.

"What was it like, Dad?"

"I thought I was going to die with my enemy instead of my family," he said, without looking up, "and then I realized I didn't have much of a family either." Music waved, as if to brush away what might sound like self pity. "My doing, that; all of it. I've kept you at arm's length since you were born."

Charlie sat as close to him as was comfortable. "Why?" he asked quietly.

Music looked up from his glass of water. "*Hard* gets to be a habit, I guess. And in case you think I've changed, I just disemboweled your brother."

"Disemboweled, how?"

"Told him the truth."

That'll usually do it, Charlie thought. "The truth about what?"

"His ability."

"I don't think Reggie has a lot of illusions about that. He's as good as he's going to get, and he knows it. He knows his limits and stays out of trouble."

"I told him he isn't good enough to be honest."

"Isn't good enough to be honest," Charlie repeated, as if the words could carry—had to carry—another meaning.

"I told him something else too."

Charlie waited. *Latin, or hieroglyphs next.*

"I told him I don't cheat."

◆

Lia drove to the yacht basin after her last class and asked at the gate for the *Music Hall.* The man told her the *Music Hall* had met with disaster. Didn't she read the papers?

"Disaster? What disaster? When?"

"Last night sometime. Burned and sunk." The man shook his head. "Beautiful boat."

"Who got off?" *Did anybody get off? Was Charlie on the boat? Did he go back to his father when he left me?*

The man at the gate rummaged under his desk for the paper, sorted through the sections, found the one he was looking for. Took another age, Lia thought, to find the page he wanted. "Ah. Here it is. 'Disaster off Molokai.' Let's see." He read with his finger. "'The *Music Hall,* out of Kansas City.' Funny damned place for a boat to be from."

"Read," Lia said.

"'The *Music Hall*'s owner, Music Halloran, and his guest, Vincent Arthur, of San Diego, were picked up by a fisherman early this morning from a reef half a mile off Molokai's north shore.' Says one of 'em had a cat."

"To hell with the goddamned cat."

"Says, 'three crew and the captain are missing and are presumed to be drowned.'" The man shook his head. "Presumed to be et, they mean. Shark waters, those. Captain's name was Walston."

"I know. A nice man. Nothing there about the owner's two sons?"

When the man's finger went back to its slow reading, Lia reached in and took the paper. "Let me see."

"Yes, ma'am."

Music and Arthur had been treated at the hospital in Hoolehua ("for cuts and abrasions") and then had chartered a helicopter back to Honolulu. The rest of the article included a short interview with

195

a colleague of hers at the University, a native Hawaiian who suspected that, *threatened* that, ancient curses were at work.

Lia looked up from the paper. "It doesn't say where this man Arthur is staying."

"Stayin' at the Ilikai," the man said, and silently swore at himself for not getting paid first for knowing it. "At least he was. Him and his daughter."

Lia thanked him and turned to go, then turned back. *Charlie had won a house.* "Mr. Halloran must have had other guests last week. Somebody local."

"That's right, he did."

"You know the man's name?"

"I could look it up in the log, but I'm not supposed to."

"Oh." She almost turned away again. "Is there a way I could encourage you to do something you're not supposed to?"

"I accept tips."

"How large of one?"

"Fifty dollars."

"Fifty dollars?"

"Maybe forty."

Lia had sixteen dollars and some change in her purse, what was left from lunch. This seemed a ghoulish thing to dicker about. She gave him a look, a curse of her own, and drove to the Ilikai, thinking, *Let's hope I don't have to come back.*

The desk clerk connected her to Arthur's room, where the phone rang and rang and rang. She hung up after fifteen of them and prepared herself to sit all night in the lobby watching elevators when she felt a light touch on her shoulder. "Hi."

It was Charlie's voice, but it wasn't, too. It was Reggie.

"Reggie!"

"Hi," he said again. "What are you doing here?" *Damn, Dad wouldn't have put it so bluntly.*

Lia didn't notice. "Looking for anybody who can tell me where Charlie is. But how's your father, first?"

"Dad's fine," he said, and grimaced. "Changed, but fine. Mr. Arthur got cut up some. So you know about it?"

196

She nodded. "Charlie wasn't aboard? You weren't aboard?"

"Neither of us. Charlie's at his new place."

"That's what I came for. Do you know where it is?"

"Kailua, Groton said. I don't even know where *that* is."

"I do."

Reggie introduced her to Bobbie and Vincent (she hadn't even noticed them standing behind him), and they in turn invited her to join them for dinner; hungry as she was, she refused. She ran for a phone book, looked up the address, and only when she was halfway up the Pali, her Volkswagen laboring in second gear, had she thought, *I could have called him.*

She parked behind Charlie's rented Firebird, looking at the house lights. What was on the other side of that doorway? *Who* is a better question, she thought. Were there two Charlies, one she could love, and one she couldn't? She gripped the wheel as if still driving, or driving away. But perhaps *what* was the right word after all because a look, a gesture, a touch would upset her life further or return it to her. Go in that doorway, she thought, and you don't come back out the same.

At her approach, a shadow scurried off the porch, down the steps past her and into the weeds, growling. The voices inside stopped. *Voices; he has company.*

"Groton?" Charlie's voice.

"It's me. Lia."

"Lia?"

Had he sounded glad as well as surprised? The window next to the door was missing too. *Oh, Charlie.*

She threw herself into the lighted square (something she'd told herself she wouldn't do), barreling into his chest so hard she felt him rock and catch them both. She felt an instant's stiffness, a slight hesitation, and then he hugged her too.

"I've been meaning to call," Charlie said. "How did you find me?"

Before she could answer, a voice behind him said, "Just be glad that she did."

She looked around Charlie's arm. "Mr. Halloran."

Music was getting to his feet to greet her.

Lia pulled free and crossed the room to take his hand, and held it, and pulled him back down onto the sofa as she sat. "Sit down, please. Shouldn't you be in a hospital?"

"I got wet is all. Then I stood around for a couple of hours. They won't let you use up a hospital room for that." Music gave her hand a squeeze. "It's nice to see you again."

Stood around. "You, too, Mr. Halloran."

"I thought we'd agreed on Music."

Lia tried her best to smile. "I'm confused about a lot more than names just now." She held out her other hand and dragged Charlie down next to her, a Halloran on either side. "I feel claustrophobic, boxed in."

Charlie tried to pull away an inch, but she held onto him. He looked across to Music, who gave him no help. "A bad place, that," Charlie said.

"So what do you do when you're in a corner?" Lia swiveled to stare at each of them. "You must get into them yourselves."

Run, Charlie thought. *Dive out windows.*

"We're not supposed to. We spend our lives learning—or think we're learning, anyway—how not to get into places like that in the first place." He raised the hand she'd left free, saying, *But look at me.*

"You've got a decent chance with my son. He knows where the corners are and which one he's in. Charlie *is* his own enemy, and there's no hope for the two of you until he gets that sorted out. But after he does, I think the two of you face better odds than most."

"Get that sorted out?" Charlie asked. "How, Dad? Snap your fingers and undo everything? *My whole life?* Can you wave a hand and remake me?"

Music smiled kindly. "I think so, yes."

Sandwich plates and mismatched glasses lay scattered on end tables under lamps. Music swatted at a bug. "'Undo everything,' you said. 'Remake me.'" He stared at his son as an architect might a building, measuring it. "I can't, of course. I did too good a job the first time."

Charlie sent Lia a look that said, *See?*

Music searched for an avenue he knew he wouldn't find, then sighed. "What I can do is tell you how I played the hand you're holding now and lost with it. Get comfortable."

"I can sit for days, Dad, comfortable or not."

Music nodded. "Of course you can."

"'Get comfortable' is the two halves of your own mind talking."

Music nodded again. He'd told his sons to listen to the table chatter, to pay attention, that men's minds were divided, and that the truth of their feelings—their fears—could make itself known in their poor jokes and small talk. Reggie hadn't understood, but Charlie had.

"I met your mother in the spring of 1937, when she was nineteen. I was twenty-one." He closed his eyes. "Good God, Charlie, she was beautiful. *Life* was beautiful. Before the war, a young man in our business had the whole world in front of him. I was working up a stake to go to Paris. I wanted to see Berlin, too—Paris and Berlin were the sirens of that era—then London some, and the exotic cities along the Mediterranean: Venice, Athens, Constantinople. *Byzantium.*" Music looked up. "Well, you know the ones I mean. Ever been?"

Charlie shook his head.

"Nor I. It's a shame. Don't miss out. I would have gone—at least, I *might* have gone—but for Margaret Losen. *Side pot*, I thought. I had *quick* in my fingers and no compunction about winning. What are you doing?"

Charlie had the phone book open and was dialing. "I want Reggie to hear this."

Music appeared disconcerted, something Charlie had never seen. He reached back and pulled the line to the phone. "This lesson isn't for your brother; it won't do him any good." He smiled at Lia and allowed the smile to smooth his face. *Like a sheet being shaken*, Lia thought.

"Margaret and I met innocently, or so I was led to believe. I hadn't any friends, you see, that a young lady could manipulate. I hadn't any brothers who'd stayed around, nor classmates, nor people I worked with for her to use as leverage. I wasn't one to go to dances much, and I didn't attend a church, and I certainly wasn't part of the social circle her family moved in, so she had to be *inventive*. Years later, after she'd gone, I'd tell myself that it was her own damned doing anyway, her own corner of her own maneuvering.

"God knows where she saw me first. It was probably in my car; you could see that coming for fifty miles. In any event, she had her father, a councilman, part of the power structure, call the chief of police, and she lied to both of them to get me thrown in jail."

Music, seeing Lia's look, said, "I swear. This was one of the few times in my life that I've been gaffed. She claimed her purse had been stolen and described me. Tall, fair-haired, good looking," Music blinked at his son bashfully, "yellow coupe, all the details that would round up only me.

"I stood in a lineup in the back room of a precinct house next to a bunch of squat, bowlegged cops, and thought I was done for. I saw myself looking at five years." He laughed softly. "It turned out to be eight.

"Anyway, when she'd got a good look at close range—right profile, left profile, from the front, from the back—she had them

200

turn me loose, then met me on the sidewalk and offered me lunch at her house to make up for the misunderstanding. My heart was lost by the time I'd eaten half a plate of potato salad and asked for a second glass of lemonade. We were married that same year, in June, in the Rawlings Street Methodist Church in Kansas City. After Reggie was born, when she finally admitted her crime, she smote me a second time. *I'd married a crook.* I knew then—we both did—that any last chance you boys might have had was gone."

Music faced Lia, not Charlie. "Her leaving, and why, you've both heard about. You haven't heard about me, about trying to buck the house percentage that faces you when you're raising two boys and not knowing how, when you're going to bed alone every night, especially the bad nights, when you can't shake the guilt of leaving your sons in the hands of strangers while you work a hotel craps game or, once, a thousand-mile poker table in the baggage car on the train from Kansas City to Chicago and back." He turned to his son. "That's when I learned, Charlie, that you've got to have a door handy, no matter which sort of game you're playing, because there's no good place to hide on a train."

"Like now, Dad?"

Music decided that didn't need answering. "You must have been eight months or a year old—still in diapers, anyway—when I noticed your affinity. You could shuffle a deck before you could balance upright. You knew the rank of hands before you could count."

"That was your doing."

"Why are you so certain?"

"There's never been anything else I could have been."

"True. You were born to handle cards. What else did you ever want to be?"

The silence lasted so long that the cricket under the porch started up again.

"Nothing comes to mind? All right, I'll tell you. You think now that you wanted to make choices. But you don't realize you already made them, much younger than most. You chose your life, this life, before you remember choosing."

"I never chose anything."

"You did, again and again, sitting down to every lesson. We make damned few choices in our life, really. That was one. This is another one of them now. Life's no good alone." He looked to Lia and repeated it, then turned back to Charlie. "Do whatever it takes to keep from playing solitaire."

"What does it take, Dad?"

"Honesty," he said simply. "Something I didn't give you. You got that on your own."

"I want chaos." Now Charlie leaned forward. "I want chance to work, to be open to it. I dealt myself a straight flush aboard the *Music Hall* and folded it. That wasn't accident, but it wasn't order, either. It was something larger."

It sounds a lot like love, Music thought. "Looking at the two of you," he said, "I'd say you've found it. Chaos, I mean."

"Is this what it looks like?" Lia asked. "Is this how it behaves?"

"It looks like your reflection," Charlie said.

"It behaves like an animal," said Music.

Groton walked in without an invitation, knocking twice on the jamb as he passed it. "It's midnight, Halloran, and you still have a houseful of people. I thought you must have a game going." When he saw Music he stopped.

"Hello, Mr. Groton."

"Hello, Mr. Halloran."

Music stood and stretched and winked at his son. "Your play."

His dad was right. "Got some chips here, Groton?"

Groton shook his head. "I never play here, and never bankroll a game."

"That's a good rule. But right now we need a couple of hundred things, a hundred on a side."

"Things?" Lia asked.

"It doesn't matter what—marbles, bottle caps, loose change, match sticks—each with the value of one. Table stakes, of course, no limit."

"What are we playing for?"

"The house," Charlie said, surprised at the question. "Your ownership behind your hundred things; my ownership behind mine. This time it stays won or lost."

"Just you and me?" Groton asked, glancing at Music.

"I just got rid of my last house," Music said. "I don't want another."

"Does she know how to play?"

Charlie looked at Lia.

"*I'm* not going to gamble a house."

"He wants you to deal," Charlie said. "Is that all right?"

"I don't know how."

Music chuckled. "One or two or all three of us will teach you as you go. It's the fact that you don't know how that makes you valuable at the moment."

"I don't know, Charlie."

"Look, honey, I'm a gambler. I can't change that."

"Yes."

"I don't think you understand. The only thing I've ever really gambled on was staying hidden, not being found out. Now I'm going to *gamble*. I'm going to put my skill against theirs. Against his," he said, pointing at Groton.

"Give the civilians a chance?"

"Give us one."

Groton, at the kitchen table, sorted his piles of pennies and matchsticks and thumbtacks into categories. Charlie glanced at them. Music smiled at Lia and winked, knowing Charlie had counted how many matchsticks, how many bottle caps, how many everythings, when they were being doled out.

Groton had gone out for new cards while the three of them rounded up two hundred things. Charlie pushed the sealed deck across to Lia. "Here's the deck. The box is hard to open; you've got to slide a fingernail under the flap. There'll be jokers and junk on either side of the cards; pull those off. Spread the cards face up so we can see the suits. Sometimes a deck is missing a card, or has one doubled. They'll be stiff and hard to shuffle. Take your time."

It was painful for the three of them to watch, but the cards got mixed after she'd sprayed them a couple of times.

"Seven stud," Groton said. "That's two down cards, one up card, and then stop."

Lia was still flustered.

"One down each," Charlie said. "Do it twice, then one up each. Start with me, 'cause Groton's dealing."

Groton watched carefully even though she hadn't yet started.

"For God's sake, Groton, I've only known her a week."

"A week with a Halloran might be enough," he said, but he sat back anyway and relaxed a little.

Lia still hadn't moved a card. "It occurs to me," she said to Charlie, "that this is a little like that piña colata. Probably worse."

"Did you ever pay that lunch check?"

She shook her head. "I forgot."

"Uh, huh. You don't want to do this, we'll figure something else out."

"What are you going to do with the house if you win it?"

"Move in. Marry you."

"And if you don't win it?"

"Move into your house, I guess. Still marry you."

"What happens to you, Mr. Groton? Where do you go if you lose the house?"

Groton, Charlie could see, was debating silently with himself, but he said, "Vince Arthur is going to make his losses right. This is one of them."

"Don't bet on it," Music said. "I'm still waiting for a check to clear."

"So," Lia said, "you don't really lose anything either way. Charlie thinks he doesn't, too. This is what you fellows call gambling?"

Music laughed out loud. "Lose everything you have, but her."

Lia dealt, pushing the cards across the table with a forefinger pressing on the center of each of them.

"It's interesting what you said about chaos, Charlie," Music said.

Lia nodded, concentrating.

"Five things," Charlie said, pushing them out.

"Call." Groton added five thumbtacks to the pot.

Music straddled a kitchen chair, his arms crossed on its back, his chin on his hands. Charlie was to his left, Groton to his right, Lia across from him. *Points of a compass.* Five stud. Charlie was showing a king, queen, off-suit. Groton was showing a nine, eight of diamonds. *He's got an ace or a nine or an eight down, Son, but you know that. Most likely the nine, but you know that too.*

"Everybody else who's ever lived and who's not religious probably thought about it—if he ever thought about it—as a wind you couldn't do anything about. Chaos happens *over there* somewhere, takes the shape of a drought or an army, and moves in your direction to make your life miserable for some reason of its own."

Lia dealt them each another card. A six for Groton, an ace for Charlie. "Wind," she said.

"Twenty things."

Groton folded.

Music watched her gather the cards, struggling to make sense of their rectangles, careful to keep the just hidden ones still hidden. "But you seem to see it as an opponent."

"Isn't that what you taught us, Dad? What else were all those drills about?"

"Well, yes. Those were designed to counter a different sort of chaos, that of inattention, of sloppiness, of forgetfulness. The chaos of error. But that's not what I meant. You talked about it as if it were a real enemy, with a brain and liver attached."

"Isn't it?"

"The Devil?" Music smiled the way he did when setting a trap.

"I didn't say that." Charlie remembered that straight flush he'd given himself. "If we're pawns, why play?"

"Why, indeed."

"Besides, you didn't leave much room in us for religion."

"Good. So?"

"Seven," Groton said, when Lia was ready.

Lia dealt the cards. It seemed to Charlie that she was getting quicker about it, that they were coming off the deck with a little more authority.

Groton got a ten, Charlie a two, and Charlie folded as soon as Groton bet.

"Seven," Charlie said, calling the next stud game. To his dad he said, "So, what?"

"So how do you see this opponent?"

"Not always the same," Charlie said.

"Oh?"

"Same *thing*, different shapes. Sometimes, as I told Lia, it's your reflection in the mirror. That's the shape, I think, you wanted us to see as kids."

Music nodded, not agreeing necessarily, but meaning, *Go on.*

"Sometimes it's the reason for art, you know, a Rembrandt instead of an orange canvas. Sometimes it's what fights with sunrises."

"What fights with sunrises?" Music asked.

"I don't know. Ask Lia. But they couldn't be so beautiful, could they, without an argument going on out there somewhere?"

Out there somewhere, Music thought. *It's that vagueness, Son, that I still worry is going to get you killed someday.*

"It's your bet, Halloran."

Charlie flicked his hidden cards with a thumbnail, an action Lia couldn't imagine could lift them far enough for him to see anything, but apparently she was wrong because he bet.

Music shook his head. "It's physical."

"You sure?"

"It has to be. I agree it comes in different shapes at different times, but always nameable ones. The last one was called Bruman. They carry knives they've practiced with as hard in their lives as you have with odds."

"It's your bet again, Halloran."

Charlie slid a palmful of objects into the pot without counting. "Twelve things."

Lia counted; there were twelve.

"What I find most often," Music said, "is that chaos is disguised as order."

"The government?"

"I was thinking more about the trouble you were in ten days ago. What got you there?"

Bad dice in my pockets, Charlie thought. "I don't know, what?"

"A straight against the odds. Your error was in noticing it. No, you *had* to notice it—your error was in acting on it."

"Goddammit, Halloran, play your hand."

"You're not paying attention," Music said, and even Lia could see that he was talking to Groton.

Charlie had a ten, four of clubs, another ten and a two unsuited. Groton had just made queens and three spades. "Did you check?" Charlie asked.

"Yes."

"Why?"

"What do you mean, *Why?* It's none of your business why."

"I'll tap you."

Groton looked down at his things.

"You have thirty-one," Charlie said.

"Milo," Music said, like a hiccup or belch slipping out involuntarily.

"I know, but jeez, Dad. He thinks *Lia's* slow."

"And knock off the code words," Groton said. "Christ, you Hallorans can *talk*." He stared at Charlie's tens and, pointedly, at his own queens. "What are you doing tapping me?"

"I'm a wind. I'm the chaos in your life." Charlie saw his dad smile.

And mine, Lia thought.

And mine, Music thought.

"Want me to tell you what you've got?" Charlie asked, then did without waiting for an answer. "You've got queens and probably sevens, two pair, anyway, or you don't stay this long, and anything better, you don't check. You've probably got four spades, too, so all in all you've got a decent draw *except you've got to put your house up* to see it through." Charlie smiled. "That's a lot to wager on a hand that's not made yet.

"Me? I've got three tens, at least you've got to figure I do. So if you catch one of a couple cards, you've got an okay chance of beating me. And no other spades are showing, so maybe you've got better than an okay chance. But of course, a ton of cards still aren't showing. Diamonds, hearts, clubs.

"Right now, you've got to guess I've got the best hand made going into the last card, and I'm making it very tough on you to stay."

Charlie's eyes got flinty. "That's why I'm tapping you. And if you'd listened to what my dad's been saying, you'd know why I'm explaining it to you."

"And if you'd listened to me the day before yesterday," Groton answered, "you'd know that soft play is my style. I'm capable of checking three queens or a flush into your hand. Call."

"Want to turn 'em over right now?"

"No. Deal."

Lia looked at Charlie, who shrugged. "Deal," he agreed.

"Down," Groton reminded her.

"It doesn't matter; all your things are in the pot."

"*Down.*"

Charlie nodded to Lia, but didn't move to look at his last card. He watched Groton's face as he reached for his. "Lia was right, earlier, when she said there's nothing at stake for us."

Groton's hand slowed, then rested on the card's back.

"We're a couple of professional gamblers. We ought to be able to devise a pot worth winning."

"I thought we had. It's a *house*, for Christsake. Your old man bet his *boat*. Is that what happens to you up there in the air you guys breathe? Is the only thing worth risking your lives?"

"Ouch," Music said.

Charlie didn't answer; it was Lia who asked, "Charlie?"

"I don't have a gun around here," Groton said, "but there's a couple of good-sized carving knives. I have some rope somewhere, or if not, I can borrow some from a neighbor. We could make nooses and tighten the knots around our necks and give the bitter end over to the other just before we show our hands. The winner yanks on it."

Charlie seemed to be considering it.

"Or this: drag in the—I was going to say *innocent*, but that wouldn't apply to your father—the bystanders. Let's figure out how to get them involved. Let's spread this *wind* of yours around to everybody."

"Are you done?"

"I guess I am."

"I've got three tens," Charlie said, "unless this last card boated me." He turned it up; it didn't.

Groton mixed his three down cards, then spread them. Two of them were spades: a flush, and a winner. "Whatever else you would have bet, you would have lost," Groton said, raking in the things.

"I have to work tomorrow," Lia said quietly, then looked at her watch. "*Today.*"

Maybe I lost the *whatever else* anyway, Charlie thought.

Once she'd resigned from dealing and stood up from the table, she didn't know what to do next. She'd come out here for a resolution. Music, as she might have guessed, saw Lia's difficulty and solved it for her. After all, she didn't know whose permission to ask to stay.

"Take the bedroom," Music said, "and get some sleep. This looks, now, like it might go on a while."

She'd done just that, hanging up her clothes carefully in Groton's closet because she'd have to wear them again, her mind empty of anything but a tired unease. She'd asked that someone wake her at nine, but she suspected she wouldn't sleep.

Charlie had only a couple of dozen markers left—*things*, he kept calling them—and she could see that Groton had stung him with more than his hand. Music had been hugely disappointed about something, but she wasn't sure what. Some ancient history of theirs, she was sure, some lesson he should have learned but hadn't.

You'd better figure out what, girl, a voice in her head said, and she nodded at it as if it were a person present. *Whatever it is has a testicular involvement.*

She honked out loud at that in this strange bedroom. A dentist had told her father once when he'd gone to have a wisdom tooth pulled that it wouldn't be easy, that the roots were so deep and twisted they had a testicular involvement.

Even as she willed herself to stop smiling, she knew it was true. The shadows inside Charlie Halloran were complicated and old. And whose doing was that, if not Music's, a man she liked, *even admired?* That, she realized suddenly, was part of her unease. *Oh, God, the tangles of family.*

She slept a little. Liam was with her, speaking in Spanish, which she didn't understand. He showed her pictographs that, if she could only decipher, would clarify her troubles.

She woke at eight-thirty, still tired and no less troubled, and dressed and went out into the living room, where the men were sitting exactly as she'd left them five hours before. Lia took in the nearly equal piles of things in front of Charlie and Groton, the unblinking concentration on all three faces, the fact that Groton was dealing from a deck anchored to the table (the compromise they must have reached), the broken window, the door ajar, the cat asleep at Music's feet.

"I'll get some breakfast on my way to school," Lia said, and Music rose to say goodbye, but Charlie only lifted a hand in acknowledgment before pushing some things into the pot.

"I'll walk you out," Music said.

"You don't need to."

"Yes, I think I do."

The greens of the palms' tops, the blues in the bay—even the brown yards—were extraordinary, *crisp and soft both*, Music thought.

He opened her car door for her, and she got in, but he didn't close it; instead, he leaned on its top edge with his arms crossed. "My son's an idiot."

"I'm not going to argue."

He gave her a real smile, his face full of the warmth her own father's had. "I like you a great deal."

"And I, you."

"Not all of Charlie's idiocy is his own doing."

"I know." She held the ignition key, but she left that hand in her lap.

"It's hard for a certain kind of man to learn to love—maybe it's hard for all men—but for a gambler, it's worse. Especially a gambler as good as my son. For him, it's harder than hard."

"*Why?*" She almost cried the word.

"Because," Music said slowly, "love requires trust, and I spent his childhood beating that out of him."

She nodded, not knowing what to say.

"That isn't what worries you, is it?"

"Charlie sees it that way, too, that something was beaten out of him. But there's something else," Lia said. "I don't know what it is." She turned the key over, looked carefully at both sides. "It might be this. Why did you say 'Milo' last night?"

"It's a reminder that he's too proud." And then, in case she didn't understand, he said, "Pride is fatal in a gambler."

"In a marriage, too."

"In a gambler," Music said, as if he hadn't heard, "that pride comes when you think you're invulnerable. That's why it's so dangerous, because you never are."

She nodded again. "He understood all that from 'Milo,' didn't he?"

"Of course."

"And you've got signs—signals with your hands, and such—don't you?"

Music leaned away from the car. "Yes. I think I know where you're going with this. It's worse than that, actually. Or more subtle. *Where* a player keeps his hands in front of him, even how he holds his head, can be a signal. *Anything*, Lia, that's agreed to beforehand is a message. And yes, we've got lots of them in this family."

"And the responses to them are automatic?"

"Pretty much," Music agreed.

"Then what do we hope for now?" Lia asked. "That he lose?"

"That's the difficulty, all right."

"Is Groton good enough to beat him?"

"No. Not under ordinary circumstances."

"I didn't think so." Lia put the key in and turned it. With the engine idling, she said, "I guess I hope, then, that Charlie's good enough to beat himself."

♦

Music went back in, sat down and watched, but his thoughts were of what Lia had just said, and of what he'd once told Vince about deliberately losing to your children. "Why not take a break?" he asked.

"Don't want a break," Charlie said. "Want to get this done with."

In the voice he hoped would reawaken old disciplines, Music said, "It'll clear your head. Lia's only a mile away yet, heading for the nearest coffee shop. Don't lose a greater pot playing for a lesser one."

"A break's okay with me," Groton said. "Half hour, hour. I could use a shower too."

Charlie looked at his father.

"Go on."

Charlie took his keys and sauntered out, but Music, standing at the door, was glad to see that when Charlie was free of the house he didn't waste any time getting to his car. The Firebird moved out quickly. Music stayed there, blocking Groton's way.

"Excuse me."

"Do you want a shower or a lesson?"

"You think I need one?"

"Everybody does," Music said. "I take a lesson myself whenever I can find somebody to give me one, which I'll admit isn't very often. Don't you think I know enough to help?"

"Why would you help me against your son?"

"Isn't it obvious? If he wins the house, he's going to lose the girl."

"No, that's not obvious."

"Well, it's so, obvious or not. Charlie can get the money to buy another house."

"You'd really help me beat him?"

"I'll really help you beat him." *But it's not going to be easy with this thick-headed numbskull.*

"What's the lesson?"

"Sit. Let's see if we agree on what we know, first, all right?"

Groton sat and nodded.

"Charlie's a better cheat than you are."

"He's not cheating." Groton got a panicky look. "*Is* he?"

"No, he's not cheating. *Pay attention.* Agree or disagree: Charlie's a better cheat than you are."

"Yes."

Of course he is. "That thought's working against you, Groton. You're focusing your energies in the wrong places. You even still half suspect him of teaching Lia to cheat and slipping her into the deck somewhere like a cold card. You're tired."

"That's why I need a break. This has gone longer than I thought it would."

"You need this more. You've had better cards; you should have won before now. Charlie's been playing second-bests and winning with them."

"Out-playing me."

"Out-*betting* you." Music let his eye wander around the room. "This house means more to you, you think, than it does to Charlie, and so the stake is higher for you. But I'm not sure. He thinks his future is wrapped up in this, and in a way he's right. I think it's equally important to you both. But he plays higher stakes better than you do. Except for that once, early on, you crumble when you have to go all in, and he knows it. Even that once, he goaded you into it."

"No, he didn't."

"*Yes, he did.*" Music fixed him with a look to make the sentence stick.

Groton stared back for a moment but dropped his eyes.

"Go all in the next time you've got decent up cards. And do it again the time after that. He doesn't expect it from you, and he'll be cautious. He'll fold anything but a monster. And if he's got a monster, you're dead anyway."

"Turn the tables," Groton said.

"More than that. Those two bluffs will sink him. Charlie can't play cautiously. For him right now, that play will be a killing blow."

"Maybe you just want this over."

"I do. But your biggest flaw is cowardice. Call it caution, if you have to. You know it, I know it, and Charlie knows it. This will gut him. Look inside yourself and tell me I'm wrong."

Groton shook his head. "You Hallorans are a strange family." He went next door for his shower.

Music, alone with the cat, said, "Family," like an echo.

Charlie caught Lia at a stop light and tapped his horn. She looked up into the rearview mirror without expression, without, Charlie thought, recognition. He tapped the horn again.

When the light changed, she drove through, and past a restaurant. Charlie passed her in the wrong lane and braked. Now she honked. Charlie waved.

Traffic behind was honking, too. She drove around him, but got stopped at the next light. *Tag.* He pulled up in the left-turn lane beside her, waited for the light, then cut her off when it went green.

He drove two blocks very fast and swerved into the curb. He shut the engine off and climbed out, holding up his keys.

She drove by, but fifty feet later her tail lights came on, and she pulled into the first spot that was open.

"I don't have time for this, Charlie," she said when he came up to her door.

"Make time, please. I'm sorry. Let's have something to eat."

"I have class."

"At eleven."

"I have to change clothes."

"I'll go with you."

"I have to think."

"No, you don't. You love me. You just don't love who I am."

She laughed.

"I mean you don't love who I am when I'm playing. When I'm in front of cards there's nothing else in the universe." At her look, which told him she knew that, he said, "I'm making this worse, aren't I?"

He was making it better, a little, but she nodded anyway.

"Let me buy you breakfast."

"Follow me home," Lia said, "and I'll make some."

They made love just inside the door on the carpet. *Needs vacuuming.* She hadn't expected any such thing, and she could tell he hadn't either, and even while he was peeling off her underwear she was wondering just how—and why—it had happened like that. She gripped his back under his ribs and didn't want to ever let go.

"You make me so damned angry."

"I know."

"And confused."

"I'm good at that. I can even confuse myself anymore."

"I love you, goddammit."

"I love you, goddammit, too."

"I was right a year ago, or a week ago, or whatever it's been since the day I first met you."

"How's that?"

"You're that mysterious force I've been hunting. *Oh!*"

"How's that?"

"That's fine."

The half-hour break Groton wanted was nearly five times that when Charlie got back.

"You ready to play, Halloran?"

"You bet."

They'd dealt six hands before Groton had a board showing enough power to make the play Music had suggested. Groton had a king, jack, five of diamonds against Charlie's queen, seven, nine unsuited.

"All in," Groton said, "thirty-nine things."

"Call."

"*Call?*" Groton glanced at Music, and Charlie, following the glance, admired his father's impassive face. He got all the information he needed from Groton except why his father had coached his opponent while he was gone. *Good move, too.* It probably would have worked, Charlie thought, except he was sitting on three queens.

Groton got another diamond, and his relief came out in a sigh.

Charlie got another—and the last—queen.

"Too bad we're out of things," Groton said.

"Yes." Charlie dealt the last card down, which Groton ignored, turning up his flush. Charlie turned up his four queens.

Groton stared at them for a moment, counting them, then got up without looking in Music's direction and walked out of his house.

"Dead, anyway," Music said to Groton's back. To Charlie, Music said, "I thought you'd planned to lose it back to him."

"So did I."

"I hope you don't end up wishing that you had."

K

♣

The movers arrived on Saturday without Groton. Parked cars needed reparking, as their van took up the whole street. What a way to get to know the neighbors, Charlie thought. *Move your car?*

Room by room the house was emptied, boxed, then carried out on hand trucks and stacked in the truck like large, square cardboard bricks. Without the owner to give them directions, they took everything.

Charlie and Music, to get out of the way, walked down to the beach, and Charlie was pleased to see that his father had left his sports coat and tie at the house. Still, a white shirt, gray slacks, and polished loafers in Hawaii might as well have been a tux. "We should get you some things," Charlie said.

"Things?"

"Casual clothes. Shorts. Flip flops."

"Flip flops?" Music's lips curled around the words awkwardly. "And maybe one of those short-sleeved shirts that looks like a bad still life?"

"Now you're talking. Mangoes. Pineapples."

Music put his hands in his pockets and stared at the children in the water bobbing like corks. The sand was scattered with young women in bikinis, but Music didn't seem to notice. "When a kid wants to change the way his father dresses himself, one of two events is about to take place."

Charlie waited.

"Either the old geezer is about to get stuffed into a home, or Dad's about to catch the next flight out."

"You always taught us to be invisible." Charlie didn't think he could sell *comfortable*.

"Protective camouflage is the phrase I used," Music said. "I don't need it."

"I guess that's right; I keep forgetting."

Music made a sound with his tongue against his teeth. "All those years wasted, if my sons keep forgetting."

"Reggie has a better memory; your lessons weren't lost on him."

"He was easier to shape. Have you heard from him?"

Charlie shook his head.

"I left two messages," Music said. "He didn't return either of them."

"He'll call, or leave a note for you at The Gardner, something."

"Maybe. I'm not so sure. It's strange."

"What?"

"That he'd be the one I'm disappointed in."

Charlie's right hand tensed, as if accepting the block of a deck and readying himself to deal. *What small things trigger us.* "Lia told me that what she remembers best about growing up is the storms in her house and the sunshine after."

"And how do you remember yours?" Music asked, still looking out at the breakers.

"No storms. No sunshine, either. We never had any weather in our house, Dad, just climate. And it's climate that determines whether you eat—say—bananas or not, build your house of wood or not. Eat *anything*, for that matter. Build a house at all." He plucked at his father's shirt sleeve. "We've moved around a lot, but we've carried our climate with us."

"I suppose that's true."

"We can't go on being disappointed in each other." *Or ourselves.* "And finding our only happiness when we're not."

"Is that what we're doing, Charlie?" Music turned, finally, and looked at his son.

"Any time any one of us meets another, it feels like a final exam."

"I guess it does. I guess maybe it *is*."

They stayed on the beach until the sunset's colors ran into the sea, until the kids and the girls had gone, then walked up the hill in the soft lights of houses.

Charlie's was dark. Cracker Jack followed them in from where he'd been hiding in the yard and rubbed up against Music until he was picked up.

"I guess I ought to buy some furniture."

"Or some light bulbs," Music said, flipping a switch that switched nothing on. "Or a hotel room."

"I'm staying here, Dad."

"I know that. But tonight?"

"Even tonight, I guess. I'll just stretch out on the floor. This is the first thing in my life that's *mine*." In the dark, Charlie could see the electricity jump from Cracker Jack's fur as Music stroked him.

"Get one for me, then?"

"What, a house?"

"A hotel room. Everything I owned, and all my cash, was on the *Music Hall*. I'm broke."

◆

Reggie's and Charlie's luggage—a suitcase each—had been aboard the boat, too, when it sank. Reggie went shopping with Bobbie to replace his clothes, get a new suitcase, buy airline tickets. His new bag was one corner of a pyramid in the suite's living room on Sunday morning.

Bobbie was on the phone with her dad, who'd flown back to San Diego three days before. She gestured for Reggie to pick up the extension.

". . . you coming home anytime soon?" Vince was saying.

"Reggie and I are leaving today."

"I'll have a car pick you up. When do you arrive?"

"Eventually."

"Ah. Something I should know?"

She looked at Reggie, who nodded. "We're eloping. To Las Vegas. But I guess now that you know, it's not an elopement, huh?"

"I guess not."

"You don't sound surprised."

Vince wasn't surprised. *Why not?* He didn't feel sad, either, as he'd thought he might at this moment. When he checked a list to see just exactly which feeling had him, he decided on *relief.* Perhaps even happiness, in a vague sort of way. "Now I can write off all the money I lost as a dowry. Is he there? Is he on the line?"

"I'm here, Mr. Arthur."

"If you ever want honest work, call me."

"They sure won't let me work in Las Vegas."

Vince had to grin at that. *I've got a son-in-law who's not allowed in an American city.* He pictured passports, barricades, uniformed men holding shotguns. He turned his attention back to his daughter. "Are you sure you don't want a wedding, honey? Gowns? Flowers? Church? Presents?"

"I just want to be married, Dad. Right away."

"Vegas."

"Yeah. They might not let Reggie sit down at their tables, but they'll let *me.* After that," she shrugged happily, which he couldn't see, "who knows?"

"Promise—" Vince began, and stopped.

"Promise what?"

"Never mind." It had been meant for Reggie anyway. *Promise me,* he'd wanted to say, *that you won't turn her into what you are.* But then it occurred to him that she'd already played a pretty decent mechanic masterfully, had played him, as the saying goes, like a violin, and had won without him ever knowing he'd lost.

♦

Charlie's dad stayed at the house after all, surprising them both. Charlie was awakened by Hawaii's daily pre-dawn shower, and when enough light had crept into the house, he saw Music stretched out on the bare floor as if at attention. His first thought was that his father was dead. The cat lay curled against the back of his head like a pillow.

Charlie's knees cracked when he stood, and when he was on his feet, his ankles popped from the weight. Cracker Jack's head came up, swiveling, and Music's eyes opened.

"Sorry. My legs sound like breakfast cereal in the morning."

"They sound like small arms fire, Son, but you didn't wake me. I've been lying here for an hour trying to move." *All night.*

"It's been years, I'll bet, since you've slept like this."

"I've *never* slept like this." Music levered himself up on an elbow, wincing. "I've slept in bad beds, Marine Corps cots, in chairs, regularly, of all sizes and shapes, and on the ground. But not like this. Not flat out on boards." He sat up. "I slept in a boxcar, once, that was more comfortable."

"I should have gotten you the hotel room you wanted."

"Beggars can't be choosers." Music sat up all the way. He pressed his hands against his kidneys. "I'm fifty-five. I should be past looking for handouts."

"Temporary difficulties," Charlie said, giving him a hand up.

"Is that how you look at it?"

"Sure. What else?"

"Stupidity. I gambled the place I live, which is all right; I was well-heeled, and not all that comfortable on the boat, as pretty as she was. But I gambled everything else—everything I own—against the ocean."

"Against a man," Charlie reminded him.

"Whom my opponent had hired. Stupider yet."

As much as he would have liked to save the old man's feelings, Charlie couldn't disagree.

"I've spent my life teaching." He shook his head wearily, maybe to work the kinks out of his neck. "And find I don't know anything."

"That isn't true, Dad."

"I don't need your pity."

"All right."

"What did I tell you kids to risk?"

"The answer you're looking for," Charlie said slowly, "is no more than twenty percent of what you've got."

"What do you mean, the answer I'm looking for?"

"That's what the textbook says, right? No more than twenty percent?"

Music nodded.

"But you taught us, too, to risk it all, *to risk anything*, under the right circumstances."

"The right circumstances being when you can't lose."

"When is that, Dad? When is there ever really such a time as that?" Charlie brushed off his father's sports jacket and handed it to him, wondering why he hadn't slept on it, or under it, or used it as a pillow. "When you're holding four aces? A straight flush? The first lesson I remember is that every hand—even a royal flush—is relative."

"So when do you bet everything?" Music asked quietly.

"You bet it all when the pot justifies the risk, when what you stand to win outweighs whatever you stand to lose. What were you playing for, Dad?"

"A quarter of a million dollars."

"Um, hmm."

"That's not enough?"

Charlie shook his head.

"Was Groton right? This family needs to risk more than money?"

"Of course he was right. Half right, at least."

"Well, then?"

"Pride," Charlie said. "You'd run out of pupils, and you wanted to teach. And, I think, you enjoyed torturing Arthur with the *Music Hall*." Charlie opened the door. "Let's go find some breakfast and, after that, some furniture."

"Milo," Music said.

"Yes. Remember Milo, Dad."

◆

"I've got a house," Charlie told the furniture salesman, "and I want to fill it up."

He surely must have wondered why this young man and his father smiled at him the way they did. He fumbled for his sales book and dropped his pen pulling it from his shirt pocket.

"What's the mark-up on furniture, ninety percent? A hundred?"

"Oh, no, nothing like that. It's—"

"It's got to be," Music said to his son.

"The same as diamonds. You keep the list," Charlie told the salesman, "and after you total it, we'll cut it in half. Then we'll negotiate a reasonable profit for the store and a commission for you."

"And delivery," Music added.

"The delivery's free," the man said.

"Damn right," Charlie said. "Why don't you look around for stuff for the guest room," he said to his dad, "while I make a phone call."

◆

Come furnish your house, Charlie had said on the phone. *We need everything, even silverware.*

"Has he even asked me to marry him yet?" Lia asked the reflection in the windshield. "And if he has, what did I answer?"

What's this, if not an answer?

Charlie had chosen one of the larger furniture stores on the island, a nice one in the Ala Moana mall. She waved off a salesman and meandered through the store, its half-rooms without ceilings reminding her of a doll house.

Lia saw Music before she saw Charlie. He was examining a cherry dining room suite; fifty yards away, Charlie was looking at brass bedsteads. She raised her hand *hello* to Music and joined Charlie in *Bedrooms*.

"Is your dad staying?"

"Not if you don't want."

"I think that would be fine. For a while."

Charlie smiled. "You can bet a Halloran's 'for a while' is shorter than anyone's. He might not stay at all. I haven't asked him."

"Mind if I do?"

"You like him, don't you?"

She nodded.

"There's hope for me, then."

"Not much." Lia took his hand. "A little."

"We need to sort that out."

"Yes."

"I'm clear in *my* mind about it, you know. About you. About us."

"Are you, really, Charlie?" Lia let his hand go and looked back over her shoulder. Music was keeping a young man at bay, asking questions she was sure he didn't care about. "I wish I were. Your family scares me."

"I know."

"You don't, really. You think it's the gambling, the cheating."

"Isn't it?"

Lia shook her head. "I thought so, at first. But it's not that. It's—" Her mouth moved, searching for a word. "It's the *control* you have over others. It's learned, partially, I think, but it's more than that, greater than that. Larger than that, I mean. Look at your father."

Charlie looked, saw what she had seen, and shrugged. "He's buying us time to talk."

"Yes."

"So?"

"So it comes so naturally to all of you." She raised both fists in frustration. "Not just the ability to guide the behavior of others, to manipulate them down the streets you want them to go, but the—the—*awareness*—of the moment, the sorting of a huge number of variables, and the instantaneous response—by intuition, I guess—to it."

"That's poker. How is that at work here?"

"Your father. He saw me walk toward him; in fact, he probably saw me long before I saw him."

"He probably did."

"I waved to him but didn't stop. From that he gathered that I was eager to speak to you, and he moved three steps to intercept the salesman without *appearing* to intercept him."

"That sounds like Dad."

"But don't you see, Charlie? That's *weird*. That's astute at a level I'm not sure there's a word for."

Charlie shrugged. "He made a good guess."

"*Don't lie to me*." She was suddenly angry, and he backed up a step from her eyes. "You know damned well it wasn't a guess. He read the signs in my wave. He read my intention, my confusion, my need. He didn't guess; *he knew*."

Charlie was silent for a moment, then said, "Yes, he probably did."

"No *probably* about it."

"No. No probably about it."

She sighed sadly. "And you. Your first reaction just now was to try to *mislead* me." She felt her tears begin and wiped her eyes before they arrived. She looked down at her dry palm. "That's what scares me, Charlie. You were trained—or born—or both—to lie instinctively." *And you always will.*

"We're pretty evenly matched," he said.

"*What?*"

"You've got a divining rod for truth. That's *your* genetic makeup. It's stronger than my deception." He held his hands up. "You'll win these biological battles."

"*I don't want to battle.*"

Yes, you do, he thought. *You're drawn to conflict.* "It would be a mess, this marriage."

Lia lowered her eyes and nodded.

"Full of thunderstorms," Charlie said.

She nodded again.

"I want you to marry me, anyway."

Lia nodded a third time. "So do I," she whispered.

Charlie wondered, naturally enough, what parts of him he'd been given by his mother and, looking at Lia now, he wondered what parts of their children she'd design. *I'm sure of this: Our child, the son of a son of a card cheat, whose mother has a Ph.D. in mathematics, will be some kind of a hell-twisted genius.*

Lia was thinking much the same thing, except the child she saw—a daughter—would take advanced degrees in a field not yet named and add *Halloran* to a list that included *Copernicus, Galileo, Newton. Our genetic engine's not a gambler's rose, love, but an instrument wanting to hum. She'll be a jumble like Mother's piano, the keys a chaos on the keyboard, the strings bent and the hammers broken. She will be born with wonderful music waiting in her dark interior.*

Charlie reached for her hand, and she surrendered both of them. "Everything's going to be fine," he told her. "I promise."

"I wish you *could* promise that."

"I can. I'll just have a quick peek at the deck. *Trust* me."

Charlie left his bride-to-be and his father in Honolulu to put together his new home. He boarded the plane late, walking quickly through the long tube that connected it to the terminal, and was ushered aboard by the stewardess who closed the hatch after him. He squeezed past his two neighbors to his window seat, where he buckled up and waited for the plane to rise. When it had, and was banking left, he stared down through the scratched plexiglass and the soft clouds at the razor-edged landscape of Oahu.

In his window and his mind's eye, he watched the early weekday traffic on its way to work like a boil of ants. *What made me think I could ever do that?* Something about them in their cars—their white faces, their round shoulders, their apparent mindlessness, maybe—brought him a picture of Dex. *All of us*, he thought, *heading for our own accidents.* He had a connection in Los Angeles for Dallas, then he would drive. For whatever reason (proximity, the sudden awareness of accidents that Dex was family) seeing Dex, too, felt more than important; it felt necessary.

Charlie would make the drive from Dallas to Little Rock with the top down, the sun hot on his left shoulder, the car's tires humming on the old sun-bleached pavement like a real American spiritual. He'd stop twice to eat and once for gas and finally would run into that same work traffic in Little Rock. The cars might as well have been the same ones he'd seen that morning—the roads the same, too, the faces behind the windshields frozen into a universal tiredness. *Not the exhaustion of their work,* he realized, *but the weariness of their lives.*

"You have a Halloran, here," Charlie would tell the woman at the desk downstairs. "I'd like to see him."

The woman would thumb through a Rolodex. "Dexter?"

"That's the one."

"Are you a relative?"

"Yes."

"Visiting hours start again at seven-thirty," she'd say. "Right now's supper."

"He's in a coma," Charlie would tell her. "I can't imagine visiting hours—or supper, either—can matter a whole lot."

She'd squint at a notation on Dex's card. "He's on the fourth floor. You'll have to ask at the nurses station."

"Thank you."

Still ascending, higher and higher over the Pacific, his head socketed against the cushion, Charlie's imagination—this new gift of his—placed himself there, suddenly.

The nurse on the fourth floor shrugged helplessly. "Sure, you can see him. Stay all night, if you want. You're only the second visitor he's had." She put a hand on his arm. "Have you ever seen anybody in a coma?"

Charlie shook his head.

"It can be spooky if you're not prepared for it. He's got no more expression on his face than a stone."

"I'm prepared for *that*." *Expressions have been beaten out of all the Hallorans in one way or another.*

"Talk to him," she said.

"Talk to him?"

"A lot of us think it might help." She smiled tiredly. "But nobody really knows."

Dex's room was at the end of the corridor near the stairs. Charlie stood at its open door for a minute, staring at the lump in the bed that had been his cousin, suddenly wishing he hadn't come, not wanting to visit a *thing*. Hair in tufts was growing back over Dex's shaved, still-bruised head. Even with the sheet tucked up to his neck, his body half-hidden by oxygen tanks, connected by wires and clear tubing to half a dozen bottles and softly humming machinery, Dex looked frighteningly naked.

That vulnerability decided him. *What Halloran can resist a sucker like this?* "Hello, Dex." Charlie closed the door and looked for a place to sit. "Got into some trouble, didn't you?" *What had Dad said? That he'd been hauled up on a chain hoist and beaten with shovels.* "This family can find some interesting ways to fold, huh?"

The same nurse knocked and pushed a plastic chair in. She nodded apologetically and left the door open.

Charlie pulled the chair closer to the bed, seeing now in the absence of lines in his face why Dex had seemed so naked. The genes, bruised too, he guessed, were twisting Dex's exterior in their spiraling way back to his beginnings. "The nurse outside is pretty," Charlie said, and sat. "But you're not.

"I felt like you look not too long ago, Dex. And you really look like hell. Dad—your Uncle Music—says I'm some sort of an evolutionary jump, the end of the line, and he's right in a way; I got to where I was beating *myself* up, saving the civilians the trouble." He meant to laugh, but it came out different. "I got to the place where

I didn't even need marks anymore. That's the hole in us, you know. This life makes us cheat ourselves."

The humming in the room had rhythm, violins maybe, and the plunk of a guitar. A radio had been left on low volume at Dex's bedside. Charlie reached across and turned it up. Sammi Smith's heart was breaking. He turned it back down, patted Dex's hand, then, surprised to find it warm, held it.

A muscle spasmed in Dex's thumb, and Charlie gripped the hand tighter. It could have been a signal for *split* or *partner.* "There's currents in a life, Dex, in the mind and the body and the heart. Maybe even in the soul. They pull against each other, and if you're not paying attention, they damn near pull you apart." Charlie looked at that blank face and felt tears start. If the nurse was right, and Dex could hear him, Charlie wasn't helping at all. "None of those worries for you, Cuz. No more worries at all." *You're in a riptide.*

Charlie went to the window just before dawn and looked out at the lighted parking lot; nothing outside had changed. He turned back to his cousin and said, "I'll tell you something, Dex. When I leave here, I'm going to Kansas City. You know who's up there, don't you? Have you seen her, Dex?"

It would mean another four-hundred-mile drive in the sun, this time with it beating down on his right shoulder, the tires humming, the day as hot and still as the small dead animals on the side of the road. *Going in a circle. No, not quite that; completing it.* As he had when he'd dealt himself the straight flush, he could see his future clearly, each decision like a card, the whole deck.

The Kansas heat would press on him like an iron. He'd wipe his hands on his slacks, resting one for a moment on the white porch rail, lift it, and see his palm white with chalk. When he touched his finger to the bell, he'd think he'd been electrocuted—go blind for a moment as the sun bounced off the screen door with a noise, a squeal, and a slap—then he'd realize it was the door opening and that he'd stepped aside for its arc, and that he was facing a woman, his mother, who must have been waiting all this time for him to make his play.

Shifting awkwardly, as if he had pebbles in his sneakers, leaning crookedly in front of her, feeling as if he didn't fit his clothes, Charlie would look at her and past her at the same time and see in the dark parlor his own face and Reggie's staring back from gold, oval frames, a bubble-square of light like a cartoon's reflecting from the eyes. A picture of his father that might have been taken a week ago would stare back too.

"Come in, Charlie," his mother would say. "Sit down with me. Have you seen your brother? Your father? *Any* of your relatives?"

Her genuine smile would embarrass him, just as if he'd been caught with bad dice in his pockets.

He said to Dex, "I suppose I have, huh?"

ACKNOWLEDGMENTS

I received a first-rate gambling education (beginning with the curious way I earned my allowance as a child) from my father, Estes Gale Hawkes, and later, from a friend, the best gambler I've ever met, Jimmy Sanders. My brother Gale helped flesh out both the *Music Hall* and her demise. John Whelan, Tasha Cooper, Robert Van Voorst, David Rife, Jack Humphrey, Clyde Peeling, Stan Wilk, Sloan Harris, and Greg Michalson have all lent something valuable. Sascha Feinstein offered—and sometimes insisted on—his usual brilliant eye and ear.